FORGET ME
NOT COWBOY

As if he realized he'd pushed it too far, he nodded, his gaze caught on hers.

And as she stared into those blue depths, the warmth of his hand beneath her palm, her earlier words came back to haunt her.

Gray McClain wasn't a friend.

Or he wasn't in the traditional sense of the word.

Because she couldn't think of a single other friend in her life that she wanted to touch. Kiss. Make love with.

Nope, she thought as she leaned into that hand as he shifted his hold to cradle her cheek.

There was no one on earth that fit that bill other than Gray.

By Addison Fox

FORGET ME NOT COWBOY
THE COWBOY SAYS YES

FORGET ME NOT COWBOY

COWBOY

Rustlers Creek

ADDISON FOX

AVONBOOKS

An Imprint of HarperCollinsPublishers

FORGET ME NOT COWBOY. Copyright © 2022 by Frances Karkosak. All rights reserved. Printed in the United States of America. No part of this book may be used or reproduced in any manner whatsoever without written permission except in the case of brief quotations embodied in critical articles and reviews. For information, address HarperCollins Publishers, 195 Broadway, New York, NY 10007.

First Avon Books mass market printing: November 2022

Print Edition ISBN: 978-0-06-313523-9
Digital Edition ISBN: 978-0-06-313524-6

Cover design by Amy Halperin
Cover illustration by Larry Rostant
Cover photograph by Yasmeen Anderson Photography
Cover images © Shutterstock

Avon, Avon & logo, and Avon Books & logo are registered trademarks of HarperCollins Publishers in the United States of America and other countries.

HarperCollins is a registered trademark of HarperCollins Publishers in the United States of America and other countries.

FIRST EDITION

22 23 24 25 26 BVGM 10 9 8 7 6 5 4 3 2 1

For the Root Literary team.
Your professional acumen is second only to your warmth and loveliness. You all prove that hard work and success is a perfect match with kindness and the support of others.

And for Holly—fearless leader, savvy professional and one of the kindest people I know. I'm so grateful to be on this publishing journey with you.

FORGET ME NOT
COWBOY

Chapter 1

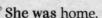

She was home.

Not the flit in and flit right back out in forty-eight hours sort of home. But the settle in and spend some time sort of home.

The stay and figure out your life sort of home.

The time to meet the ghosts of your past sort of home.

Harper Allen looked at the main street of Rustlers Creek as she drove the last few miles off the highway and wondered at the increasing knot that twisted her stomach. A knot that had started to tighten as her flight into Billings from Seattle touched Montana ground.

Why was it so hard? Or maybe a better question was, why did it have to be?

She reflected on all of it as she took in the pretty, appealing look of downtown. Had it always looked like this? So quaint? So clean? So . . . welcoming?

And she had to acknowledge that much of it had to do with her sister, Hadley Allen Wayne, a woman better known far and wide as the Cowgirl Gourmet. Hadley was a major reality star, a fan favorite of The Cooking Network, where she'd made her career. One that now included books, a cookware line and—she saw the bright shining building at the end of Main Street—a lifestyle experience with her newly opened Trading Post.

It was fascinating to see that as her sister's life had grown bigger and bigger over the past several years, her success and fame hadn't only affected her. Her husband, Zack, had certainly been affected. A state that had nearly ruined their marriage before they worked it out back at Christmas.

But Hadley had made an impact on all of Rustlers Creek, too. The entire town had been transformed by her work, the crew that regularly set up camp in town swelling the population for several months out of every year. And then there were the visitors. Several major hotel chains had actually put in locations to accommodate the influx of people that came in and out of Rustlers Creek, something that had only grown since the Trading Post had opened a few months ago.

And then there was the latest, Harper thought, shaking her head as she turned at the end of Main Street. She'd found the online listing while looking up a state-mandated food law in Montana and realized that Hadley had created something of a tourism mecca in their small piece of heaven here in Big Sky Country. Several surrounding towns, including Granite Ridge and Whisper Falls, had gotten in on the deal, creating B and B packages, orchard visits and a horseback riding experience through the myriad of trails that made up this part of the state.

All as a result of her big sister's love of cooking.

They were just shy of a year and a half apart in age, but their birth order had definitely shaped their relationship and their personalities. It had also shaped how each had reacted to their mom's death when they were thirteen and twelve. Hadley was a nurturer and someone who showed her love for others by doing.

What she also was, Harper admitted as she took the turnoff for Wayne and Sons ranch, was a major force in entertainment. One who'd generously offered Harper a chance with her new coffee company. A venture Harper had embarked on after leaving more than a decade working in tech in Seattle. A job that, while not necessarily inspiring, had given her a sizable nest egg and an idea for a new kind of business.

One that built on customer interests, algorithmically taking the things they loved and creating drinks especially for them.

Her initial work at the local shop in Seattle—one she'd purchased on a whim the week she quit her big tech job with its highly lucrative salary—had already become something of a test case for the idea, and it was working. She'd stolen business from the four surrounding chain locations in a matter of months.

And now she was here, back in Rustlers Creek, to put it all to the real test. Building out a business that could be shipped nationwide, with the help of her smiling, enthusiastic sister and the happy souls who wandered into the Trading Post.

"Come on, Harper. Come do it!" Hadley's excitement spilled over as she nearly toppled her wine while they sat at their father's worn kitchen table around 11:00 p.m. on New Year's Day. "Come home for a while. I want to spend time with you and we can get something really cooking at the Trading Post. I need a signature blend, after all."

"You want me home?"

"I do. I miss you."

"The way you and Zack have been entwined around each other, I didn't know you could miss anything."

She grinned at her own joke as she lifted her wine to her lips, but knew it was one threaded with happiness and relief. Hadley and Zack had found their way back to each other, their marriage nearly ending over years of misunderstanding and personal struggles on the subject of children.

It was a close call, she reflected as she drove down the long drive at Wayne and Sons, and Harper couldn't deny how relieved she was. If Hadley and Zack—a couple who loved each other to distraction—couldn't make it, what hope did anyone else have?

A point that seemed important, even if she'd lost her own hope years ago. A woman got one chance at her grand romance, Harper knew. One great love that filled your soul as easily as it destroyed it.

For some like Hadley, they were supremely lucky and got to keep it.

And for others . . .

She let the thought hang as she pulled into a spot near the house. Her gaze drifted over the vast land that stretched out in every direction.

He might be out there, even now. Because when you came back to a place filled with the ghosts of your past, Harper mused as she parked her rental car, you could run into them anywhere.

DR. GRAYSON MCCLAIN removed his gloved hand from a deeply intimate spot on a deeply pregnant heifer and stood back to assess the animal. "She's a bit distressed but should deliver just fine. My examination likely didn't help with the distress part. She'll resettle in a bit."

"You seem pretty sure about that," Zack Wayne said as he got to his feet from where he'd crouched beside Gray. "She's a bit later than the rest of the herd."

"It's late March, Zack. We're still well within birthing season." Gray took in Zack's anxious face. "What has you so bothered?"

He'd known Zack Wayne for a long time and

considered the man a friend. He also knew him to be one of the best and most responsible beef producers in the state of Montana. So the sour expression that filtered across Zack's dark brown gaze, and the sun-worn grooves edging the man's eyes, was a surprise.

"I'm trying to spare Carter from any of the pregnancy discussions this year."

"He and his wife are having a baby, not a cow." It was an obvious point, and Gray couldn't help but wonder if Zack was transferring a bit too much of his concern over the herd onto their ranch foreman. "Carter can handle it."

"I'm not so sure. He seemed real suave and smooth for most of the pregnancy, but ever since Bea moved into her last trimester he's gotten a hell of a lot more skittish."

"He'll be okay."

Zack didn't appear persuaded. "His latest worry is that we'll get a late spring snowstorm when Bea goes into labor."

Of all his possible concerns, Gray figured Carter was more accurate on that front than any other worry the man might think up. But as someone who'd practiced medicine for fifteen years—albeit the large-animal kind—he'd learned that it was the things you never anticipated that were the ones to blindside you.

And that Mother Nature was a hell of a lot more sure of herself than humans gave her credit for.

But that blindsiding part of the equation? Well

hell, Gray thought as he stripped off his rubber examination gloves. Wasn't that really the definition of life in a nutshell?

"Look. Gray." Zack closed the fence door to the pen where they had the expectant heifer settled and turned to face him. That dark expression struck once more and Gray went on high alert.

What *did* have Zack so bothered?

"What's going on?"

"Harper's back. I mean, she's back in Rustlers Creek, but she'll be here on the ranch quite a bit, too. She and Hadley are working on her new venture."

And there it was. Blindsided on a perfectly respectable Tuesday afternoon, Gray thought as Zack continued speaking about his sister-in-law. Even if the words had grown garbled and fuzzy and faraway sounding, he still managed to catch most of them, any morsel of information about Harper Allen something he couldn't resist.

Somewhere, Gray surfaced enough from his Harper-haze to key back into Zack's words. "What venture is that?"

"Harper's bought a coffee company. She's determined to change the industry and she's working with Hadley on an exclusive blend for the Trading Post."

"Coffee? Harper? What happened to her computer science and programming work?"

"That's the amazing part. She's using it all to create custom blends. Her customers in Seattle are going nuts for it. And she's come up with some really good brews."

Zack's enthusiasm for his sister-in-law's new business venture was evident, but even with the description, Gray was still having trouble picturing Harper Allen in a barista's apron, blending coffee like a mad scientist.

Yet, even as he considered her new venture, it made an odd sort of sense.

Hadn't there been that summer she'd decided she was going to learn to mix a list of the ten most challenging cocktails and had set about dissecting every recipe with the most minute attention to detail.

They'd been damn good, too, as Gray recalled. He'd still never had a better old-fashioned than Harper's, no matter how many he'd tried.

"I'm happy for her, then," he finally said, the words feeling like cement against his tongue. "That's great people are responding so well."

The Allen-girls magic, Gray figured. Hadley had it in spades, with national acclaim to back it up. But Harper . . .

While seemingly quieter on the surface, she carried a magic all her own. He'd been drawn to her from the first, all those years ago when it was awkward and frowned upon to be a senior trailing after a sophomore. He'd hidden his feelings then, well aware the son of Burt McClain didn't get a pass on anything, and that a seventeen-year-old male chasing after a fifteen-year-old female would only be seen through the most negative of lenses.

So he'd waited, only spending time with her when they both worked their jobs with the town's vet. Harper worked with the grooming crew and he worked directly with Doc Andrews, and that had been all the time he'd been allowed to see her or talk to her with any level of intimacy or privacy.

It had only been later, when she'd come home from school and he was already hard at work on his veterinary degree, that he'd finally been able to act on his feelings. Feelings, he'd been deeply relieved to know, that were mutual.

"So you're going to be okay with it?"

Once more, Gray keyed back into Zack's words, those long-ago memories needing to stay right where they were. Hadn't he learned a long time ago, you got nowhere traipsing down paths that weren't for you?

And falling for a woman, no matter how magical, wasn't in the cards when she was the bright, vibrant daughter of one of the town's most respected men and you were the son of one of its least.

Yep, Gray had learned that lesson the hard way. And as he pushed off the thick bars of the corral, he stared Zack dead in the eye.

"I'm fine, Zack. And I've been more than okay with it for a long time."

HARPER SAT AT the long bar counter and watched her sister work. It always struck her as odd when she was here at the ranch that she sat at the very same counter where her sister regularly broadcast to millions of people. Sat at the same counter that was on display on the front of hundreds of thousands of cookbooks, in homes all across America.

And sat at the same counter where she'd cried her heart out to her sister on more than one occasion.

How did those things coexist?

It was the strange juxtaposition in her life that the one place she'd run from all those years ago had somehow become the very place she couldn't avoid.

Even before she'd made the decision to buy the small coffee company in Seattle, that had been the case. Her small, dot-on-the-map hometown had been transformed into a place people *wanted* to come to.

And all because of her sister.

"How was the flight in?" Hadley expertly chopped chives for a baked potato bar she'd already set up on the opposite side of the kitchen, her gaze seemingly on the very sharp knife she used as well as Harper's face, both at the same time.

"Good. I always forget how long that drive seems from Billings."

"It's a lot of wide-open space here."

"Not so much when you drive through downtown. Things look different." Harper considered those first impressions she'd had as she drove through Rustlers Creek. "Fresher, somehow."

Hadley scooped up the chives with the edge of her knife and dropped them into a small serving bowl. "A coat of paint'll do wonders."

"So does that Hadley Wayne shine."

Her sister actually blushed at that, a feat that wasn't all that hard to do with her strawberry blond hair. "That's silly."

"It's true. The whole world is in love with you, rightly so." Harper picked up her bottle of water and lifted it in toast to her sister. "And the whole town shines right along with you."

"I really do love how the business supports other people. The way others in Rustlers Creek have benefited from my success. It makes all the fuss seem a bit more worth it, you know?"

"What fuss?"

"The whole 'TV shit show' as Zack calls it."

Harper stilled at that. She and Hadley had spoken in depth about the challenges Hadley and Zack had faced in their marriage, and Harper knew a lot of it had grown difficult under the scrutiny of filming a TV show. Was it still a problem?

"I thought Zack was over being upset about the show?"

"He was never upset about the show, exactly. But he's still got eyes and a working ranch. He has a healthy skepticism about the whole Hollywood aspect of our lives and he's not wrong."

"Now you're the one who sounds skeptical."

Hadley shrugged as she pulled out a length of plastic wrap to cover the various bowls she'd prepped for the potato bar. "It's less skepticism and more an understanding of what I nearly lost. A pretty set and lots of people who watch my show could never replace my marriage, and all the Hollywood stuff is really just a fancy mirage. I always knew that, but almost losing Zack pressure tested that belief. Zack and me, you, Dad, Zack's family. That's what's real. What matters."

She understood what her sister was saying and knew that while not completely identical, working in the tech industry had a lot of that same mystique. The mythos of what went on inside a modern tech firm, the thrill of venture capital funding for the latest technological promise, and the hope that the business you worked and sweated for would become a Wall Street unicorn—all of it had consumed her life for the better part of a decade.

And where had it gotten her?

Disillusioned with it all and happier about walking away than she ever could have imagined.

Wasn't that part of what had bothered her so badly these past few months? She'd left Montana after things went to hell with Gray, convinced she was starting out on a new adventure. One she'd sunk her all into—everything she was.

And again, Harper thought with no small measure of frustration, where had it gotten her?

Damn near sick with an ulcer and disillusionment about ever finding happiness with anything, anywhere.

And she hated it. She was a reserved person by nature, but she wasn't maudlin and she wasn't hopeless. So why . . .

Why had she felt exactly that way for longer than she could remember?

She considered her sister as Hadley moved around the kitchen. Because they were so close in age, they'd always had a sort of emotional and conversational shorthand, much the same way people spoke of twins having a bond. And yet, Hadley had kept her in the dark about her marriage and all the challenges she and Zack had faced.

Harper respected the decision—sisters or not Hadley was entitled to her privacy—but she could also admit to feeling left out. Or worse, sad that her sister had faced those scary times all alone. She was still struggling with how to verbalize those feelings and was conscious enough of how close her own emotions were to the surface to know now wasn't the best time to address how she felt.

But she *would* find a way to talk about it.

"Is there something I can do to help?" Harper had been waved off from prep work when she'd first arrived, but suddenly sitting still didn't suit her mood. Action would feel better.

Anything but sitting still, wrapped in the same

thoughts she hadn't been able to escape from for way too long.

"I'd love some help getting the potatoes out of the oven while I take care of breaking up the meat in the slow cooker." Hadley pointed to some large kitchen mittens near the stove before heading off to the opposite end of the kitchen.

Grateful for something to do, even if it was minimal, Harper pulled the disposable container out of the oven, rapidly counting off the number of baked potatoes wrapped inside.

"Just how many people are you feeding tonight?"

"This is your welcome home dinner. It started off with just you, me, Zack and Dad and sort of picked up steam."

Since there had to be at least twenty potatoes nestled in the disposable pan, Harper mentally counted off who could be coming. "So I assume that includes Charlie and Carlene."

"And Mamma Wayne," Hadley added, immediately bringing to Harper's mind Zack's flamboyant and entertaining grandmother. "And Bea and Carter. And Charlotte. And I think at least one of the triplets."

Zack was the oldest of six, with a brother who followed him in age, then his sister, Charlotte, who had gone through school with her and Hadley. And then there were the last three Wayne children, triplet girls who had to be in their early to midtwenties by now. "It still seems like a lot of potatoes, Had."

"You know me. I like to make extra."

"Is that what we're calling this feast from Idaho?"

Even though she heard the skepticism in her own voice, Harper had learned early and often that her sister's love language was feeding people. And Hadley had enough recipes up her sleeve that she'd know what to do with leftover baked potatoes, likely making them into a potato salad that would be even better than the loaded option they'd all enjoy tonight.

It was only when Hadley bustled back over from shredding the meat in the slow cooker that Harper took in a suspiciously guilty quality to her sister's eye contact. Or lack thereof.

"What aren't you telling me?"

"It's nothing, really. It's just that . . . Well, you know me. I mean, everyone needs to eat. And when I talked to Zack before, he mentioned some work they were doing out in the barn."

"Hadley?" Harper asked her sister expectantly. "What's going on?"

"It's just that it was a busy day today and we needed one of the cows looked at who is having a difficult pregnancy. And it's tough work and no one should eat alone. And—" Hadley broke off as the distinct sound of voices—*male* voices— sounded from the hallway outside the kitchen. Zack's voice echoed first, but Harper could tell he was speaking to someone as they trudged in from the garage.

And then she heard it.

That deep, resonant voice that still haunted her saddest dreams and most fevered ones, too.

"I really don't want to intrude, Zack. This is your family dinner."

"You know you're family, too. And Hadley insisted." Zack stopped short as he walked into the kitchen, but it was the quiet, drawn face that stood beside her brother-in-law that stopped Harper's heart for no fewer than three beats.

Gray McClain stood beside Zack, all six feet two inches of rangy male. His dark hair stood up in spikes on the side of his head, where he'd no doubt run his hands through it several times as he worried over his latest bovine patient.

But it was the deep, velvety blue of his eyes that really caught her up short.

A blue she still saw in every one of those dreams that haunted her far more often than they should.

"Hey, Harper," Gray said, nodding his head.

"Gray." She uttered that lone word, grateful her voice didn't betray any hint of the tightness that practically strangled her vocal cords.

"It's good to see you."

"You, too." She nodded, suddenly struck by the urge to beat her sister senseless with one of her eight million kitchen gadgets, love language or not.

But it was only as she kept her gaze trained on Gray, even after her brother-in-law leaned in for a hug, welcoming her home, that Harper realized something else.

At least those maudlin thoughts had taken a

holiday, vanishing as if they hadn't been her constant companion for months on end. Because, Harper realized, when the ghosts of your past finally did show up, all you could do was put on a smile and brazen your way through it.

Chapter 2

Gray took in the large dining room table and the conversation that flew from one end to the other and back and wondered how anyone heard anything at all. Or formed a response when there were at least three other conversations taking up space in the air, vying for someone's input and attention.

Of course, none of the individuals in the midst of those conversations had their guts churned up and laid out on the table for everyone to see.

Even if everyone was far too polite to say anything about it.

He'd known coming to dinner was a bad idea. But Zack had insisted, and then he'd insisted that Hadley had insisted and, hell and damn, Gray was caught. Especially when the only thing that awaited him at home was a night of watching some of the rodeo he'd recorded the prior week-end and a sandwich made with a few pieces of deli meat he'd slap between bread and maybe a beer.

A fact Zack might not know but Hadley likely did, which was why she'd insisted on the dinner invitation as well as the leftovers she'd ply him with before he left.

It was sweet and kind and vintage Hadley and he adored her for it.

Even if sitting a few feet away from her sister was a barely veiled form of torture.

God, she looked good.

Although he knew she'd never been a tall woman, she was smaller than he remembered. Slight, almost, but that firm chin still spoke of strength and attitude. Not much got past her quick, alert hazel gaze, either. The combination would have seemed harsh—and perhaps it did to some when all that whip-quick intelligence turned on you—but Gray had always seen something else.

He'd always seen the tender vulnerability beneath.

The tough exterior that hid a thoughtful woman who saw and felt the world around her.

Deeply.

Harper Allen, the only woman he'd ever loved, and the only one who'd ever made him question every single thing about his life. All the things, really, that he preferred to keep buried and locked away, unwilling to look at any of them too closely for fear of getting singed by the memories of a shitty childhood and a horrible pair of parents.

You spend the second half of your life getting over the first half.

It was an Irish proverb he'd heard once, and the idea had stuck, far more powerful than he could have imagined. And, in his case, 100 percent truth. Even if, at thirty-four, he was pragmatic enough to hope he wasn't halfway done.

"Heard you and Zack spent quite a bit of time today with one of the heifers." Charlie Wayne interrupted Gray's thoughts and he was grateful for the intrusion.

"We did. She's doing fine." He shot his friend a wry grin across the table. "Just running a bit later than Zack's timetable."

"Aren't we all?" Zack's father shot his son a wink before turning back to Gray. "I've been telling him for years spring calving is actually a season, not a handful of days. Even when it seems like every one of those little buggers arrives at once."

Zack's father had survived a personal rough patch, frustrated by his inability to actively work the ranch any longer, but sitting there, talking to Charlie, Gray recognized a cattleman. Charlie Wayne had likely forgotten more than anyone currently working in husbandry even knew. It was in his bones and it was gratifying to speak with an older man who understood every aspect of the business he'd devoted his life to.

Instead of talking to one who was bitter about every aspect of the world around him.

Shaking that off, unwilling to spoil the moment, Gray smiled at the sentiment. "But you are right. In the thick of it all, they do feel like they're coming all at once. You've got a nice-looking group of calves this year."

"All Zack's doing." Charlie waved a hand toward his son. "He's the genius behind all of this. I now get to sit back and enjoy watching it happen."

A recently acquired state, if Zack's raised eyebrows were any indication, but Gray just nodded and gave the older man his respectful due. "Something you've surely earned, sir."

Charlie let out a loud hoot at that, clearly aware of the communication arcing between Gray and Zack. "I was a crazy son of a bitch for damn near half a year. Put everyone through hell while I was at it." He turned to his wife and laid a hand over hers. "I'm just glad everyone waited around until I got my balls unslung over it all."

"Dad!" Zack frowned at Charlie before shooting his mother a helpless look.

Carlene only smiled. "The man speaks the truth. I'm just grateful he's putting those balls to better use."

Zack turned a mottled shade of red at his parents' antics, and Gray couldn't help but laugh at it all.

Charlie planted a big kiss on his wife's cheek

before smoothly moving the conversational ball. "How's your land coming along?"

"Good. I don't spend nearly as much time on it as I'd like but it's coming along. I've gotten several areas fenced in and a good start on the stables and paddock. I should be able to start bringing in my rescues by summer at the latest."

"I'm glad Beaumont sold you that piece. You can do something serious with twenty acres and it's given him a bit of breathing room."

Although Chance Beaumont's business situation wasn't a huge surprise around Rustlers Creek, and certainly not to the table, Gray didn't miss the way those varied conversations quieted or the attention that shifted toward him and Charlie.

Chance's father, Trevor Beaumont, had run Beaumont Farms into the ground. The sale of the parcel of land to Gray was enough to keep the bank off Chance's back for a few months, but Gray knew the man was struggling to move his business forward. Although he left Chance to his own counsel, they'd known each other since they were young. Trevor and Gray's own father were thick as thieves. The man was in tough straits, no doubt about it.

A fact he wondered about when he caught Charlotte Wayne's sharp gaze from farther down the table, her interest in his and Charlie's conversation quite clear.

Before Gray could linger too long on it, Harper spoke. "What's coming by summer?"

Her question was quiet, spoken in a low tone, but in the easing conversation around the table it shifted everyone's attention firmly to the two of them.

"I'm starting a blind horse rescue. I've wanted to do that—"

"Since you worked for Doc Andrews." She finished the sentence for him. "That's amazing that it's finally happening for you."

"Things are falling into place."

They had been, Gray thought. He'd come to a place in his life where he felt good in his business and equally good in his personal interests. Owning his own land was a piece of that, supporting his dreams of a rescue organization, just as Harper said. He hadn't found any sort of lasting romantic relationship, but he'd grown content with what he had—occasional dates that turned into something more interesting for a few weeks or months. Sure, they might not last, but he'd had his heart pretty well ruined once before and he wasn't looking to repeat the experience.

Even if there were times, especially lately, when he'd roamed that piece of land that was now all his and admitted that freedom had some decidedly lonely aspects to it.

HARPER WASN'T SURE why she was so affected by the news of Gray's land purchase and the start of his horse rescue organization, but it had hit her far harder than she'd expected.

The result of watching someone's dream come true?

Or more an understanding of just how important that dream was and how long he'd obviously worked to make it a reality.

While rescue organizations did good work, their cost and upkeep, as well as finding qualified team members to support the effort, were challenging. Add on the expense of caring for large animals and it was a dream with a large price tag.

"I know euthanasia is a part of the job. I've prepared myself for it and know that there's a merciful aspect to it, when handled with respect and care. But these horses, being put down just because they're blind? There's another way."

"What can you do about it?"

"I'd like to create a rescue. Give them a place to live out their later years and support their needs. Help maybe make them adoptable to the right farm and family. They're animals and they're adaptable with the right patience and the right circumstances around them."

That conversation they'd had, so many years ago as they cleaned up in the vet practice where they worked, had stuck with her through the years. The conviction he'd had so young, as well as that deep-seated need to give care.

Hadn't that been one of the biggest surprises as she got to know him? They'd spoken of his dreams for the rescue and his desire to become a large-animal vet.

She'd talked of her science classes and the computer class she particularly enjoyed, and he'd always listened to her, never teasing her that she was riding the geek train or boring him with talk of computer programming languages.

And then, once they'd gotten past those things they cared about—the conversations that created a bond in the first place—they'd shared the harder stuff. Her losing her mom and him living with the reality that his had run away from her marriage and her child.

They were deep, serious conversations for people the world believed too young to have them.

And in them, she'd found understanding in an unexpected place. Where everyone else expected tears or sullenness or just unending grief, with Gray she'd found a place where she could share her thoughts. Yes, her own sadness, but also a sounding board over the confusion of whether it was right that she still wanted to go to the school dance or the Friday night football games. Or that she'd yelled and screamed in happiness at the pep rally the prior week and laughed when she'd figured out a tough string of code in her computer class.

Yes, she missed her mom. Terribly at some times. But she also still found ways to smile and laugh and be happy. Did that make her a bad person?

It was Gray who'd told her that it made her strong and resilient and that her mom would want all of it for her. And after a while, after several conversations where she *wanted* to believe him, she woke up one day to realize that she did.

At fifteen she'd understood very little of it, but as an adult who'd lived the years that had passed since, she'd come to understand he'd given her a gift beyond measure. One she'd been able to keep, even after all the things that had been said between them.

All the things that had come *after* they'd been together.

All the things that couldn't be taken back.

Well, his kind words and understanding over her mother couldn't be taken back, either. And she'd hoarded each and every one of those talks way down deep inside, like a miser with gold. Only in her case, Harper knew, it had been about healing. About finding a way past the hurt and the pain to get to the place where she could move forward.

He'd told her she was strong.

And then he'd laid her so low she'd had to fight and scrape for every bit of that strength to move forward.

But she had.

So why were the memories always so close here? Or maybe said another way, why did they have so much power? She'd moved on. Truly moved on and made a life for herself nearly eight hundred miles away. It was a good life, with successes and accomplishments and opportunities that stretched her and helped her grow. It had become so easy to look at the frustration and the ennui of her profession over the past few years and forget all the good things that had come before. But she'd loved her life and her work for a long time.

She'd become up-and-comer Harper Allen in Seattle. She'd made a group of friends and a career and a life that was bigger than she ever could have imagined while growing up in Rustlers Creek. A town so small that not only were there more people living in three square blocks of her Capitol Hill neighborhood in Seattle, but that was also so small she'd ultimately gone to high school with kids from four additional surrounding cities. Even with all that space and land, she'd *still* only graduated with eighty-four other people.

There had been more people in her entrance class at her tech start-up than all of her fellow graduating seniors in high school. It had taken some getting used to, but through it all, Gray's words would echo in her ears.

That she was strong and resilient.

Which was why she'd live those traits now. She'd come home for a few months to spend time with her family, to support her sister and to revel in that support in return. The past few months, since making the decision to buy her new business, she'd felt that same old joy and excitement. The launch of something new. The opportunity to stretch her creativity and her mind to build something from scratch.

Coffee 2.0 wasn't just her business, it had become a new, fresh focus for her life.

She wasn't the same Harper Allen who'd left Rustlers Creek all those years ago.

And if she still had a small piece of herself that loved Gray McClain unreservedly, well, she'd just use all that strength and resilience to bury it way down deep.

After all, she'd done it for the past decade. There was no reason to think she had to stop now.

GRAY SHIFTED THE bag in his hands, assured by the heft of the rustling brown paper that he'd be eating well for almost a week. Hadley always made sure she sent home leftovers with everyone after a meal and he was well aware she usually added a few extra portions to his stash.

It was kind and sweet and something she'd done for years. Which made this weird, embarrassed reaction to the bag of leftovers odd in the extreme.

He knew how to feed himself.

More, he'd actually developed a few skills in the kitchen. He made a mean baked ziti and he had a pretty good handle on a Sunday pot roast, too. He wasn't some confirmed bachelor who made do with takeout every night.

So why was she sending him home like a pack

mule with enough food to feed half the cowboys in the Wayne and Sons bunkhouse?

"Everything okay?" Charlie Wayne had come into the small alcove in the area between Hadley's kitchen and the side door most everyone used to enter and exit the ranch house, a bag of his own dangling from his hand. It didn't look nearly as full or weighted down.

"Yeah, sure." Gray shook his head. "Just thinking about that exam earlier. I meant to tell Zack he should call me if anything changes overnight."

He hadn't been thinking about the impending calf at all, but if Charlie noticed the quick fabrication, he was too kind to say anything. "You know Zack has you on speed dial. But I'm sure she'll be fine until morning. Carter just called, since he and Bea checked on her on their way home."

"Good. That's good then. I'll be heading out."

Charlie smiled before slapping Gray on the arm. "My daughter-in-law has a big helping of brownies for you before you go. Better not leave without it or she'll hound you for weeks that you left something behind."

"That woman is a menace to my cholesterol."

Despite his grousing, the warning had him moving, since he knew Charlie was absolutely correct. And since he'd already had this weird reaction to the leftovers anyway, he might as well just get it all handled at once and take his lumps. He could always bring the extras into his small office tomorrow and share the spoils. Hadn't his office manager, Marta, complained and accused him of being a sugar hoarder the last time he'd mentioned some of Hadley's desserts?

Another brown paper bag was waiting on the counter as he walked back into the kitchen and he ran straight into Harper.

Even with a kitchen the size of half a football field, her long stride out of the pantry was right in his path. With her head down and his focus on the bag on the counter, they'd slammed right into each other.

Which meant he had a heavy bag of food in one hand and an arm scrabbling for purchase around her midsection with the other. The scent of her filled him anew, after hints had floated his way all through dinner, and he breathed deep without even thinking. She was brilliance and light and he'd always associated her in his mind with early morning sunshine and fresh orange juice.

Which was far more fanciful than he'd ever been about anything in his life, even if it was still true.

And something he'd always kept to himself since he had no doubt no woman on earth, any-time ever, wanted to be thought of as smelling like breakfast.

Suddenly aware neither of them had moved, he became acutely conscious of the press of her body against his, the soft roundness of her breasts pressed to his chest. He immediately dropped his arm, stepping back as the distinct notes of coffee drowned out some of that re-membered sunshine.

"Sorry about that." He pointed toward the counter. "I forgot your sister's take-home trough of brownies."

"She pushing food on you?"

Harper's smile was simple and easy, unre-strained from the heavy history that had hung between them all evening. It was one that he was helpless to resist.

"Doesn't she always?"

"You should see what she does to my father. I swear the poor man has so many frozen casse-roles in his freezer he takes at least three a week to school and hosts teacher lunches in the break room."

"I hear he's all the more popular for it."

"My sister's love language is food."

"Then it's safe to say she spreads love far and wide."

And as the words came out, he had to admit they were true, even if he'd just bitched to himself about the copious amounts of leftovers.

Conscious he'd been staring at Harper since they extricated themselves from one another, he caught sight of the coffee in her hands. "Coffee 2.0" was written on the face in a stylish script that was at odds with the name. "Is that yours?"

"Yep. I wanted to show Hadley the new pack-aging."

Harper held up the bag and Gray considered it

once more. There was something fresh and clean about it, even as it hearkened back to a different time.

"I like how the name is so modern but you've used the sort of script you'd find in a fifties coffee shop."

"That was the point."

"It works."

Harper held up the bag, assessing. "Do you think so?"

"I do."

"It's a bit moot, to be honest. I mean, in Seattle coffee is practically a religion. The real test is when I try to take it elsewhere and see if people respond the same way."

"I overheard a bit of your conversation with Charlotte at dinner. You create the blend with an algorithm?"

Although he had been keenly aware of everything about her at dinner, he hadn't been the only one interested in the way she'd spoken of her new business. He knew the power of technology and had seen how much it had transformed his work over the past decade. To think that she could do the same with a product that had been around for centuries was rather amazing.

"It sounds sort of geeky, but that's the whole promise of Coffee 2.0. It struck me that while there are different blends, it could be possible to create something specifically for someone. It was random, but it struck me one morning while I was waiting in line for my daily fix. The guy in front of me was having it out with the barista on how hot the water needed to be on his pour over and how many ounces of one bean he wanted and how many ounces of another."

"So you're doing the world a service?"

"Saving it from yuppie assholes with a caffeine addiction?" That smile was back, big and broad, before Harper waved a hand. "I'm not quite *that* good. And I'm not sure there's any product on earth that can fix that problem. But I do think I can help people have something special in their daily indulgence that they can enjoy just for themselves."

Curious, Gray reached for the coffee in her hand. Their fingers brushed lightly as he took the bag, that simple touch reverberating through his nerve endings. Ignoring the sensation he had no business feeling any longer, he focused instead on the words imprinted on the back of the bag.

He knew it was marketing-speak, but the label spoke of that first cup, the spark of starting your day with something just for yourself with a taste that had been enjoyed throughout history. It was silly to feel this shot of pride at the words, at holding her work in his hands, yet he did.

All those many years ago, when they'd talk of who they were and what they enjoyed and what they wanted out of their lives, he'd always known Harper had deeper reserves than likely she even knew.

Wasn't her new venture an example of that?

She'd built a life for herself in the tech industry.

Although he'd limited himself through the years on how much he'd ask Zack and Hadley about her, he'd kept up. The few questions he did allow himself and the natural gossip that spread around town when people talked about the kids from Rustlers Creek who'd "made good" had kept him well-informed.

She had a big job and a lot of responsibilities. If he'd understood properly, she'd even built an add-on to a social network that allowed for an online shopping experience in virtual reality. He'd searched online for that and had been so proud to see what all those coding discussions in high school had ultimately produced in an adult professional.

And then he'd had to close the search bar and live with the memory of her smiling face, shining back from a series of photos that had accompanied the online article. Harper at her desk in an open-air office. Harper standing in front of a classroom, teaching a group of at-risk youth about coding. And the last, Harper dressed to the nines, arm in arm with a tuxedo-clad guy at a charity function in Seattle.

He'd lived with those images in his mind ever since, well aware there was little benefit to going searching for her again.

So he'd worked hard, once more, to put Harper Allen behind him. She wasn't a part of his life any longer and to dwell on those photos—or any other aspect of her life—was the dumbest thing he could do.

Even with all that work and effort to put her behind him, standing there in the Wayne kitchen, staring down at her next big creation, Gray felt something tighten and then close in his throat.

And suddenly he knew he had to leave.

To get out of there and away from the temptation that this woman had been from the first time he'd seen her. When he had no real idea of what life could hold beyond frustration and anger and disillusionment. When he didn't know there was someone in the world who could look at him like he mattered.

No, Gray amended to himself. Not just mattered. But who believed he could be their entire world.

Chapter 3

Harper walked around the Trading Post with her sister, inspecting the setup in the restaurant area built into an entire side of the store. The whole display was impressive, and Harper wasn't sure what she was more enamored with. The fact that Hadley had created an experience that was so immersive for her Cowgirl Gourmet brand, or that she'd somehow managed to convert a part of downtown Rustlers Creek that had been built at the turn of the previous century.

"This place is amazing, Had."

"I'm really happy with how it's all come out."

"Happy?" Harper let out a low whistle. "I know you're not about the money, but Hadley, you're printing it in here. Seriously, it's insanity. I saw four people alone with baskets that had to have two hundred or more dollars worth of goods in them."

"That's not what it's all about."

Harper shrugged. "Side benefit. And something you should be proud of. People want a part of this and you've made it accessible. And wow, did you make those people really happy. Those women were so excited you were here and that you took the time and spoke with them. You made them feel special and that's a gift. Besides, others make a profit off of you. You're entitled to make one yourself."

Hadn't that been one of the first lessons she'd learned in business?

She wasn't a greedy person and she spent a lot of her personal hours working on projects that helped those who were less fortunate find a path forward, but she'd also learned early on in her career that if others were going to profit from her talents, she should, too.

"You done yet?" Although the words could seem harsh, the teasing glint in her sister's eyes was assurance enough she wasn't upset.

"I get carried away."

"Preach the girl power. Seriously." Hadley reached out and laid a hand on Harper's arm. "But it's really about the other part you said. About making people feel a part of things. That's what's so important to me."

"If those smiles were any indication, consider it done."

It had been fascinating to watch. Empirically, she knew her sister was a celebrity. Hadley had been in the public eye long enough now that Harper had been with her when others had noticed her sister. But to see it up close and personal like that?

It was something to watch.

She'd peripherally experienced celebrity in her own professional career. The tech industry definitely had some celebrities of its own and she'd had exposure to that through the various projects she worked on.

But to know that it was her own sister who attracted that sort of attention. It was . . . well, it was sort of amazing.

"You were awesome back there, too. You knew all the right things to say."

"Those women made it easy. And it was great to hear their feedback. What they liked about the Trading Post. What I could do different."

"I didn't hear anything but high praise."

Hadley laughed at that. "They were exceptionally kind. Carlene and I had a woman in here a few weeks ago who would have rearranged every single one of our shelves if we'd let her. According to her, we had poor flow and a confusing floor layout."

"How'd Carlene handle that?"

"It helped we had a rush in the café and she was needed." Hadley ran a hand over the long counter where they stood. "So what do you think?"

"I love it."

"Not the sanitized version. Really. What do you think? I want to know."

While she'd been here back at the holidays right around the grand opening, there'd been so much going on it was hard to focus on any one area. Now that she had the time and the space, their late afternoon visit ensuring it was just the two of them and the staff who were cleaning up for the day, Harper did as Hadley asked.

Large windows framed the dying early spring light. It cast a glow over the front of the store, filtering back in small wisps to where they stood at the restaurant counter. The entire area had a welcoming feeling that Harper could picture no matter the season.

The bright, endless sunshine of summer. The crisping days of fall. And what she'd already experienced at the holidays—those cozy nights when it was still early enough to do things and dark enough to feel the cold kept at bay with a warm drink and a comfortable seat at the table.

Allowing her gaze to travel beyond the café, Harper really couldn't agree with the nosy, intrusive visitor from a few weeks before. The layout was fantastic. People flowed from housewares to cooking items to an area devoted to the show and Hadley's cookbooks. Her sister had even found a way to replicate the look and feel of the exterior shots of the house at the opening of *The Cowgirl Gourmet* with large, framed images of the ranch that sat high on the walls.

It was Western chic but it was something else.

There was an attainable quality to what her sister created. In a funny way, it was how she felt about her coffee. She wasn't looking to build something exclusive or exclusionary. Instead, it was meant to be something everyone could partake in.

Everyone could enjoy.

Hadn't she learned that lesson early? With Gray?

Although Rustlers Creek was hardly a metropolis at fewer than two thousand residents, she and Hadley had grown up with a degree of privilege she didn't necessarily understand but had known all the same.

Her father had been the principal at Rustlers Creek High School since she was in junior high. And he'd been a teacher for nearly two decades longer. They'd lived in a modest, but nice home near the center of town. She'd had a new backpack each year and fresh school supplies and new shoes and clothes. All the things she'd taken for granted as just the way you lived.

The way things were.

It had only been when she'd met Gray that her eyes had opened in ways she'd never expected.

Where their initial conversations had been about their interests and observations about things at school, she'd been struck the day she'd sat down with him on their break at their vet job to eat lunch and he hadn't had anything.

"Aren't you hungry?"

"Nah, I'm good." He sat across from her and

stretched out his long legs to the side of the small break room table.

"You sure? I heard your stomach growling earlier when you helped me leash up Mrs. Seiler's sheepdog for grooming."

"I'm good. Really."

She'd grown pretty adept at knowing when to back off. Whether it had come from her own pain in losing her mother and being with people who didn't know how to hold their comments or just an innate sense of not wanting to intrude on others, she had no idea, but she usually left people alone, no matter the subject.

But something stuck in her chest.

Hard.

She *had* heard his stomach growl. And she knew he got paid more than she did helping out Doctor Andrews. So why was he being so weird about eating?

Even if she was pretty sure he wasn't eating because he didn't have the money.

Although she'd rapidly lost her own appetite, Harper opened her brown bag and found the sandwich that she'd made that morning and the banana she'd snagged off the counter bowl. And nestled on top of both was her sister's latest creation. Gingerbread.

For all her increasing understanding that something was going on with Gray and his not eating, she obviously hadn't held back the grimace.

"What's wrong?"

"My sister. She's started on her Christmas baking early."

"You don't like baking?"

"I love baking. But I don't like gingerbread." Pulling the offending cookies—beautifully decorated with white icing—out of her bag, she stared down at them.

And for the first time in her life, felt shame.

She had a bag full of food and he had none. And here she was, complaining about the cookies.

"Would you like to try one?"

"After you've given them such a glowing review?"

It was silly and stupid and in the midst of feeling like she had no idea what to say, she knew that he'd found the *exact* right thing to say.

His joke was something that gave them both dignity, and while she had never thought about that before, in that moment she understood it with stark clarity.

"Just because I don't like them doesn't mean they aren't good. I just don't like those fall flavors."

Harper held the bag out to him and watched as he hesitated for the briefest moment before he took one. And then he bit in, taking a big bite of the rounded head, and Harper saw something else.

Something that looked a lot like relief.

"They're delicious."

"If you say so."

"Come on. You're not pumpkin spice obsessed like the rest of the world?"

"You mean that gross stuff they're advertising you can put into your coffee?" She actually felt a small shudder run down her back. "No thank you."

Gray held up the remaining leg of the gingerbread man. "It's good." He popped that last piece in his mouth and chewed. "Really good."

She shoved the bag across the table. "Then you're saving me from lying to my sister. I'll tell her they're delicious."

"But you didn't eat them?"

Now it was her turn to smile. "And now I don't have to."

And he didn't have to go hungry, either.

It had become a game for her, each week what she could find in the house from her sister's devotion to the twin arts of cooking and baking. If Gray knew her plans, he didn't say anything. Instead, she always brought food to work and complained that "Hadley was trying something new out on her and her dad." A few times she even managed to sneak extras for him to take home, when she knew it was something he liked.

In those meals she'd found a way to talk about all the things she didn't have words for. How she felt the first time Hadley made one of their mom's recipes. Or what she really thought about her dad's protests that he wasn't going to start dating again. Or even what she didn't want to

eat for Thanksgiving since it was the holiday that
made her miss her mom the most, even more than
Christmas, and wasn't that weird?

"Harper?" Hadley's smile was kind, but it was
hard to miss the concern in her gaze. "You okay?"

"I am."

"You looked like you went somewhere for a
minute. A few minutes, actually."

"I did. There are a lot of memories here."
Harper looked around before returning her gaze
to Hadley's. "More than I realized, I guess."

"You doing okay with it?"

The urge to brush off the question was strong,
but this was her sister. Hadley had been there for
her through the breakup and all the years since.
And she at least deserved an honest answer.

"I think so."

"I think that's what's hard about small towns."

"What do small towns have to do with it?"

Without missing a beat, Hadley pointed out the
front window to the small shop across the street.
"Right there. Mom used to take us for ice cream
after ballet and it's why I won't serve any here.
I won't take a single bit of the Parkers' business
away from them, and I stock their cards on the
counter and have all the servers encourage people
to head there for a scoop."

"That's nice."

"It's also a memory. One I have every time I
come here."

"But that's a good thing."

"When the memory's good. But it's hard to live

inside a postage stamp when the memories aren't so great." Hadley's voice lowered, their conversation just for the two of them. "I am so happy you're back. But I'm also aware that it means you have to see Gray. That you have to confront those memories. If I'm pushing too hard or making too many impromptu dinner plans, you need to tell me."

"Is this about last night?"

"No." Hadley shook her head, her green eyes wide before her mouth curved in a distinctly sheepish smile. "Yeah. Zack might have mentioned last night that I laid it on a bit thick with the family dinner and the invitation to Gray."

Anger sparked, quick and sudden, and Harper held up a hand. "He's your friend. And he's always welcome at your house. In your home. Don't change that because of me."

"I won't. I mean, I'm not. But—" Her sister broke off, before seeming to press on, shifting tacks. "I could have waited at least a day. Or two. Or even a week. You just got here and you were stuck having a big, loud family dinner."

"I'm not part of the family?"

"Of course you are. I just mean with Gray, too."

"Don't change your life because of me."

When Hadley looked about to argue, Harper rushed on. "I mean it. Whatever happened all those years ago between Gray and I? It's over. Water under the bridge. And I didn't come back here to make anyone feel awkward or bad."

"I'm trying to apologize, Harper. For being shortsighted and overbearing."

"You weren't. I mean, you aren't." Harper shook her head. *God*, why was this so hard? These weird emotional land mines that seemed to pop up without warning. She'd braced herself for the possibility that it might happen, coming back home for an extended stay.

She'd just never expected it from her own sister.

GRAY CONSIDERED THE leftovers waiting for him at the house as he made the last turn onto Main Street and felt something restless spike in his gut. He'd gotten over whatever that weird feeling was when Hadley laid half a freezerful of leftovers on him. He'd even brought the desserts into his practice, earning him serious points with his small staff before they'd all headed out for a busy day.

So why was he still smarting from that strange sensation that had come over him?

He wasn't some bachelor charity case.

Which made the fact that he was considering a banana split for dinner slightly laughable, but true. Especially when he calculated the chocolate shake he wanted on the side.

It wasn't the sort of meal he made a habit of, but he'd had a busy day and he could use the sugar boost. The calf Zack had been waiting on finally made its arrival, along with two others at Wayne and Sons around six this morning. After wrapping up there, he'd headed a few towns over to take care of an aging mare with a disjointed hip.

When it was clear her prognosis was an end to her long life—his most hated job as a vet—he'd done the sad work and then left a grieving family to their pain. He'd then wrapped up what felt like an endless day by heading toward the outskirts of Bozeman to evaluate one of the horses he was considering for his rescue.

So yeah, he'd earned the sweet treat.

He found a spot a few doors down and parked his truck, the gleaming lights of the Trading Post shining as he got out and walked toward the ice-cream shop, Parkers' Parlor. The Trading Post was yet one more of Hadley's projects that had turned into another beacon of prosperity on the main drag of Rustlers Creek. People came from shockingly far away to go to her shop. It gleamed like a bright jewel and had already added to the success of the other businesses in town as a result.

Apparently, once people visited the Trading Post and ate a meal in the café, they spilled out and pressed on through the town Hadley loved so much. A small wine bar had opened in time for Valentine's Day and a new B and B was set to open on the town square come June. There was even talk of a new restaurant going into the old abandoned mill at the opposite end of Main Street that would provide a new fine dining option in a town known more for its bar with peanut shells on the floor than epicurean fare.

The Cowgirl Gourmet had put her stamp on her hometown and they were all prospering for it.

Which made the sight of a head bent over a

small dish of ice cream through the window of Parkers' a gut punch he wasn't expecting.

What was Harper doing here?

He scanned quickly but didn't see anyone else he knew, most specifically her sister and brother-in-law or any of the varied members of Zack's extended family. To the best of his knowledge she was staying over at Zack and Hadley's. Was she taking in the sights by herself? Late in the day, no less?

Since his stomach had long since moved from growling to actively bulldozing itself in an attempt to find sustenance, he kept with his plan and walked into the ice-cream parlor. And was immediately assailed with the rich scents of vanilla, sugar and heavy cream.

There were a few people scattered around at the small tables, but Parkers' was pretty empty for a school night.

"Hey, Gray! What can I get you?"

Dusty Parker had been serving ice cream since Gray was a boy, probably longer. Gray had seldom had the treat when he was a kid, ice cream an indulgence Burt McClain wasn't fond of, therefore no one else needed to have any of it, least of all his son. It was only once he had a bit of money in his pocket that his old man wasn't swiping away that he managed to get a treat from time to time.

"Hey, Dusty. Banana split and a chocolate milkshake."

Dusty nodded, clearly in full understanding of the restorative properties of the desserts he served. "Heard you had a rough afternoon out at the Becker property."

"Not as hard as the Beckers," Gray said, touched at Dusty's easy sympathy.

"Go on and take a seat and I'll bring everything out to you."

Gray did as he'd been told, heading for Harper's table. Her gaze was still on her ice cream, just as he'd seen her outside the window, and something struck him as he had a quick moment to take her in without her knowing.

She was still the woman he remembered. Her pretty, petite features, offset by rich hazel eyes, lush lips and a chin that was slightly too square. It was that square chin that had added to her beauty, counterbalancing those pixie features in a way that sculpted her face into something strong and winsome instead of something too delicate to be worth someone's attention.

Even as he saw the woman he remembered, he saw the changes, too. A decade had aged her, refining her features into those of an adult woman. There was a sharper aspect to her cheekbones, the cheeks below hollowing a bit with the fading of her younger self.

And as he stood there and stared, seeing the woman *and* the girl who'd lived in his memories for so long, he couldn't remember ever thinking she was more beautiful.

She didn't have Hadley's celebrity looks—that sort of polish that shone under lights. Instead, Harper Allen had something he'd always found deeper and more compelling. Something that spoke of mysteries and layers, a puzzle he'd never quite figure out.

It should be frustrating, that lack of fully knowing, but it was intriguing, instead.

And for a time, it was a puzzle he'd had all to himself.

Aware he'd stared a few beats too long, Gray closed the rest of the distance to the table. "Mind if I join you?"

Harper looked up, the thoughts that had obviously kept her occupied and oblivious to the noise in the ice-cream parlor fading. "Gray. Hi. Sure."

She scrabbled to pick up the small service napkins littered on the table, creating a place for him. "What are you doing here?"

"Having dinner."

That slight hazing of her gaze was back, only this time he saw the confusion. "Dusty serves food now?"

"No." He had no idea why but a strong, cheerful smile seemed to spread of its own accord. "I'm just eating like the five-year-old I try to hide inside."

"I'm impressed you *can* eat like the hidden five-year-old inside. Mine is always quite persistent that she can handle it, then makes me regret it all evening."

He patted his stomach, that smile still tugging at his lips. "Mine's easily subdued with a chocolate milkshake."

It was a ridiculous conversation, but it somehow eased them into things and gave Gray the opening he needed to find out why she was there by herself. "What are you doing in town? I thought you were staying out at Zack and Hadley's."

"I am. I just—" Her gaze drifted to the Trading Post, its lights visible through Parkers' front windows, before shifting back to him. "Hadley had a few things to do across the street and when she mentioned how we used to come here as kids I decided to come over for a scoop."

"Everything okay?"

"Everything's fine."

Since it was quite obvious everything wasn't fine, he considered how to play the moment when Dusty bustled over with his banana split and chocolate milkshake. "I brought extra spoons," Dusty said, his face set in innocent lines Gray didn't buy for a minute.

"Thanks, Dusty, but I have my ice cream," Harper said.

Dusty let out a hard "pshaw" before pointing toward her dish. "You had one scoop of chocolate. That's hardly a filling treat."

"Why does everyone push food on me?" Her comment was low and Gray didn't miss that Harper had waited to make it until Dusty was well out of earshot.

"Food is love and all that?" Gray pushed his banana split toward the center of the table, its wide dish dwarfing her half-eaten chocolate dish. "And Dusty is right. That small dish really is a crime against humanity."

"It's a treat."

"Do like I do and make it a meal." He reached for one of the spoons, handing it over. "Here."

She took the proffered utensil and he was absurdly pleased to see the smile edge her lips. Gray let her go first, even more pleased when she took a real spoonful, laden with ice cream, banana and whipped cream.

"Mmm. That's good," she said after she swallowed and Gray reached for his own bite, his growling stomach audible at the table.

"Sorry."

"Eat." She waved a hand. "Long day?"

He considered his response around his first bite of banana split, not wanting to share sadness amidst the sweet, but ended up going for the facts. "Longer and, unfortunately sadder, than I'd expected."

"Oh, I'm sorry. You had to put an animal down?"

"Yes. The Beckers' twenty-two-year-old mare. She had a great life, but—"

"But it was time." She reached across and laid a hand over his. "I'm sorry."

The casual movement—one that was done so easily—caught him off guard, and he stared down at their hands. It was care, so simply given, and in it he saw a power he never expected.

And support he'd never received before after a long day of work.

"Thank you."

Seemingly flustered as she saw his gaze so

firmly locked on their joined hands, she picked up her spoon once more.

Still deeply touched by the gesture, he sought to smooth out that sudden awareness of each other.

"It wasn't all bad, though. I also saw the first horse I'm going to bring to my rescue."

"Really?" That hazel gaze lit up, her quick interest adding the smooth he'd gone for. "What is its situation?"

"He's a former racehorse. A quarter horse who's been stabled near Bozeman. He's had a pretty good life best I can see in an examination, but he had an accident that took him off the track about a year ago and he's been blind ever since."

"Who has him now?"

"The stables who've raised him are committed to very ethical practices with their animals, but they heard about what I'm building and would like him to have a better life. One that's a bit calmer than the excitement around a racing stable."

"He'll be a good horse to start with. It sounds like it might be easier on your staff to learn and build their skills with a horse that has had his type of training, too."

Gray was impressed with how quickly she'd keyed in on his very thought process. "That's what I'm hoping."

"Do you have staff yet?"

"I've been interviewing interns from the University of Montana. I also have several high school students who work with me at my practice after school and as their summer jobs. Three of them have expressed an interest in working with me at the rescue. But I still need to find a program lead." He smiled, thinking of his own high school job. "One that's not driven by the start of football season."

"Have you thought about Ms. Delaney?"

"The gym teacher?"

"Yeah. My dad mentioned she was retiring. I'm almost positive she was an equestrian in college." Harper considered her spoon, remembering the conversation she'd had with her father about people around town she might remember. "Like Olympic level."

"There's no way it would be that easy."

She shrugged before sneaking another bite. "Maybe it can be."

Gray remembered their gym teacher, but not well. A vague memory of a tall, regal-looking woman filled his mind's eye but that was about all he could muster. "If she just retired, do you really think she wants a full-time job?"

"Wouldn't you retire as fast as humanly possible when working with hormonal teenagers?"

"Fair point. Though, if I'm honest"—he scooped up another bite—"I get all those hormones myself in my summer and after-school workers. Most are pretty well-behaved."

"Um, maybe because you're paying them."

Once again, she hit the mark dead-on, that

ever-perceptive and rational nature of hers cutting to the heart of the matter.

"I'll call your dad and get her number."

When she only nodded around a mouthful of sundae, he decided to go for broke.

"You've helped me so I'd like to do the same."

"For what?"

"What had you so upset when I walked in?"

"I wasn't upset, per se." She waved a spoon to stop the argument she clearly saw brewing in his eyes. "Really, I wasn't. I had a conversation with Hadley that unsettled me. Hence each of us going to our separate corners for an hour and my decision to linger over my problems with sugar."

"What unsettled you then?"

"Being home is a lot. On top of starting a business and quitting my job."

"Okay. I see that."

"And then Hadley started in on this whole thing about being sorry she tossed a family dinner at me my first night here and it just made me feel—"

When she stopped, obviously searching for the right word, he gently asked, "Was the fight about me?"

"It wasn't a fight."

"Was the *unsettling conversation*," he amended, "about me?"

"Yes and no."

"Well, what was it? Yes or no?"

"Hadley made it about you but I said it wasn't."

"So what was it about?"

Harper set her spoon down, her gaze roaming around Parkers' before drifting to the window and the lights of town beyond.

"Here, Gray. I'm home. Hadley thinks she knows what that's like or what it's all about for me, but she doesn't know. I left. I made a life for myself. I moved past it all. And now I've tucked my tail between my legs and slunk home."

"Do you really feel that way?"

That hazel gaze that had haunted him for nearly half his life stole his breath as it slammed into his. "That's exactly how it feels."

Chapter 4

Why had she gone there?

What crazy, mad, sugar-fueled demon had perched on her shoulder and allowed those words to come out of her mouth?

Harper stared down at the nearly depleted bowl of banana split between them and knew it was a cop-out to blame her sudden rush of honesty on dessert.

Or dinner, as it might be.

She was mad and upset and unsettled and still sporting a serious case of embarrassment that Hadley would think she couldn't invite a family friend over for fear it would make Harper feel bad.

And *yes*, she and Gray had history.

And *yes*, it was nice of her sister, putting her first.

But seriously?

Was she so badly off that she couldn't be in the same room with a man she hadn't exchanged more than fifty words with in over a decade?

The worst part was, she couldn't actually tell Gray any of that for fear of embarrassing him and making him feel weird when he was at the ranch. Which only added to this—oh God, was she actually going to say it again?—*unsettling* morass of feelings that kept swirling and didn't seem to have any place to land.

And which also reinforced the fact that she really didn't want to tell him for fear it would ruin this lovely flow of conversation they still seemed able to fall right back into.

And hadn't she missed it?

For all they'd been to each other and all they'd shared—and incendiary chemistry had always been high on her list—they'd had other aspects of their relationship, too.

It wasn't all naked hot sex, though now that she thought about it, she had to admit that she'd been diligently avoiding thinking just how nicely he'd filled out. He'd never been small, even in high school, but what had been a large, almost awkward frame had sprouted muscles that covered every inch of him. She'd had a sense of that when their relationship had progressed into something more mature after she came home from college, but even then, he still hadn't hit his full adult frame.

But here?

Now?

Wow, she had to admit his work uniform of jeans and button-down shirt did an easy job of showing off all that solid strength.

And with it, came the memories of the way those broad shoulders felt as they flexed beneath her hands. How that already deep voice grew low and husky when his lips were pressed up against her ear. How those long, clever fingers knew just where to touch to drive her crazy.

They'd had all that, once.

And now that she was home, it was all so close to the surface.

So really, Hadley could just cut her a damn break. How else was she supposed to feel?

Especially when she knew, down to the very depths of her toes, that she didn't come home to rekindle a romance. Her life and her business were in Seattle. Gray McClain was here, and he was sitting on a new land purchase and an expanding business that verified that fact.

Besides, they'd had something once. A real something that he'd walked away from. She had no business—Harper doubled down in her mind, amping up on the reserves of resistance she'd need for the next few months—going anywhere near those feelings for him that were so easy to conjure up.

To remember.

They might still have pieces of those kids who'd found understanding in one another all those years ago, but they'd had plenty of time since to become adults who had nothing in common, and worse, no common ground to build on.

"I'm sorry it was unsettling."

"Thanks. I'm over it. Or am getting close to it with all this sugar flooding my veins in a happy rush. Besides, Hadley and I usually have a fight around day three anyway."

"You do?"

"Hell yes. It takes that long for each of us to fully retreat to our respective corners and sibling hierarchy. We'll fuss at each other, get over it and move on."

"That seems very mature of you."

"A lovely thing to say, since not more than fifteen minutes ago I was mentally sticking my tongue out at her each time I looked at the Trading Post through the window."

"I bet you looked cute doing it."

As flirtatious comments went, his was hardly a bomb to the hormones, but Harper felt it all the same. That steady awareness of one another that never fully faded.

With the reality of that hanging heavy over her—oppressively, really—she gently wiped her lips and set her napkin down on the table. "I should be going. A good pout is acceptable but hiding out from my sister isn't."

He stood along with her, a gentleman to the core, and Harper again felt that rush of hormones as his fingers touched her shoulder where he helped her shrug into her coat.

"Thanks for the ice cream, Gray."

He'd stepped back as soon as he'd helped her into her coat, but now as they stood there, he reached out and settled a hand on her forearm. Despite the thick down of her jacket, she felt that touch like a brand over her skin.

"Thanks for sharing dinner with me. The Beckers' mare was weighing more heavily than I realized. I appreciate having someone to talk to."

"Of course."

It was a simple matter to accept the thanks. To say goodbye and leave the shop. To cross out into the early spring cold and walk away after a conversation with a friend.

So why were her steps so heavy as she trudged back to the Trading Post, unwilling to turn back to look at the solitary figure sitting alone in the window?

MARTIN ALLEN CONSIDERED himself an uncomplicated man. He'd married young, to the love of his life. He'd raised two beautiful daughters. And he'd been an educator for his entire adult life, which meant he spent his days around children in an environment where they showed both the best and worst sides of themselves on a regular basis.

So when he'd woken up at fifty-eight and wondered what the hell he was going to do with himself for the rest of his life, it had caught him by surprise.

He'd had more than two decades to make peace with the idea that he wasn't going to grow old with Maria. And if his emotions on that subject weren't always peaceful, time had shifted them to a place of acceptance.

His girls were thriving. Hadley's life continued to amaze him in ways he never could have imagined. He had a famous child—he smiled at the thought and imagined how tickled Maria would have been at the very idea. While Hadley's success was something he was proud of, her ability to keep her priorities in check and always in place glossed that pride to a high sheen. He'd always believed it, but the troubles she and Zack had survived the past winter—and a lot longer, he'd found out after she'd finally come to talk to him about it all—had proven she knew what was most important in life.

Everything else, all the fuss and trappings, and yes, he acknowledged, genuine *fame*, added those extra moments to life that made it sparkle and shine, but which weren't the keys to happiness.

And wasn't that the root of his concern for Harper?

He was so proud of his baby. Her work in Seattle had produced amazing things. She even carried part credit on a virtual reality teaching device that was training surgeons with a degree of precision so accurate they could mimic the work of microvascular surgery in a skills lab. For all his own knowledge and his twelve years teaching science before moving into an administrative position, he only understood about half of what Harper said in any given conversation. A fact that also polished his pride to a high gloss.

And now he had her home.

And while he'd suspected she had gone to Seattle all those years ago to both advance her career and to find herself, now that she was home, he was worried she'd never discovered the latter to her needed satisfaction.

Was it losing Maria at such a young age?

No matter how much he'd tried to be there for his girls, no amount of understanding or attention or affection could change the fact that they'd lacked a mother during their teen years. For all the joy and sadness the three of them had shared, it had always hurt him, in a place he buried deep, that they'd had to do it all without Maria.

A somber fact that all the scientific knowledge in the world couldn't change.

And then there'd been Gray.

Martin and Maria had met, fallen in love and married young so he'd had no reason to question when his girls found serious relationships at a young age. But his father's heart had always clutched a bit harder when Harper would talk about Gray McClain.

Martin had no issue with the boy, his hard work and ethical behavior a standout among the young men who attended Rustlers Creek High School. But as a school administrator, Martin knew the kids who came from trouble. And Burt McClain wore the moniker like a badge.

Martin had mitigated his own natural tendencies to paint Gray with the same brush, well aware he wasn't in a position to change the boy's home life but that he wasn't going to judge him for it, either.

Which had made Gray's ultimate decision to end his relationship with Harper, long after his father's influence should have mattered, a disappointment.

Something else he'd have discussed with Maria if he could. Something he did discuss with her, late at night, in the conversations he still carried on in his head with his late wife.

And wasn't that part of the wondering, too?

Here he was, a widower since he was in his late thirties, and he was still talking to his dead wife. While a big part of him hoped that never changed—he'd loved Maria with everything he was and all he'd hoped to be—the cold fact was that he'd lived two decades without her. And, if his latest doctor's visit was any indication, he had several more to go in that same state.

He was grateful for his health, but he increasingly wondered what he was going to do with all that robust, teeming-with-life health the doctor was so proud of.

It helped—he smiled to himself—that he regularly took the rich, fat-laden casseroles Hadley insisted on giving him to work. Cheese, mayonnaise and about an acre of Tater tots did a body a lot better when spread around to share with others.

And still . . .

He was lonely.

It was the elephant in the room that he didn't want to acknowledge, but it was there all the same. Taking up far too much space and air.

He snagged a beer from the fridge, glancing at the top shelf—yep, another casserole was tucked in there—and closed the door without inspecting the contents. He loved his daughter to distraction, but she really needed to lay off the food. Since filming for her show would be starting up in about six weeks, he knew the steady brigade of meals would slow down as well, and he couldn't believe he was counting down the days. It was a loving gesture and he loved Hadley for it, but it would be nice to . . .

Shaking his head, Martin admitted the real problem. It wasn't his daughter and it wasn't the food deliveries. It was him.

And his elephant.

The doorbell echoed from the front of the house and, intrigued, he set down his beer and headed toward the front door, opening it to find Gray McClain standing on his porch.

"Gray."

"Mr. Allen." Gray nodded his head.

"It's Martin. Marty," he amended as he extended the door to allow the man in. "Come on in."

Gray came into the house, his bearing formal and stiff, and without warning Martin remembered the way the poor guy used to suffer when he came to pick up Harper. No matter how many times he'd told the young man that to call him by his first name, he was never anything but Mr. Allen.

It was a sign of respect and he could hardly argue with it. But there was something in that stiff, almost regal bearing that had always tugged at Martin, too. He'd spent his entire life around kids, and he always recognized the ones who had to grow up too fast.

Gray McClain had always fit that bill.

"I'm sorry to bother you, but I was hoping you could help me with something."

They'd exchanged basic pleasantries the other night at Hadley's, and Gray hadn't said anything then, so he was intrigued by the request. "I was just contemplating dinner. You want to join me for a beer and whatever it is Hadley stuffed in my fridge this afternoon while I was at school?"

Gray's grin was lopsided and a little sheepish. "Please take this the right way, because your daughter's cooking is amazing, but she sure does feed a lot of people. I still have leftovers from dinner the other night."

Martin slapped Gray on the shoulder before gesturing him back to the kitchen. "A fact I was just thinking about myself. Come on—we'll see what we've got, and if it doesn't suit, we'll call out for pizza."

AN HOUR LATER, with a loaded pizza nearly demolished on the table between him and Martin

Allen, Gray popped the top off a fresh beer. He'd only had one so far, but it had been an oddly pleasant hour to share a beer and a pizza with a man he'd always been slightly intimidated by.

A reality that had everything to do with him, and nothing to do with the man sitting opposite him.

"Your latest crop of 4-H students are showing a lot of promise," Gray said around a swallow of his beer. "Decker Nelson is clearly following in his father's footsteps. His love of the animals is bone-deep and he's got a maturity to him that's hard to beat."

"He doesn't know it yet, but I just recommended him for Montana State's Animal & Range Sciences program." Marty smiled. "The kid's got a bright future and I think he's a shoo-in for a scholarship."

"If I can add any weight to that, please let me know."

Marty nodded before patting his stomach, all while eyeing the last piece of pizza. "Wow, that was good."

"I won't tell Hadley." Gray smiled.

"I owe you two sets of thanks, then. One for Decker and one for keeping my secret."

They sat in companionable conversation for a few more minutes, lamenting spring training for baseball season and the upcoming NFL draft, before Martin circled back to the reason for his visit. "You said you needed my help. What can I do for you?"

"I'm not sure you know, but I'm opening my

own animal rescue. A focus on blind horse rescues, specifically, but I'll likely take on a bit
broader remit once we're up and running."

"It's good work. Needed work," Marty added.

"I think so, but it's proving a bit harder to staff
than I expected. I was talking to Harper last
night, and she suggested the gym teacher who
just retired."

If Martin Allen had any reaction to the fact
Gray had spoken with Harper, he didn't show it,
but Gray felt the hole open in his gut all the same.
Although he and Marty had always had a cordial
relationship, Gray's work with the Wayne ranch
ensuring they saw each other from time to time,
he knew that his relationship with Harper had
left a mark.

Hadley had found a way past it, keeping that
steady cordiality between them that never suggested she harbored any ill will against him.

With the town's most respected man and be-
loved principal, Gray hadn't been quite so sure.

"You mean Jacqueline Delaney. She did retire,
just at Christmas."

"I wasn't so sure she'd want to go back to work
after retiring, but Harper was persistent. Said you
never know."

Again, Gray wanted to bang his head against
the table for mentioning Harper again, but he
needed to keep the conversation as level and easy
as possible.

"It's a good idea, especially because she retired

early. Said that the kids deserved a younger teacher for gym. The woman's in better shape than most thirty-year-olds, but we respected her wishes." Marty reached for his beer, considering the label. "It's been a loss for the school, but this could be a great option for you. I'd prefer to call her and ask her permission first, before sharing her number, if you don't mind."

"I'd appreciate that. And I understand your needing to ask her first."

"So, you saw Harper?"

If he thought he was getting off easy with a shared pizza and a phone number, Gray realized with considerable chagrin, he was out of luck.

"I did."

"That didn't take long."

Marty was direct, a trait Gray always associated with the man. A sort of level honesty few people seemed capable of giving to others.

"I stopped into Parkers' last night for dinner on my way home."

"Dusty's serving dinner now?"

"Nope just ice cream." If he was sporting a bit of embarrassment about Marty's direct questions, he might as well go for broke. "Clearly I'm on a streak this week. Ice cream last night and pizza tonight. All I need are corn dogs and cotton candy tomorrow night and I'll complete the eight-year-old food Olympics.

"Harper was in there getting a scoop when I stopped in and we talked for a few minutes."

Since he was already in the thick of things, Gray pressed on. "I know she deserves better than the likes of me. That's why I walked away all those years ago, and I'm not going back on that, sir. I wouldn't do that to her."

He sat uncomfortably under the other man's perusal, Martin Allen's gaze as direct as Harper's and equally unwavering. Gray didn't see any judgment, but he knew it had to be lurking in there somewhere. Burt McClain and anything that touched him left a measure of stink no one could fully ignore.

Which meant it was time to take his leave.

"I appreciate the dinner and your time. But I'll let you get back to your evening."

Marty nodded and stood, walking him back to the front door. The silence was oddly heavy. It was only as they got to the open door that Marty spoke.

"I lost my wife a long time ago, so I never had a chance to discuss our adult daughters with her. But I think I speak for both of us when I say this."

As endorsements went, Gray figured it meant something if Martin referenced his late wife, even as he puzzled at the reference.

"The likes of you, Gray McClain, best as I've always been able to tell, are the makings of a good and decent man."

Gray shook Martin Allen's offered hand, grateful for the words but unable to let them lie. "The name McClain doesn't mean much here in Rustlers Creek. The name Allen does. Please know I mean what I said."

The door closed at his back and Gray couldn't shake the subtle sense of disappointment drifting through from the other side.

Chapter 5

Harper considered her notes on the proper water temperature for steaming milk, adding it into a string of code she was playing with on customizing lattes. While there were a lot of elements she was willing to alter in the hunt for the perfect custom brew, she'd decided early on there were some areas she didn't want to change.

The milk in a perfect latte was steamed to 140 to 145 degrees Fahrenheit. Coffee brewed between 195 and 205. Not only didn't it make sense to alter those elements, but she risked fundamentally altering a recipe in a way that was just bad, not custom, if she played with function over form.

Hadley might have several tricks up her sleeve to create a perfect meal or dessert, but Harper and her father had lived through a lot of experimentation on her sister's journey to becoming the Cowgirl Gourmet. Eggs cooked at a certain temperature. Milk scalded at another. Chocolate melted at yet another.

Some things you just didn't change.

Sort of like her and Gray.

The thought snuck in as she keyed in a few lines of code, so forcefully out of sync with her work that she had to reread her inputs a few times to make sure she'd captured her intentions correctly.

It had been a week since their discussion over ice cream, and she'd yet to come to any sense of equilibrium over the time they'd spent together. So she'd done what she always did when she couldn't get her head in order.

Work.

Which was a funny thought because she'd always found a degree of fun in her work that never made it feel like drudgery. She did something she loved and was fortunate enough to have a skill that was in constant demand.

Which was also a strange complement to her and Gray, if she were honest.

His love of animals and his skill in caring for them had ensured he was always employed. Sometimes for long hours and at the expense of his personal time, as their ice-cream shop meeting last week had suggested. But she'd met few people in her life who took their work as seriously as he did.

Hadn't that been one of the most difficult things to understand about their breakup?

He'd claimed that there was just too much of Burt McClain in him to have a successful relationship, and Harper knew the opposite to be true. Gray *wasn't* his father. Nor was he like the man who'd thought it okay to take his son's earnings, all while starving him in the process.

And even if she took his emotions at face value—feelings that might not be rational but were real all the same—she couldn't deny there was so much more to what they had than young, ill-advised lust.

Their relationship hadn't just been a passionate force in her life. They'd had a true bond, created over mutual interests and attraction, before they'd been in a position to act on it. Instead of something created out of heat, they'd had to create something *over* all that banked heat. A way of building intimacy that wasn't about the physical.

It was ground she had trod over and over through the years, wondering in her quiet moments—the ones where she allowed herself to remember—where they went wrong.

"Just remember, they call it salted earth for a reason."

"What's that?"

Harper let out a small squeak—at the interruption and the embarrassment of being overheard—when she turned to find Zack's sister, Charlotte, standing behind her with a broad smile on her face.

On a squeal, Harper got up from where she'd

settled herself at Hadley's kitchen table to greet one of her oldest friends. "Hey there!"

Charlotte's embrace was warm and welcoming, her tall, lithe form chic and enviably slim beneath Harper's hold. "Oh, it is so good to see you. I've missed you so much. And we didn't get nearly enough time at dinner last week to catch up."

"Right back at you. Although"—Harper stepped back but kept Charlotte's hands in hers—"if I didn't love you so much, I'd be massively jealous at how Armani looks draped over five feet ten inches of gorgeous."

A light blush tinged Charlotte's cheeks. "I work in PR. And whether or not it should be this way, the outfit is at least half the message."

"Nah, I don't think so. Your words are the message. You just keep everyone's attention when you say them."

That blush deepened before Charlotte dropped into a chair at the table. "Aren't you sweet? Especially on a day when not a single word out of my mouth seemed to persuade anyone to do anything I wanted them to."

"That's why I like my computer. It doesn't talk back."

"From what I hear, you've got the mad skills to make it talk back. In a variety of languages, no less."

It was Harper's turn to blush and she took the seat beside Charlotte and closed her laptop lid. "Not today. And since I've been staring at that screen since noon"—she glanced at her watch, horrified to realize it was nearly five and she hadn't noticed—"I need to get out with a friend. You game?"

"Exactly what I was hoping for when I drove over. You up for an evening at the Branded Mark?"

"Do peanut shells belong on floors?"

"They do at the Branded Mark. Besides, I'm hungry for one of their burgers."

"You look like that and you eat burgers? Seriously, if I didn't love you, I'd hate you."

Charlotte's quick grin was a match for one Harper had seen through the years on her brother-in-law's face. "Then I'm getting extra fries."

"Bitch."

"Yes, I know. It's a tough job but someone's got to do it. Which also gives me the perfect opportunity to ask you what ground you've been salting."

"Oh, I—"

Harper knew their banter was nothing but fun—and if there was anyone she could share her earlier thoughts with, it was Charlotte—but she held back.

As to why . . . Harper resolved to think about that later.

"Just complaining at my computer and, in this case, glad it can't talk back."

Charlotte accepted the excuse with a simple "Okay," and Harper wondered why she suddenly felt guilty for lying. A question she was still asking herself a half hour later as they walked into the Branded Mark.

She was entitled to her own thoughts. Even if they were circular and endlessly unhelpful to either her peace of mind or her ability to find some equilibrium now that she was back home. And just because the denizens of Rustlers Creek—her sister's sister-in-law especially—knew Harper's history with Gray didn't mean she had to put it on display.

Even as a small voice gnawed at her to say something. To share the details of her conversation with Gray over ice cream.

They found some empty seats near the dance floor after Charlotte had navigated several hellos and quick conversations on the way to their table. Harper recognized a few people but realized that more faces seemed to belong to strangers.

Had she been gone so long she couldn't remember the people she grew up with?

Charlotte set her menu down. "I don't know why I'm even looking. I'm still having that burger I was thinking about back at the house."

"We'll make it two."

"Good. Then I can ask you my question." Charlotte leaned forward over the table. "I might be ignoring the overheard complaints you tossed at your computer back at the house but I'm not ignoring that look on your face. What has you looking so sad?"

"Is it that obvious?"

"No." Charlotte smoothed a hand over the cover of her menu. "And to be fair, *sad* isn't quite the right word. But you're more reserved than

I've seen you before. Which leads me to ask what has you upset."

"Being home is—" Harper folded her own menu, tracing the impression of the words *Branded Mark* in the cover. "Home has more memories than I think I was ready for."

"It's hard to stay and it's hard to come home. Irony at its finest."

It wasn't what Harper had expected, especially knowing Charlotte had started her own PR firm a few years back. "You want to leave?"

"Not leave, not really." Their server set down the beers they'd ordered on their way to the table, and Charlotte diverted their conversation in favor of ordering. It was only when their waitress was heading back to the kitchen that Charlotte picked up the thread. "It's just that not much changes in a place where everyone knows you, even including something dumb you did in grade school."

Harper had a vague recollection of something silly Charlotte had done on Valentine's Day when they were in elementary school but wasn't able to conjure it up from the recesses of her memory. She nearly asked before something held her back.

Hadn't she felt everyone's eyes on her for the past week since arriving in Montana? Worse, weren't those gazes extra sharp when it came to how she'd react to Gray?

For some reason, traipsing down that road for Charlotte felt like she was prying.

So she opted to ignore fourth grade politics in favor of commiserating with her friend. "That's the strange thing, though. Life, experiences, the world around us. It all changes every day. I think those changes are just harder to see when you're in the middle of them."

"I guess you're right. Hadley and Zack almost lost their marriage because of not seeing those changes."

Harper was struck by how similar Charlotte's thoughts on Hadley and Zack's marriage were to her own, but was prevented from saying something as their waitress set down their plates. After she left Harper used the change in topic to dive in. "Can I ask you something about that?"

Charlotte dipped a fry in ketchup. "Sure."

"I realize it's their marriage and all. And they're entitled to their privacy. But did it bother you any that Zack didn't confide in you?"

"Yes!" Charlotte pointed a finger before reaching for another fry. "And sort of no. But that's a brother-sister dynamic. And one that has five years between us, too. Does it bother you Hadley didn't say anything?"

"*Bother* is a harsh word." Harper looked down at her own plate, toying with the lettuce leaf she'd set to the side. "It's not my business, and I really do mean that. But if I'm honest? Yeah, a little bit. More because I had no idea my own sister was so unhappy for so long.

"I'm so glad they've fixed their problems and are focused on their future, truly I am. But—"

"But it feels like you missed something. Something big."

"Yes, it does."

It was ridiculous to feel this way. She meant what she'd said—her sister's marriage wasn't her business—but she'd also meant the sentiment that she ached to know Hadley had spent so much time frustrated and miserable in her marriage.

All while she could have been there for her. A supportive force, even if she had no ability to fix the problem.

Nor did she have a right to butt in.

A fact she kept reminding herself every time her pride prickled up at the thought that she'd been in the dark for so long.

"My mom has a saying," Charlotte said. "Little kids, little problems. Big kids, big problems."

"What does she say about adults?"

"That's the thing. To her, we're still the big kids."

"How'd she handle the near breakup between Zack and Hadley?"

"Since she was dealing with my father's antics, I think she was a little preoccupied. But I know it bothered her, too. That they had to go through something so difficult. And that it got as tough as it did there for a while."

Hadley had briefly mentioned the challenges her father-in-law had gone through the prior year. The reality of no longer being able to actively work the ranch from the back of a horse hadn't sat well with Zack and Charlotte's father and he'd made life rather miserable for everyone around them.

Would her father ever do something like that?

Although her dad didn't have the obvious, robust health Charlie Wayne did, he was an active man. He was also one without a life partner facing the later years of life with him. Although she'd always felt weird about the idea of him moving on from her mother, her mom had been gone a long time.

Had she been fair in feeling better about him being alone than being with someone?

Something suspiciously like embarrassment lodged in the middle of her chest. And wasn't that the strangest part about grief? Her mom had been gone for nearly two decades and those swift arrows of heartache could still knock her off-balance.

Not only did she feel off-kilter, but she found an odd echo to the conversation with Charlotte.

Would Hadley have confided in their mother about her marital troubles?

It was something she'd wondered about her own heartache all those years ago. Would it have been easier to bear losing her relationship with Gray, knowing she'd had her mother there to console her?

Much as she'd like to believe things would have been better, if she were honest, Harper knew it wouldn't have helped.

Gray McClain had done a number on her heart.

And while a mother's hug would have comforted in the moment, that blow had been something that simply had to be borne.

It just sucked that she was still bearing up underneath it, even today.

JACQUELINE DELANEY STARED at her cell phone and wondered why she was so nervous. She'd spoken to Martin Allen nearly every day for thirty-two years.

Thirty. Two. Years.

Or at least the days of those years that fell between September and the following June.

She'd only thought about him the rest of the time until school started back up each September.

What could he want? She'd only been gone from the high school for a matter of months. And she left copious notes for the teaching graduate who came in after her. She'd even given enough notice that they'd been able to overlap for several months so the new, perky young gym teacher could get the lay of the land and settle in to her first Montana winter.

It was cold as hell opening the gym each morning when the temperature was hovering around zero and it took a certain amount of fortitude to do it day in and day out. If Jackie were honest, she hadn't necessarily believed Stefani-with-an-*I* could handle it.

But Stefani had been made of far sterner stuff, and Jackie had been forced to change her initial opinion.

Sort of what people did to you when you first arrived?

Fresh off the equestrian circuit following a shot at a gold medal in the '88 Olympics. She'd earned bronze and the achievement of a failed marriage in a span of six months before moving on to the life change of a teaching position at a rural high school, the prize after she came out of competition *and* not-so-wedded-bliss.

It wasn't a decision she regretted. Far from it as it had given her a life and a home in the farther reaches of the Western wilderness. A place she'd believed she'd needed to transplant her Boston blue blood after her debacle of a marriage and the additional humiliation of being cheated on by the scion of one of Boston's oldest families and his best friend from prep school.

A fact that wouldn't make anyone blink in today's times. Hell, Jackie amended, a fact like that wouldn't have sent a well-heeled young man into a fake marriage any longer, either.

Thank God for that.

But in the late eighties, Thornton's sexuality had been a secret. One he'd desperately tried to keep—from her and everyone else. A feat made easier by her competition and travel schedule.

Now, looking back at it at fifty-five, she was forced to admit that she'd built a living for herself, but had she really built a life? She'd dated off and on through the years, never finding quite the right match. The sort of match, she'd imagined, that would make you give up your personal space because having that person in it made the giving up feel like sharing instead.

And she'd never really found that.

She enjoyed men but perhaps her earlier experience had spooked her more than she'd ever wanted to admit. Did she have bad judgment? Had she given off some suggestion that she didn't care about making a life with someone? Having a forever?

Or maybe—as she'd feared once she passed forty and oddly accepted once she passed fifty—she was just not the marrying kind.

Which brought her right back around to Martin. Everyone at the school had called him Marty, but she'd never gotten past their first meeting when he'd bumped into her in the teacher's lounge, introducing himself as Martin Allen, the high school's biology teacher.

He'd been Martin to her ever since.

And since he'd been married and well-known around the school as deeply in love with his wife, she'd kept whatever traitorous thoughts about how attractive he was to herself.

Even if she had wondered for years just how deeply blue his eyes were. Like the edges of a Montana sky in summer, just before the sun dips below the horizon at sunset. Or maybe they were more the color of the Côte d'Azur she'd seen once on a summer vacation. Maybe both were right, since his eyes shifted colors when they were inside at a pep rally or outside on a spring afternoon running field day activities.

But even with all those thoughts and considerations and comparisons, she never breathed a word to anyone. Not before his wife died, not after Maria passed and *really* not after their widowed principal had become something of a fascinating topic of gossip in the teacher's lounge.

Instead, she'd dealt with the strange layer of guilt that had descended after the woman he'd loved so much succumbed to cancer. Surely it was wrong to feel this way about a married man. And then to feel that way about a widowed man with two young daughters.

Even if she had long forgiven Thornton, she'd still borne the pain of being cheated on. And her feelings for Martin Allen had always felt like cheating, too.

Maybe that's why her emotions were upsidedown, and it all felt so stark and surreal to have a message from him with a request to call him back.

What did he want?

His message had been vague. Polite, asking how her retirement was going, before saying that he needed to discuss something with her.

Something?

What something?

She'd only listened to it about fifty times. Maybe sixty. And she still didn't have a clue.

She'd also run out of reasons to ignore the message. Her week-long visit back East with her mother had been dutiful, as always. Rather pointless and still vapid enough to nearly induce head banging against the thick cherry posts of the bed in the room that was still, more than thirty years later, referred to as "Jacqueline's chamber."

Her mother had inquired about her health. Had asked why she'd decided to retire so young. And further asked when she'd be moving back from "that godforsaken hellhole" where she'd chosen to make a life.

Beyond that, their conversation had revolved around the latest charity luncheon her mother had coordinated, the upcoming summer musical program she was chairing for the symphony and a two-week trip to Europe Jackie's parents were planning in the fall. After, of course, all the "horrid tourists" went home.

Since she'd learned about a year after moving to Montana that dwelling on the visits she made back East only left her nasty and irritable, she pushed it all down in a damn fine example of New England stoicism.

She used that same granitelike fortitude to also push down the feelings of unrequited attraction that had swamped her for the past three decades she'd lived in Rustlers Creek.

And hit the number on her phone that belonged to Martin Allen.

GRAY SWUNG INTO the parking lot and out of his truck just as Chance Beaumont pulled up beside him. Despite living on the same piece of property—even if the bank said parts of it now belonged to each of them—Gray had been coming from a long day in the opposite direction. It didn't make any sense to pass downtown to head out to the ranch and then back in again just to drive together.

Besides, as every good single man knew, having access to his own set of wheels was paramount in the never-ending dating game that could be fun at times and a plague at others.

Of late, it had felt decidedly like the plague.

And he couldn't even lay it at Harper's feet.

He'd felt like this before she got home to Rustlers Creek, but her presence certainly hadn't helped his monumentally shitty attitude. Which was why, when he got Chance's text around four that afternoon to see if he wanted to go out, Gray was all in.

He might know everyone in Rustlers Creek, and a Thursday night at the Branded Mark wasn't exactly drawing in crowds of people he didn't know, but at least it was something to do.

Something to take his mind off Harper.

And really something to take his mind off that unnerving conversation he'd had with Marty Allen last week.

I lost my wife a long time ago, so I never had a chance to discuss our adult daughters with her. But I think I speak for both of us when I say this.

The likes of you, Gray McClain, best as I've always been able to tell, are the makings of a good and decent man.

Gray made it a point to live a life above reproach, both because it was how he wanted to behave and because he'd seen a bad enough example in his father.

An example he had zero desire to emulate, repeat or ever be compared to.

But that didn't make him a "good man." Far from it. It made him a man who did what he had to do to get by.

A man who'd once been the boy who'd made his mother leave, well aware of the stink attached to their family name.

"We're better off without her," Burt lamented one night, coming home surprisingly early, even though Gray had figured he wouldn't see him until morning. His father wasn't drunk enough, but he was in a weird, ranty mood.

But at least there was food.

Gray didn't think they were better off, but since his old man had brought him some food from the diner that he was currently shoveling into his mouth as fast as possible, he didn't respond. He knew that look in his father's eye. That tyrannical sense that the whole world had more than him, and therefore Burt McClain was entitled to take whatever he wanted, no matter the price.

He'd done that with Gray's teacher, hadn't he?

Gray had heard it himself. The way Mrs. Hammer complained out in the hallway to another teacher about her parent-teacher conference with the "McClain boy's father" and how he gave her the creeps.

He might be ten, but Gray knew what that meant,

even if he didn't understand all the particulars. But once he'd heard them talking about his creepy father and "what he was possibly teaching that boy," Gray knew he'd had to do something. So he'd told his mother that he hated her and he wanted her to go away. To go far away from them and leave Rustlers Creek.

She was already fragile and he'd found her crying more and more lately. Gray figured if he used nasty words like his father and really pushed it, he could push her over the edge.

Could get her to leave.

So he did it. He yelled and screamed and told her he never wanted to see her. That his life would be better if she went away.

And then one day she was gone.

And no, they weren't better off without her. But she was better off without them, and that was all that mattered.

It was all that still mattered, Gray knew, as he stuffed back down whatever had dredged up one of the worst memories of his life. He *would* shake this off, and he would have a beer with his friend.

"Hey, Doc." Chance greeted him as he swung out of his own truck. The vehicle was polished to a high shine, one more thing he knew about Chance the rest of the town had little understanding of.

About two months after moving in, Gray had headed up to the main house, needing to borrow a few tools Chance had kindly offered as always available to him. He'd seen Chance washing the truck, curious, since the man had done the same a few days prior.

"Dirty already?"

"Not really."

"It's supposed to rain later."

"Heard that." Chance buffed a small spot on the front hood. "But it doesn't matter. A clean truck's a sign of a prosperous man. A dirty one's what my old man drove day after day."

Chance stepped back to peruse his work, and Gray headed off to get the tools, struck once again by the lingering sins of the father.

Realistically, Gray knew he wasn't the only person who had the ripe good fortune of living with bad memories every day. But it was something else when it was advertised up close and personal from someone else. He and Chance hadn't spoken of it again, but the indigo shade of blue on the man's F-150 was always buffed to a high polish. Just like the man's cowboy boots and the fresh haircut he kept in check every other week at the small barbershop a few doors down from the Branded Mark.

Chance Beaumont might be battling back a load of debt on his family ranch, but he wasn't going down without a fight. And he was damned determined to look the part of that prosperous man he so desperately wanted to be.

"Hey, yourself. You ready to get your ass kicked at pool?"

"Aren't you a funny guy? Especially since I'm

planning on drinking for free all evening when I ~~ckin your uoo ut nlnc bull.~~"

It was about as close to insults as either of them got, and Gray felt the stress of the week slide off his shoulders as he headed into the bar with Chance.

A state he should have known was too good to last when he felt Chance stiffen next to him, then stopping as they nearly ran into a group of cowboys forming a large circle at the bar.

But it was only as he followed his friend's gaze that he realized the real reason they'd stopped.

Harper Allen and Charlotte Wayne sat at a table about fifteen feet away.

Chance gathered himself quickly and headed in their direction, Gray reluctantly following. How could he not? The women looked gorgeous in the muted lights of the Branded Mark.

And both looked pissed as hell their party of two was about to double.

Chapter 6

❧❧

Harper fought the shot of excitement that sizzled in her veins as she caught sight of Gray and instead pasted on a careful and slightly disdainful expression as he and Chance Beaumont headed their way. The history between Charlotte and Chance was long and bordered on vaguely silly from time to time, but it was deep-seated and seemingly ageless.

And there was no reason to make more of this than necessary. Chance had only walked over to their table to goad her friend beyond all levels of sanity.

A feat, if she remembered correctly, he managed with a surprising degree of regularity.

Had that continued into adulthood?

Based on the sour look on Charlotte's face, Harper could only assume yes.

Even if their byplay did give her a few moments to consider Gray without Charlotte's laser focus.

He looked good. Tired again, just as she'd seen him last week at Parkers', but good all the same. The darker circles under his eyes didn't diminish the power of all that blue, and she was struck by how electric his gaze looked in the muted lights of the bar.

"Mind if we join you?" Chance's voice was all easygoing twang, but there was a subtle strain under the words.

Was he expecting a no?

"Do we have a choice?" Charlotte shot back, the strain in her voice a match for the lines that fanned out around Chance's eyes.

And then those lines grooved deeper from Chance's quick grin as he ignored the question *and* the lack of welcome. "Excellent." He sat down and swiped a fry off Charlotte's plate in one smooth move that Harper would have called practiced if she didn't notice the way his free hand tapped at the table as he sat down.

For all the years she'd observed Charlotte and Chance together, she'd always assumed it was genuine dislike that kept them at odds.

Was it possible there was something more?

In a somewhat gleeful and definitely relieved moment, Harper had to admit that she didn't feel nearly as exposed by her overheard comment earlier about salted earth. Nor did she feel like she was on quite as much display now that Charlotte was the object of all that attention.

"How are you doing, Harper?" Gray refrained from snatching anything off her plate, his gaze clear and direct before he hitched a thumb at the other two members of their expanded party. "They'll circle each other like dogs for the next ten minutes until Chance's beer takes effect."

Harper couldn't hold back a smile as she took a sip of her own beer. "Is this your opinion as a qualified veterinarian?"

"Oh, most definitely," Gray said in mock seriousness. "And a general observer for more years than I'd like to own."

Harper leaned in closer before she even realized her body's intention. "Do they do this often?"

"Best as I know, not as often as you might think. Charlotte's been pretty busy with her business and Chance spends a lot of time at the ranch."

"We can hear you talking about us," Charlotte shot back across the table.

"Then you know how entertaining you both are," Harper parried, unable to hide the smile at her friend's clear discomfiture. Charlotte Wayne was a beautiful woman, and Harper had observed when they were young how often her friend got hit on by every guy in shouting distance. Harper could only imagine that had gotten impossibly worse as she'd aged into the beauty she was now.

Which made the way she and Chance "circled each other," to borrow Gray's phrase, that much more interesting. Chance didn't fawn over her like the guys Harper had observed in the past. Nor did he puff himself up in her presence. Despite his continued stealing of Charlotte's meal, his conversation was actually quite engaging. And *interested* in what she had to say.

"Heard you snagged that PR job for Foley's Feed."

"Who told you?" Charlotte asked, her tone suspicious as she dipped a fry in ketchup.

"Foley."

"We haven't signed the contract yet."

"Formality," Chance said around a mouthful of half the burger he'd helped himself to.

"You a legal genius now, too?"

"Nope." Chance wiped his mouth on an extra napkin before wiping his hands. "I just know Foley talked to three other PR firms besides yours and said your proposal was the smartest, the most aligned to his brand and the most reasonably priced."

Charlotte was immediately indignant. "I'm not cheap!"

"Reasonable, not cheap. There's a difference."

Since the bell had seemingly rung for round two, Gray pointed to the empty space in front of him. "I'm going to get a beer. Want to come with me?"

Although the show had clearly gotten interesting, Harper was more than ready to leave the two of them to it. "We can get a fresh round for the table."

That same intimacy she'd felt when she'd inadvertently leaned closer to Gray to watch the sparring match persisted, the crowded place-

ment of the tables and the number of people in
the Branded Mark on a Thursday night ensuring
their bodies touched all the way to the bar.

It was . . . nice.

More than nice, actually.

When had she been out last? Really out, just for
a fun evening with friends?

Because whatever else Gray was to her, he
was a friend. Hadn't their easy camaraderie and
the innate way her body knew him when she'd
leaned closer during Charlotte and Chance's argument been proof of that?

*Of course, you don't want to sleep with your other
friends, so maybe you need to figure out a different
definition.*

The thought was sly, swirling through her
mind and shooting sparks through her nerve
endings before Harper could check the impulse.
Or consider the fact that the distinct notes of desire had settled in the wake of those sparks, heavy
and low in the belly and between her thighs.

She did not need sparks with this man. Or
that feminine pull of desire that she'd never been
all that good at controlling around him. *Carnal
knowledge*, that damnable voice whispered again
through her mind.

And like Eve, Adam and the apple, once tasted,
you could never go back.

Using all her mental availability to tamp down
on those feelings, she missed the happy laughter
and quick shout to watch out when a large cowboy collided with her at the bar. Or perhaps better

said, his elbow slammed into her eye socket, the move decidedly more painful for all the lack of attention she was paying.

"Hey!" Gray was on top of the guy immediately, his moves only stilled when the cowboy looked so mortified he could have punched himself.

"Ma'am. Oh no! I am so sorry, ma'am. Are you alright?"

Gray's arm was around her shoulders, the gesture sweet and protective and more than a little territorial, her traitorous nerve endings acknowledged, clearly oblivious to the pain coursing through her left eye.

But with reality rapidly returning, she reached out and patted the guy on the arm. "You didn't mean it. And you're just out laughing with your friends. I need to watch more carefully where I'm going."

"Or some oversized cowboys need to watch where they're tossing their elbows."

She reached up and patted a hand over Gray's chest. "Please excuse my friend. I really wasn't paying attention."

When Gray seemed ready to speak again, she patted harder, tightening the hold of her other hand where it wrapped around his back.

"I'm fine. And made of sterner stuff."

One of the bartenders who'd observed the accident was already handing over a fresh towel wrapped with ice. Harper reached for it but was beaten by Gray's long arm, stretching across the bar before he added a muttered thanks after her louder one.

And then she was being led to a far corner of the bar, away from the loud music and din of happy laughter. There was a small alcove near the bathrooms that still housed a few pay phones and a long bench that had replaced the cigarette machines.

"Sit down and hold this to your eye."

"Gray, I'm fine. Really, I—"

He shut off her protests, taking her hand in his and lifting it higher so that the ice-filled towel fully covered the top of her face.

The cold did feel good, the area around her eye smarting from the cowboy's elbow. Surprised by the continued seething as Gray sat beside her—even though it had been more than clear the cowboy was deeply sorry for the accident—she wasn't sure what to say. So she sat quietly, allowing the ice to do its work.

"Let me take a look at it."

"Gray, I really am fine. I was raised in Big Sky Country. I can handle an accidental elbow from a deeply apologetic cowboy."

"Let. Me. Look."

Since that swirly seething had added teeth, she lowered the towel and allowed him to reach over, his fingers moving tentatively around her eye socket. After several light test probes and the continued questions of "does this hurt?" "what about this?" and "can you feel this?" she finally batted his arm away.

"I am fine, Gray McClain. Besides, you should

be happy I'm even answering. It's not like your usual patients give you affirmative answers to your questions."

He finally smiled, the grim look vanishing from his face. "They're usually better patients, too. With nary a whit of sarcasm when I do an exam."

"Well, when I grow a tail, I'll lose the sarcasm. How about that?"

He'd already craned his head around the back of where she sat, as if to investigate the possibility of that tail, when he seemed to catch himself. Since she realized her joke had given him a prime reason to look at her ass, Harper had to admit that the small alcove suddenly felt a lot smaller.

Darker.

And a hell of a lot more deserted.

He moved back into place next to her, his gaze firmly back on her eye as he made a few more tentative touches to her face, this time to the ring of bruising that was sure to radiate outward from the heart of the elbow jab.

"Do you have any sensitivity here?"

"No."

"Any sensitivity to light?"

"Since it's dark back here, I'll tell you tomorrow after I go outside."

"Harper, this isn't funny. You could have something more serious. That was a big guy with a big elbow."

She laid a hand over his, where his fingertips still pressed against her eye socket. "I'm quite sure I don't have a detached retina, nor am I risking long-term blindness. But if it still hurts tomorrow, I'll go to the doctor. Okay?"

As if he realized he'd pushed it too far, he nodded, his gaze caught on hers.

And as she stared into those blue depths, the warmth of his hand beneath her palm, her earlier words came back to haunt her.

Gray McClain wasn't a friend.

Or he wasn't in the traditional sense of the word.

Because she couldn't think of a single other friend in her life that she wanted to touch. Kiss. Make love with.

Nope, she thought as she leaned into that hand as he shifted his hold to cradle her cheek.

There was no one on earth that fit that bill other than Gray.

It was madness to lean in. Even greater recklessness to lightly shift his thumb so that it drifted from resting against her cheek to lightly graze her lower lip. And it was sheer insanity to replace his thumb with his lips as he closed those last few centimeters between their bodies.

And then he was fighting the battle of the damned as he tasted Harper Allen after more than a decade away from her.

God, she was perfect, was all Gray could think as he tasted what was still so familiar, yet had changed, too.

She still smelled like Harper, overwhelming

his senses with that light, airy quality he'd never associated with anyone but her. She was breath and air to him and always had been. But as his free hand shifted to settle at her waist, he recognized the differences, too. She'd never been a big woman, but her curves had both slimmed and filled out, the changes clear to someone who had touched every inch of her.

Who'd fantasized about those moments over and over in all the years since.

Her hip bones were a bit sharper than he remembered, while the press of her breast against his arm was fuller. She had a woman's figure, with all the shape and texture and curves that came with age.

And God help him, he liked it. Every single inch of her, which he'd never believed could be more perfect, had become so.

The hand that had pressed over his shifted to rest on his shoulder, her fingertips drifting lightly over his nape. Her mouth was open beneath his, her tongue against his in an erotic press of their bodies that nearly had him shuddering.

Where had this come from?

How could need spark, so fast and so immediate, with so little provocation?

And how could that need be so greedy—so all-consuming?—with so little time spent together. He considered himself a sexual man, but he'd never been so beholden to his desires that he lost his head. Or his ability to reason. Or any of that fierce control he needed to survive.

But with Harper . . .

No, he thought as his mouth shifted over hers once more. *Only* with Harper was it like this.

Only with Harper did his body betray him into even considering abandoning all that control.

Which was the only thought that could bring him back to himself.

Pulling his mouth from hers, he stared down at her, the light sheen of moisture on her lips under the dim hallway lights nearly dragging him back for more.

Nearly pulling him back to her.

A loud punch of laughter from the bar interrupted them further, and he finally moved, standing to put distance firmly between the two of them.

He couldn't be trusted to sit so close to her.

Nor could he be trusted not to reach out once more and skim his fingers over her cheek or trail a line from the inside of her elbow down to her wrist.

In the end, Gray knew, he really just couldn't be trusted with her.

"How's your eye?"

"Fine," Harper squeaked out, slightly breathless, before she reached up to touch the edge of her rapidly reddening eye. When she spoke again, though, all hints of vulnerability were gone. "I really am fine."

"Good. Glad it's okay. Keep the ice on it for

a few more minutes. I'm going to go get those beers like I promised."

She nodded and lifted the ice back to her eye, but didn't say anything else.

Gray turned and headed back toward the long, scarred-wood bar and the peanut shells crunching underfoot and the laughter all those carefree people were sending up to the rafters and back.

And wondered why he was utterly unable to feel a single bit of it. A fact he'd just proven to himself with astounding clarity.

When others were laughing, he was more comfortable watching from the sidelines. And when others stepped out to mix it up and have themselves a good time, he held back.

The only place he'd ever—in his whole damn life—been able to feel anything was when he was with Harper.

And like a science experiment from school, he'd gone and proven that outcome to himself once again.

HARPER LET HERSELF in through the garage door at Hadley and Zack's house and wondered why she hadn't just stayed at her father's tonight. His house was closer to town, and she knew he wanted her to spend some time at his place as well while she was in Rustlers Creek. But in the end, it had seemed easier to ride all the way back to the ranch with Charlotte.

Besides, all her things were at Hadley's.

And so was the big bed in one of her sister's four spare rooms that would offer sweet, blessed oblivion as it swallowed her up.

Because her eye hurt like hell and her heart hurt worse.

And worst of all, she'd had to spend another hour and a half sitting in that damn seat at the Branded Mark acting like nothing had happened with Gray. She'd been fawned over by Charlotte for the black eye, and Chance had needed to be restrained until both Harper and Gray had let him know that not only was the black eye a true accident, but that the fresh round of beers sitting at their table were courtesy of one deeply embarrassed cowboy.

A sweet guy, who'd finally screwed up his courage to come over once more, brave Gray and Chance's dark looks and apologize for his clumsiness.

Harper assured him that she was fine, that she was made of sterner stuff and that if she didn't see him march back over and talk to the very attractive young woman eyeing him from a nearby table that Harper would personally kick his ass herself. That last instruction had finally gotten him moving, and even Chance finally smiled at the blend of youth and inveterate horniness of twenty-one-year-old men.

Which meant she'd succeeded in smoothing ruffled feathers and little else, since she was so fucking keyed up with her own personal brand of thirty-two-year-old horniness she was never going to get to sleep.

Damn Gray McClain and his kissable lips and his mind-blowing tongue and his shoulders that seemed to smooth out beneath her palms for days.

Damn him even more for the way he'd made her remember.

Or better said, the way he'd damn well fucking *verified* every one of the memories that kept her awake and restless in her own bed at night.

Good Lord, the man could still kiss. The hot, erotic press of his tongue against hers, subtly mimicking the way his body would thrust into hers when they had sex, without being gross or vulgar about it.

Oh no.

Not Gray.

He kissed in a way that spelled out, with clear promise, what he'd do to her when he had her naked in his arms. Like he was confident enough in his own skills he didn't need some lewd kiss to make her realize all that still awaited her when the promise of that kiss turned into the heated joining of their bodies.

And damn him, here she was, standing in a darkened kitchen, her body practically vibrating, imagining all that would have happened if they'd had the good sense not to come back to their senses.

The lights flicked on like harsh reality and

Harper slammed a hand against her eye, squealing as she shielded herself from the sudden pain when she'd squinted against the light.

"Sorry! Sheesh, I'm sorry." Hadley raced back to the wall panel and hit the lights, leaving the only illumination the soft yellow light that came from the overhead above the stove. "What's the matter with you? Are you loaded?"

"Sadly, no."

"Then what had you screaming like that?"

Harper moved into the light of the stove hood and pointed toward her eye. "That."

"Oh my God!" Hadley rushed forward, her concern nearly as oppressive as Charlotte's and Chance's when Harper had gotten back to the table.

"I'm fine."

"What happened to you?"

"I met the elbow end of a wildly gesticulating cowboy who is now sorry, deeply promising to honor his mother always and, if the small prayer I sent out into the universe on his behalf worked, is currently getting lucky with an eligible young woman."

"You did what?"

"If I can't have any, I'd like someone else to benefit from my pain."

Hadley leaned up against the counter and crossed her arms. "Sounds like a hell of a lot more happened than a black eye. Spill."

"Nothing happened."

"Nope. Not buying it. Besides, who prays for other people to get laid?"

"Lovely, benevolent humans like myself."

Hadley shot her one raised eyebrow—a gesture that suddenly had Harper jealous when she couldn't easily return it in kind—before she turned on a heel and headed for the fridge. Dragging open the large freezer that filled the bottom of the unit, she dug out an ice pack.

"Impressive. You didn't even have to hunt for that."

"We get a lot of black eyes around here. I have at least four more in reaching distance."

Hadley handed over the ice pack after wrapping it in a towel. Clever sister that she was, she didn't speak again until Harper had it firmly pressed against her eye.

"So what else do you have to tell me? Since it's more than obvious the most interesting thing that happened to you tonight wasn't a black eye from an apologetic cowboy."

"Not true," Harper muttered, keeping half of her face hidden by the towel.

"And now your nose is growing, which means your face is really going to look funny. Have fun explaining it all to Dad tomorrow."

"Dad?" She lowered the towel. "For what?"

"We're meeting him for lunch at the Trading Post."

"Maybe I have to work tomorrow."

"Maybe you can work around it."

Harper wasn't sure why the quick retort bothered her. Hadn't she just been thinking that she wanted to see her father? Had even considered staying at his place tonight. But the presumption that Hadley could make their plans . . .

"Way to steamroll, Had."

"Steamroll what?"

"I could have had plans tomorrow." And just because she didn't, Harper reasoned to herself, didn't mean she *couldn't*. Even if the point was entirely moot and she was taking her bitchy, decidedly nonbenevolent mood out on Hadley.

"Okay."

"Don't give me that snotty older sister tone. All I'm saying is it would have been nice to ask."

"If you'd looked at your texts, you'd have known that not only were you asked to go but that Dad specifically asked for tomorrow at lunch because he's got some plans this weekend to get ready for a school function."

She might be a lot of things, but petty wasn't usually one of them. Nor did she actually care if they went to lunch, dinner or out for a drive when it came to visiting with their father.

So why did she still feel like the light of battle had suddenly swept over the kitchen and she was stuck in its big, flashing red crosshairs?

"It still felt presumptuous. 'Work around it,'" Harper mimicked in a high voice.

Although they had a close relationship, they were equally adept at a good old-fashioned verbal knockdown. Since Harper had been aiming for it, it wasn't a huge shock when Hadley's back pokered up good and straight and her voice took on the lady-of-the-manor tone. "Which takes me back to my earlier question. I'll say it slowly to get through that thick head. What the hell happened tonight?"

Harper threw the ice pack at the counter, easily landing it in the acre of sink with a heavy thud. "Maybe you'll just have to get used to not knowing. The same way the rest of us did while you and Zack worked through your marriage for fucking *years* on end without telling anyone."

Although the tone never changed, Harper didn't miss the clear wariness that stamped itself in Hadley's green gaze. "What does that have to do with a black eye?"

"It means you have no business asking me anything when you shut us all out. Me. Dad. Charlotte. Carlene and Charlie. No one knew, Hadley!"

"Is that what tonight was about? Going out and talking about me?"

"No. Hell." Harper shook her head as sheer sadness flooded her sister's face, heightening two spots of color high on her cheeks. At that look, an ocean of regret at even bringing the subject up opened in Harper's stomach.

"No, that's not why I went out with Charlotte tonight. And it's not something we even really talked about beyond addressing the fact that none of us knew." When Hadley only stared at her, that gaze still wary and now hurt, Harper rushed on. "But it's been something I've been feeling. The knowing that you had such a shitty go of it and you never said anything.

"You never told me, Had." Harper moved closer, the rush of battle fading. "You never told anyone."

"I was embarrassed," Hadley whispered before Harper pulled her close in a hug. "And ashamed."

Harper pulled back at that. "Ashamed about what?"

"Zack and I had a good marriage. We *have* one. And thank God we do," Hadley said on a heavy intake of breath before she reached up to swipe at her tears. "But while we were going through it, I kept wondering where it went and why I couldn't tap into any of that good. Why I couldn't tell him I didn't want children any longer."

Harper knew the underlying issue of not trying for a child had been the ultimate cause of her sister and brother-in-law's problems, but it had taken nearly losing their marriage to finally understand that. After losing a child late in a pregnancy, Hadley had ultimately felt that she didn't want to try again. A feeling she'd hidden for a long time as she processed it herself.

"I know I can't tell you your feelings, but there shouldn't be shame in knowing what you want."

"No, I know that." Hadley wiped again at the tears. "And I especially know it now, with distance and healing. But in the end, I had to come to grips with the fact that I didn't trust my marriage and my relationship with Zack enough to tell him. To take the risk that we were on different pages and work through it. I chose to ignore it instead and did quite a bit of damage."

"I'm glad you both came out the other side. Together."

"I am, too. More than I can ever say."

Hadley reached out and took Harper's hand. "Since I learned my lesson and I'm not going to ignore things any longer, I need to say something to you."

Harper squeezed her sister's hand, amazed the storm had passed so quickly. Even as she was grateful for the calmer seas, she braced for whatever it was that Hadley wanted to ask her.

"I know it's a lot to be home. You quit your job, started a new business and now are here for a few months. If I'm pushing too hard or being too much, please tell me to back off."

"Is this about our discussion at the Trading Post?"

"Yes and no," Hadley said. "Yes, in that we started the conversation and didn't finish it, but no, because it's something I've been thinking about."

"Okay."

"You left here and I've never resented that or been angry about it. But I'd be dumb to think that leaving was just about making a new life for yourself in Seattle. It was also about leaving Gray."

Without warning, the feel of his lips pressed against hers, the heat of his body consuming her in that small alcove in the Branded Mark, filled her thoughts. Not like their kiss had been far from her mind, but with the half-hearted fight with Hadley the memory hadn't been quite so present.

Only now it was back and she could *feel* the imprint of his lips burning against hers.

"Thank you for that."

"Of course, it doesn't mean I don't want details."

Humor had replaced the tears in Hadley's eyes, a match for her broad smile.

"I'll keep that in mind."

And with that acknowledgment, Harper recognized another. The truth was, she wasn't ready to share her feelings. Or the experience of kissing Gray again after all these years.

Along with that certainty came another.

It had been easy to question Hadley's silence over her troubles when Harper was the one standing outside looking in. Maybe too easy. Because now that she was facing her own confusing situation, it didn't feel quite so simple or straightforward.

And for a little while, she wanted to hold the memory of kissing Gray all to herself.

Chapter 7

Gray hammered a row of nails into a stall wall, pleased when he finally stood, pressed on the fresh wood and felt no give at all. He wasn't ready to build houses, but he'd managed to do a lot of the basic work around the farm and it had allowed him to put more money toward the launch of the rescue.

The strength of the stalls would go a long way toward creating a safe space for his horses as well. All animals needed to feel that security, a reality even more true for a horse who'd lost one of its senses. Whatever conviction he had about the purpose of having an animal rescue, creating a place where animals could live quality lives was important to him.

Hadn't that been a driving force his entire life? Whatever challenges he'd faced in his own home, animals had always provided him comfort and support and a soothing sort of acceptance he'd struggled to find with people. He'd never dared have a pet, well aware his father would have found a way to use the animal against him. But he'd always found a way to spend time around animals, and his work at the vet clinic when he was in high school had been his dream come true.

A dream that had become his reality every day.

Marty Allen had called him the day before, apologizing for the delay in getting back to him but confirming that their former gym teacher, Ms. Delaney, had been traveling but was back in Rustlers Creek and would like to talk to him about the job. The news had been welcome, especially since Gray had gotten a call about an hour before Marty's asking if he'd come review another equine candidate for his program.

It was all coming together.

Gray left the stall he'd completed and moved across the barn to grab a fresh piece of wood, ready to start on the next framed out stall when he heard a long, low whistle behind him.

"Got yourself something fancy here."

Gray stilled before forcing some deep breaths in and out of his lungs. It wasn't much, but it was the coping mechanism he'd learned years earlier as a way to deal with his father. It had been a necessity when he was going up against someone bigger and stronger than he was.

As time had passed, the purpose had shifted.

Because once he'd become bigger and stronger, he risked losing his temper and becoming just like the man he loathed. And now, no matter how close Gray's memories were to the surface, Burt McClain had aged out of the physical threat he used to be into nothing much more than a pitiful old man.

A pitiful old man, Gray thought as he turned around, *who must want something.*

"Not fancy. Functional."

Burt spit a stream of tobacco juice onto the floor. "Always were into correcting me. It's awful fancy for a place you're going to shove a bunch of animals into."

Just like the deep breaths, Gray had learned not to argue. He'd made his point and that had to be enough.

"How have you been?"

"How the hell do you think I've been?" Burt's face curled up into a sneer.

"Seeing as how I haven't seen you since before Christmas, I have no way of knowing."

He'd heard his father had picked up some work near Missoula, along with a woman he'd been dating. Since Gray was happier when the old man wasn't around, he hadn't dug for more information.

"Again, the contrary bullshit. What bug's up your ass, boy?"

"No bug. No bullshit. What do you want, Dad?"

"I ran into some hard times these past few weeks. Was working up in Missoula and got in a little over my head on a bad bet."

Gray kept his voice very even. It wouldn't do to play into his father's hand too soon, especially since the outcome was going to be a fight. "What's it to me?"

"I'm your father." Burt spat another stream of tobacco juice. Although he hadn't raised his voice yet, a distinct flush crept up his neck. "I need your help and I came here, not too proud to ask for it. A son should do his duty."

"I did do my duty. For a long fucking time I did my duty. I'm done doing it."

"Ungrateful son of a bitch."

Gray stilled and looked at his father. The man who'd towered in his mind for so long had diminished nearly beyond recognition. What had once been a solid frame and powerful chest had grown thin, nearly concave. Those shoulders that had once seemed broad had lost their muscle tone, curving down at the ends like the weight of the world rested there.

And maybe it had.

Whatever else he thought about his father, he understood—deeply—that Burt McClain hadn't spent a well-lived life. And now, at sixty-five, every one of those poorly spent years reflected off him like a mirror.

It was with his own long years of frustration and resentment—and the reality that he really didn't care any longer—that Gray gave Burt his answer.

"Yep. I sure the hell am. I learned how to be one from the very best teacher."

HARPER ADJUSTED A knob on the coffee machine in the Trading Post's open kitchen and waited for that distinct hiss of steam before setting it into her frothing pitcher. She'd been experimenting for the past hour, contentedly listening to the snippets of conversation she caught around the store.

The delighted customers.

The friendly staff.

And the congenial hum of happiness that seemed to fill the place from floor to ceiling and back again.

That happy hum sort of infused itself into a person, Harper thought with a small smile, just like the steam she was currently pumping into milk. And for about the millionth time, she marveled at what her sister had created.

Every time she didn't think Hadley's work could surprise her, she ate those words. The group of octogenarians who'd descended on the café around noon had been just another example. All six women had traveled from Dallas, the jaunt to Montana their choice this year for the annual girls' trip they'd been taking since they met in their twenties.

Sixty years of vacations, Harper had thought

with no small measure of amusement as she'd offered a hand to the staff, helping take orders and
working hard to make the visit special for the
women. But it had been Hadley's joining them
for dessert that had sealed the deal.

She'd sat and talked with each woman, quickly
learning their names and asking after them as if
they were old friends. Midway through dessert
Hadley had waved Harper over, introducing her
and pressing her to tell the women about her coffee company. Where she'd expected everyone to
be annoyed that Hadley wasn't giving them her
full attention, the opposite happened.

They'd peppered her with questions, asked
her about her work, fawned over her black eye
before sighing over the cowboy who gave it to
her and cheered her on when she'd mentioned
quitting her job and buying her coffee company.

"A strong woman raised two strong women.
You can always tell," the sassy blonde octoge-
narian sitting closest to Harper had said. The
compliment was so warm and genuine that
Harper felt the telltale tightening in her throat
whenever she thought of her mother before the
woman laid a hand over hers.

"A lovely thought, but I can proudly say my father had something to do with it, too. He raised
both of us after our mom died. He always put us
first and always told us we could do anything
we wanted. Be anything we wanted."

"A gift beyond measure," the woman had
added with one more squeeze of Harper's hand.

The moment had been special—more than Harper could have ever imagined—and it had meant something to be included.

It had also added to that happy little hum.

She let the steam gurgle through the milk for another few seconds, watching the foam build on the surface before lifting the steaming rod and pulling the pitcher away. She shut off the steam and crossed to the mug she'd already filled with two espresso shots.

Although she enjoyed experimenting with her various blends, Harper wanted to be proficient at making an enticing cup of coffee, too. She didn't want to ask anything of her staff she couldn't do herself, and she was hoping to find a few details they could make unique to Coffee 2.0. Playing with the designs in the milk foam was one of the skills she was determined to learn.

"Excuse me?"

Harper looked up from the milk flower she was creating to find a woman across the counter, her features vaguely familiar. Harper cycled through who the stranger might be, her latest game as she came into contact with more and more people she had known when she was young.

"Can I help you?"

"I think so. Are you Harper?"

"Yes." Curious now, Harper set the frothing pitcher down and crossed the small space to the counter.

"I'm Jackie Delaney."

"Oh! Ms. Delaney." Harper smiled, remembering their gym teacher. "How are you?"

"Good. I'm good. But please. Call me Jackie."

For the first time Harper got the sense the woman was nervous, and her curiosity spiked a bit. Ms. Delaney . . . Or Jackie. Nervous?

The gym teacher she'd remembered from high school was kind but very no-nonsense. Which she'd likely have to be, dealing with a bunch of teenagers all day. But it still struck her as off that the woman would be nervous at all standing inside the Trading Post.

Deciding to channel a bit of that happy hum to help ease whatever had caused the nerves, Harper jumped in. "My dad mentioned you retired. How are you enjoying it?"

Something flickered in her warm brown eyes before Jackie's smile grew broader. Whatever had her smiling also seemed to smooth out some of those nervous edges. "Do you want the truth or the polite lie I keep telling people?"

"Since the truth sounds way more interesting, lay it on me."

"Retirement is a bit boring."

Harper considered how to play it and, in the end, went for the truth. "That's because you're way too young to retire."

"Aren't you sweet."

"My sister wouldn't agree." Harper grinned. "She never thinks I'm sweet. But I stand by my comment as 100 percent true. So good for you all the same."

A strong woman raised two strong women. You can always tell.

That lovely comment whispered through her mind again, and Harper smiled. She felt strong today. Strong, capable and in control of her decisions.

The kiss with Gray had been a distraction, nothing more. They were two healthy, unattached adults, and they acted on a moment of intimacy. It had been a way to satisfy her curiosity, really. See if things were still as she had remembered.

The fact they were even better was not something she was going to dwell on.

With that foremost in her thoughts, she concentrated on Ms. Delaney fully and pointed toward the coffee. "Can I get you anything?"

"A coffee would be nice."

Although the Trading Post never really slowed completely, like any other store they had times where overall traffic lulled. Harper had learned over the past few weeks that they'd likely be quiet for another hour or so and then things would pick back up until closing. It had given her the chance to linger a bit, and she was happy for someone else to practice her skills on.

"Latte okay?"

When Jackie only nodded, Harper got busy on her creation, so focused on getting the milk frothed that she didn't hear her father until he was on the other side of the counter. "Hey, sweetie."

"Dad." She looked up with a bright smile, surprised to see him. "Two days in a row. Aren't I a lucky girl?" She finished up with the milk and was pleased when her flower came even more naturally to her than the first.

Maybe she was getting the hang of this.

"I'm the lucky one." He leaned closer over the bar. "Although I am still concerned about that eye. You doing okay?"

"I'm fine and it's fading every day." It was sweet that he worried, and Harper felt a small shot of pleasure at his concern. "Let me just finish this up and I'll get you something. Then we can talk a bit."

"I'd love to talk and we can in a while. You focus on what you're working on since I'm here to meet Jackie."

Harper glanced up from where she was making the final flourish on her foamed milk flower and took in her father's face before shifting to Ms. Delaney.

No, *Jackie*, she amended.

And saw the same nerves in her father's eyes she'd seen in the gym teacher's.

"You're meeting each other?"

"She's interested in hearing about the position with Gray's new rescue."

"Oh. Wow." That vague memory of telling Gray last week about Jackie's retirement flitted through her mind. "That's great."

"He followed up with me after the two of you talked, and I reached out to Jackie. We decided to meet up for a bit before going over to his place to see his setup."

"Great. Good. That's really great."

Since it was great—what wasn't *great* about it?—she picked up the latte and handed it across the counter. With a small head nod she turned back toward the kitchen to get going on her father's drink.

And couldn't help but wonder what, exactly, was going on.

And why her father seemed nervous, too.

GRAY WAS OUT of sorts. He rarely let his father's visits bother him but something about today had stuck. That greedy perusal of the barn. The request for money. Even the tobacco stains he'd mopped up off the floor had gotten under his skin.

Why?

Why didn't it ever change? Why was he so damned needy to want it to change? It wasn't going to.

Ever.

So why couldn't he get his head out of his ass and stop thinking about it?

He closed up the barn—there was enough done that it made sense to put a lock on the entrance—and moved out into the early spring evening. He had some paperwork to do, but for the moment, he wanted nothing to do with the inside and his thoughts.

Instead, he stared out over the wide-open land

that stretched out from the barn. It was time to walk a bit and get some air.

Even if the thoughts weren't going anywhere.

And even if the steady drumbeat beneath those swirling thoughts about his parent had taken a new tone. Always before he'd believed that he and Harper didn't have a future. That Burt's influence and reputation was something that would only sully and soil her in the long run if she stayed in Rustlers Creek. That she needed to leave and make something of herself. Use her talents and find out who she was meant to be.

Hitching herself to some small-town vet from a bad family wasn't the answer to her future, no matter how badly he'd wanted her.

No matter how deeply he loved her.

And wasn't that truly at the heart of it all? He loved her. And he knew he'd loved her from about the third minute they worked together all those years ago. That sweet girl who was light and air and the breath in his lungs had stolen his heart from the first.

And he'd never been the same.

But now that she was back, having conquered the tech world and heading toward conquering a new industry, he'd begun thinking about her.

Thinking about them.

They weren't the same people they were a decade ago. Yes, age had affected them both, but some of those hurdles that felt so huge if she'd stayed—the size and shape of all the opportunities she'd have missed—didn't have the same weight any longer.

Did he dare hope that things could be different?

Did Harper even want that?

And most of all, did he even have a right to ask, knowing he was the one who'd broken things off and sent her away all those years ago?

Or did he accept that she would go back to Seattle and her new company and her life once this time with her family had come to an end?

He was a decisive man so this level of questioning wasn't in his nature. But did he really dare pursue her?

Ungrateful son of a bitch.

His father's accusation filled his mind once more, and with it the reminder that no matter what he did, he was still Burt McClain's son. And was he really any better than his father, deciding that simply because he wanted Harper he should have her?

Just like his childhood resolution to drive his mother away, Gray had made a decision for him and Harper once, and he'd made it knowing he'd have to stick to it for the rest of his life.

What right did he have now, trying to change the game?

The fact was, he didn't have any.

He meandered across the field, considering all he still wanted to do to the property. He'd continued to use Chance's staff to mow the land, an arrangement that worked for both of them. It had given him another way to support his friend, yet get his own benefit out of the deal.

While he was excited to be a landowner, he still had a lot of work to do in order to get the ranch set up and working around the day job that kept him busy for most of his waking hours.

Compromise, Gray thought. *And the very practical matter of having a life and a dream.*

Which only brought him right back to Harper.

She had dreams, too. And it wasn't his place to step in the middle of those just because she was back home for a while.

When her voice floated toward him, he thought he'd imagined it.

"Gray!"

Turning, he saw her striding across the field, her steps long and seemingly rushed.

"Wait up!"

The sun was low in the sky, casting long shadows across the field as she crossed toward him. He loved this time of year. The sun was rapidly warming day by day and he could feel all the promises that came with this time of year. New growth. New life.

New possibilities.

Even with his internal admonishments to stick to his initial intentions when it came to Harper Allen, Gray couldn't deny he felt those possibilities swirling in the air between them.

His smile fell as she closed the last few feet and he recognized the anxiety lining her face.

"What's wrong?"

"I—" She exhaled a heavy breath. "Is it that obvious?"

To others, likely not. To him?

He'd learned a long time ago to read her. He knew when she walked in if she'd had a good day or a challenging one. If the feelings about her mom had crept up and swamped her that day, or if she was managing and feeling excitement about her own life and future.

It had been easy, he admitted to himself, his awareness of her so acute that he could sense those moods with the set of her jaw or a glint in her eye when she said hello.

"Not obvious, but, well—" He broke off, wondering how to play this. "You're here. You haven't exactly sought me out since you've been home."

"I guess not."

"Is everything okay?"

"Yes." She nodded, squaring her shoulders in a gesture he wasn't even sure she realized she'd made. "Yes, absolutely. Which is only a little lie."

"Why don't we walk back to the house and I can make you a cup of coffee?"

"That sounds nice, but do you mind if we walk out here for a bit? The land is gorgeous, especially so this time of day. The fresh air feels nice."

Since the request so mirrored his own desire to get out of his house for a bit he was quick to oblige her. "Sure."

They began to walk, their steps quiet against the soft ground. Harper asked a few questions—abstract topics that Gray figured were her way of easing into what she actually wanted to talk about.

Which made her next comment both expected and not at all what he thought she would say.

"I think my dad is dating the gym teacher."

"Ms. Delaney?"

"Jackie, she told me to call her."

Gray smiled, old habits dying hard. "She said the same for me. But it's a stretch to rearrange my brain. Like calling your father Marty."

"You met her?"

"I *know* her, Harper. So do you. She timed me when I ran the mile and refereed when I played dodgeball on rain days."

He really didn't want to be amused at her situation, but of all the things he'd expected when Harper arrived, concern at her father's social life just hadn't been it.

"They came over earlier. Your father promised an introduction, and I didn't really think much of it when he drove her out here."

"Oh. Well, that was nice of him."

Gray turned to look at her, curious to see the mixed expressions on her face. Anxiety, yes, but a sort of soft smile that wasn't a match for her words. "Are you sure they're dating?"

"You think they're not?"

"I can't say I gave it much thought." When she said nothing in response, he probed a bit more. "Does it bother you?"

"No." She shook her head. "But maybe it does, and *that* makes me feel like a horrible person."

Harper turned toward him so quickly he bumped into her. The lines of her body warmed him immediately, the soft press of her against his hip—that simple brush of bodies—nearly had his brain short-circuiting. He reached out a hand to steady her, more of that warmth flowing over his palm where he held her forearm.

Images of their kiss at the Branded Mark slammed through him, sense memories blending and merging with the feel of her arm beneath his hand.

The heated kisses.

The urgent need that arced between them, as effortless today as it had been a decade ago.

That toothy, clawing need that never abated when he was with her.

It had only grown more intense since their kiss and was already spearing through him now that she was here beside him.

"You're not a horrible person."

"I feel like one. I feel selfish and childish, and there isn't any reason for it. My father's a grown man, and he's entitled to be interested in dating someone." She blew out a hard breath. "Really he is."

Her reaction was sweet and Gray couldn't hold back the smile. "He's your father. And for good or bad, our parents have a way of removing our ability to think rationally."

The expressions continued to trip over her face, from frustration to thoughtful consideration, all vintage Harper. She had a quietness to her nature that made it easy to think she wasn't prone to heightened emotions, but he knew that wasn't the case.

As his gaze drifted over her face, he realized he was still touching her. Dropping his arm to his side, he shoved his hand into his pocket to avoid reaching out to do it again.

"How'd you get so smart and levelheaded?" She blew out a hard breath.

"I've been outside all evening because my father paid me a visit before your dad was here. I'd hardly call myself smart."

The response was out without any thought to check his words, and it was only that whip-quick shift in her attention that made him realize how easily he'd offered that glimpse into his life.

She was the only person with whom he'd ever dared to share the details of his home. His father's quick and ready temper. The years he'd spent never knowing how much he'd have to eat or if his father would even come home for days on end. The fierce need he'd always had to get out of Burt McClain's shadow and influence.

When he and Harper had first met, that desperate need to get away—to grow up and just *leave* his home situation—had been his whole focus. But once he did turn eighteen and gained his own level of autonomy, Gray had realized it wasn't that easy.

Burt was still his father.

And while he might have had the ability to

leave his father's home, he couldn't actually change his parentage.

Hadn't that ultimately driven his decisions around his relationship with Harper? That realization that his life was here and hers was meant to be somewhere else.

It was a decision he'd made when he was still a lot closer to those feelings of helplessness about his father. When the oppressive feelings of being a McClain seemed like a brand on his forehead in and around Rustlers Creek.

And now? Gray thought.

While he still struggled with his relationship with his parent, he'd also come to some level of balance with it as well. He knew how to handle his father's visits and demands for money.

And he knew how to find his own equilibrium again when those visits inevitably came.

"Gray, I'm sorry. How are you doing?"

"Fine." He shrugged, aware that the response seemed more dismissive than he intended. Especially since he had shared the fact that his father had visited at all. "Really, I am. His visits are unsettling and after a few hours that feeling fades."

Those thoughts from earlier came back, and Gray added, "He's really just a sad old man now, and that's a different sort of unsettling, too."

"We never think things will be different. And then one day we wake up and realize they are."

"What do you mean?"

"It's like when we're in the middle of something,

it feels so big. And so—" She broke off, seemingly to organize her thoughts. "So all consuming that it's all we see. But in time you realize there are all these other forces working. Time passing. Others changing around you. And life just doing its steady work, day by day. And all the things that feel like they won't ever change actually do."

She shrugged. "If I'm being fair, that's more what I'm reacting to about my dad. He's been alone for a long time. And he's still got a long life ahead, I very much hope," she said on a small laugh. "Why would I begrudge him a chance to live that life with as much happiness as he can find?"

Gray smiled at how neatly she'd worked through what had bothered her as they'd strolled through the property. It seemed fitting she'd come to some conclusions as the half-built stable came back into view.

"You now sound ready to marry him off."

Where she could have been horrified by that, she only smiled as they came to a stop near her car. "I'm not quite that well-adjusted. But I also need to be a bit more open-minded on the idea that he actually has a social life."

"For what it's worth, Ms. Delaney seems like a great person. I'm really hoping she takes the position."

A small light filled Harper's hazel gaze. "You going to keep calling her Ms. Delaney if she does?"

"Old habits are hard to break."

As the words drifted out, the dying light haloing her from behind, Gray knew to the very marrow of his bones the truth of those words.

And for all her ready acceptance and wisdom of how time passed and did its work, hundreds of thousands of seconds hadn't done a damn thing about how he felt about her.

Chapter 8

"Will this snow ever go away?" Harper stared out Hadley's kitchen window, distinctly aware that the child who still lived somewhere inside her was deeply horrified by her aversion to the snow.

But the adult who'd been cooped up inside for three days?

She was all in on fervently wishing for a day of spring warmth.

"It's supposed to be in the sixties by noon." Hadley seemed unfazed by it all as she moved down the line, reviewing each of the various trays on her massive kitchen counter. She'd prepped, primped, taken photographs and scribbled intensely on a notepad for the past hour, and where Harper had initially been curious to know what her sister was doing, three solid days of cabin fever had even killed her curiosity.

"Just because you've been productive since the snowpocalypse doesn't mean you have to rub it in."

Hadley looked up from her notepad, blinking her eyes like a very cute, flour-covered version of the absentminded professor. "What am I rubbing in?"

"Never mind. I've lost you to the lure of recipe land." Harper left the window and crossed back to the counter. "What are you looking for? The trays all look fairly similar."

"No they don't." Hadley blinked again, clearly confused at the question. "They're different sizes, different rise levels and varying ingredients making up the cinnamon swirl."

"Whoa." Harper held up a hand and recognized she'd not been nearly as observant as she normally was. "Let me rephrase my question. What are you trying to discern here?"

"I want to make sure these will bake up well on-screen. Everyone loves a good sticky bun recipe, and the shows where I make dough always do really well on video views and recipe downloads after the fact, but it's a lot of brown and beige on the pan."

"Look at you, all grown-up and kicking ass at your chosen profession." Harper smiled as she leaned in to buss Hadley's cheek. "I had no idea dough was such a fascinating topic."

"You should see me when I really get going on yeast."

"Uooh." Harper feigned mock interest. "You are a woman of many talents."

Although she had no interest in ruining the mood, Harper knew there was another reason she was restless. She'd held on to her thoughts on her father and Jackie Delaney since that day in the Trading Post, and while she wanted to talk about it with Hadley, she'd also wanted to feel more in control of the topic.

And less like a recalcitrant child who didn't understand why a parent had a right to move on after losing their spouse.

"Do you know Dad might be dating someone?"

Hadley's interest was captured at that and she set her pen down. "No way! What do you know and why haven't you mentioned it?"

"Well, I didn't want to upset you."

"Upset me about what?"

If she hadn't already felt rather small about her attitude on her father's possible love life *and* her seeming inability to identify different rise patterns, Hadley's easy acceptance and obvious excitement would have sealed the deal.

"You're really not bothered?" Harper finally asked.

"Are you?"

"Gray asked me the same thing."

That bit of news—out before Harper could

check it—had her sister laying down the note-pad next to the pen.

"When did you talk to Gray about it?"

"I told you, a few weeks ago. After I found out about Dad and Ms. Delaney."

"Dad's dating Jackie?"

Jeez, had everyone in her life managed to transition to adulthood without her? Who naturally called their former teacher by their first name?

"I think. I mean, he's hung around with her a few times. And they both seemed really nervous when I served them coffee at the Trading Post."

"And just how long have you known this?"

"A few weeks ago. That same day you had those really sweet ladies from Texas in the Trading Post. I stayed through the afternoon, prac-ticing some of my coffee skills and blends in the café. Jackie came in during our lull and ordered a coffee and then Dad came in a few minutes later. And they were meeting each other."

"Wow. That's fantastic."

"Are you really okay with it?"

"Well, yeah. Sure." Hadley stilled for a minute before continuing on. "She's not the first woman he's dated, you know."

"She's not?"

"Well, no. I mean, he's not some lothario or anything. But he goes on dates from time to time."

"You never told me."

"It seemed weird to try and tell you over the

phone. And it also sort of felt like something he could share if he wanted to. But when his dates never turned into much, there wasn't a lot to tell, either. And then it really felt like it was his business and not for me to make a fuss over."

Harper's gaze drifted to the trays on the counter, oddly able to understand Hadley's point, even as she felt decidedly left out. She'd dated over the years—no one who'd fired her up enough to make a special fuss over—and when her dates with a guy ultimately petered out, it didn't seem worth making a big deal about it on a call home.

But the whole conversation was a distinct reminder that she had left, too.

What had looked uniform before on Hadley's trays, Harper realized as she looked at each one, *was* actually quite different. From the sizes Hadley had pointed out to the way she'd twisted the dough in varying shapes. Even the way she'd sprinkled the types of sugar, from fine to large crystals, was different.

Just like life here in Rustlers Creek.

Hadn't she expected, on some level, to come home and find things the way she'd left them? As uniform as her memories of the town and the people in it.

But things *were* different.

People changed. The town changed.

Life changed.

"I've been gone a long time," Harper finally said, her thoughts drifting to the evening she'd gone out with Charlotte to the Branded Mark.

That's the strange thing, though. Life, experiences, the world around us. It all changes every day. I think those changes are just harder to see when you're in the middle of them.

For all her worldly words of wisdom, Harper had to admit, she certainly hadn't taken her own advice to heart.

"Yeah, you have," Hadley said as she moved closer. "But it doesn't mean that we're not happy you're back. Really happy."

"I know that. It's just—" Harper's throat tightened and she had no idea why.

Why was she being so weird about this?

Like way down deep weird when she had zero right to be.

She left Rustlers Creek. It was an active choice, and even if it came in the aftermath of her breakup with Gray, it was still something she'd wanted for herself.

For her life.

She'd anticipated there would be some strange feelings coming home. But for the past few weeks since she'd arrived, her feelings had all felt so jumbled and close to the surface.

The bottled feelings over the fact Hadley hadn't shared her marital troubles. The strangely childish feelings about seeing her father move on from her mother. Even the warmth she'd experienced the day she spoke with the older women from Texas at the Trading Post.

She wasn't a person who lived with her emotions all out in front of her. It wasn't her natural comfort zone, and losing her mother at such a young age had only reinforced her natural inclinations.

After her mom had died, everyone had wanted to know how she was. How she was doing. How she was holding up.

What answer was there to a question like that?

Because she had zero interest in turning into a sobbing puddle in the middle of the grocery store as she and her father did the weekly shopping. Nor did she suddenly want to talk about her mother on the town square at the holidays, when all she really wanted to do was lose herself in the tree lighting and the festive atmosphere and pretend she was going to have a merry, happy holiday like the rest of her friends.

People meant well—she did believe that, despite her prickly attitude—but she'd always hated the opinions and concerns and all that *well-meaning-ness* that inevitably came from others. What was meant to be comforting had only been intrusive to Harper's mind.

So she'd shut it out.

And then once things had broken so thoroughly with Gray, she'd really wanted to leave.

Or run away.

Because she'd lived with all those concerned stares throughout her teen years, and she'd been absolutely positive that she wasn't going to do it as an adult.

"It's just what, Harper?"

"I don't know." Harper shook her head, trying

to come up with the right mix of words for her sister. Because Hadley did worry about her. And unlike those well-meaning questions that were caring yet detached, too, her sister was her biggest and fiercest champion.

"Really, Hadley, I don't. I'm happy for Dad. He's been alone a long time and it would be nice to know that he's not alone. Or not alone by choice. So whether it's a few dates or a real romance, that's for him to decide."

"That doesn't mean it isn't hard." Hadley's tone was soft, her green gaze understanding. "And I'm not sure there's any amount of distance that prepares you for your parent dating. I've had more time to get used to it, but I'd be lying if I said it wasn't odd the first time I saw him with someone who wasn't Mom."

"Did he seem nervous?"

"On his dates? You mean before?"

"Yeah. He and Jackie both seemed really nervous the other day."

"Maybe he really likes her." Hadley shrugged.

Harper envied her sister the reaction. It wasn't lack of care, but she could see in the easy acceptance of the idea that Hadley didn't have nearly the reservations Harper did.

Hadley poked the edge of one of her sticky buns, the dough springing back after she touched it. "Time will tell there. In the meantime, I want to hear more about Gray. And how he knows all about this and I don't."

"Maybe you should go back to your beige doughballs."

"They're sticky buns!"

"You want to make sure they're camera ready, don't you? And I think I have a new algorithm to work on."

Harper started backing out of the kitchen, walking squarely backward into Zack. Her brother-in-law's hard *oomph* seemed like a bit of a stretch since the man's chest was like a wall of granite, but he was gentle as he held her still.

"Where are you going?"

"I have a very important algorithm to work on."

"Better you than me."

"Harper!" Hadley's voice followed her out of the kitchen and down the hallway toward the stairs, but Harper was already on the move and had no interest in circling back.

Hadley might be full of all that well-meaningness but Harper needed to process her emotions.

And all those pesky feelings.

And, maybe, she needed to make a trip across town to visit her father now that the snow was melting.

MARTY LOOKED AROUND his kitchen and wished he'd thought to pick up flowers. But since he was currently counting his good fortune that snow was *finally* melting and the roads to and from the house were actually navigable, he'd take that as a win and try not to worry about flowers.

Especially since Jackie was coming over for lunch.

For the first time in a long time, he was deeply grateful for the large selection of food Hadley regularly left in his freezer.

Not that he wasn't grateful, he reconsidered on a shot of guilt. But it was nice to finally feel like it wasn't some sort of consolation prize that he had food in his fridge from his daughter.

It felt like he was prepared.

He'd selected a nice cut of steak—Wayne and Sons beef, of course—and had prepared a light stir-fry and salad.

Would she like that?

And why was he so nervous again? They'd had that coffee date at the Trading Post and the trip out to Gray's ranch to discuss his plans for his animal rescue. They'd also spoken every day on the phone, but their opportunities to go out had been limited based on his schedule at school and the late spring storm that had dumped several feet of heavy, wet snow across the state.

If he were being fair, he'd couched the lunch invitation as a way to discuss her new opportunity with Gray instead of as a date. And even their calls had been suspiciously devoid of any discussion of why they were actually talking. They were just . . . talking.

Getting to know one another.

And despite the fact that he'd known Jackie Delaney for more than three decades, he actually didn't know much about her at all.

If he were honest, between the fact that he was the school principal, had a famous child and had lost his wife at a young age, he'd come to realize over the past two weeks that he'd done far too much talking about himself and his life while at work and had discussed far too little about anyone else's.

The knock pulled him out of that uncomfortable revelation and he headed for the front door. The well-worn hallway rug layered over the hardwood was quiet beneath his feet and he had the abstract thought that maybe he could do a bit more with his home.

He'd gotten the rug after Hadley left for college, electing to give her the old one for her dorm. And since that had been about fifteen years now, maybe he could look into getting a new rug.

And maybe some new pillows for the couch.

And hell, while he was at it, maybe it would make sense to get a new couch.

The doorbell rang again and Marty picked up the pace. *Shit.* He needed to worry about his home decorating skills another time.

He opened the door, an odd sense of relief warring with the nerves jangling through his system. "Hi, Jackie."

"Martin." She smiled and held out a wrapped cake on a plate decorated with horses around the rim. "I realize you likely have homemade desserts whenever you want, but I wanted to bring something."

Martin.

She always called him that, and he liked how it rang on her tongue. Her subtly lingering Boston accent rolled the notes of his name slightly and it reminded him that there was a distinct elegance about her no amount of time in the Western wilds of Montana could change.

"I'm sure it's delicious."

He welcomed her in, escorting her to the kitchen. "No coat?"

"Despite all the snow still on the ground, it's sixty degrees. I'm chalking it up to that very weird definition of spring in Montana."

"It is that. You didn't experience that growing up in Boston?"

"Sometimes. Massachusetts definitely gets the wild spring snowstorm, too. But there's something about the volume of snow we get here. It's scary and incredibly impressive all at the same time."

"I've never lived anywhere else so I don't have a point of comparison. But I'm not sure I can ever remember a spring that didn't have the sort of storm we had this week."

"My arms are still sore from all the shoveling. And I don't have that big a driveway. How does your daughter manage it on a ranch?"

Marty grinned at that. "The ranch hands help quite a bit. And Zack's invested in plows and enough large equipment so they get by."

He glanced down at the cake still in his hands

and quickly placed it on the counter. "There was one year, when I was a kid, we had over a hundred inches of snow in Rustlers Creek."

"Seriously? I can't imagine that much snow."

"It's twice what we normally get. The mountains usually get around three hundred inches but that's in the Rockies. We're too far out for that." He exhaled on a hard breath, shaking his head. "And I can't believe I'm boring you with stories about the weather. Come on, sit down."

Jackie glanced at the seat he'd offered, her gaze drifting over the plates he'd set out. "Wine for lunch?"

"Only if you'd like some."

"I'm retired now. Sign me up."

He smiled as he poured the wine he'd opened a bit earlier. He'd taken the day off himself, opting to take an actual vacation day instead of working from home once the decision had been made to close the school for one more day. It was an entirely novel idea to have a glass of wine at noon on a Thursday.

"I'd ask you to tell me how wonderful it's been without all that daily responsibility, but you're not going to be retired for much longer."

Jackie took the glass he extended, holding it out so they could clink a toast before settling back against the counter. "It was a bit of a novelty at first and then for a few weeks it felt like a luxury. But after that it quickly grew boring. I like having a reason to get up and some purpose to my day. Thank you for recommending me to Gray."

"It's my pleasure."

Jackie took a sip of her wine. "Oh, this is good." She set the glass down, seeming to consider something.

"I remember Gray from when he was in high school but haven't kept up with him. His practice is doing quite well."

Marty thought about how to answer. He could give Jackie the basics—Gray McClain was a good man and he ran a quality practice—but it seemed that she deserved a bit more. Or at least some understanding of how his own life was intertwined with her new employer's.

So it was with no small surprise when she continued on.

"I had a few run-ins with his father when I first moved here."

"Burt?"

"Yeah. He seemed particularly aware of, as he put it 'new blood in town' when I got here."

Something ugly swirled low in his gut, and Marty kept his voice very even. "Did something happen?"

"Physical?" Jackie seemed to catch herself as she keyed in to his cool demeanor. "No, and I'm sorry if I gave that impression. But he was forward. Inappropriately so one night when I was out with a few other women in town. He was unpleasant enough that I knew he was a man to avoid."

"Has he ever bothered you since?"

A strange iciness had settled in his midsection,

the feeling so intense it had vanished any lingering sense of nerves or anxiety at having Jackie in his home.

"No, Martin. Really, he hasn't." She shifted her gaze fully to his. "I really didn't mean to alarm you. My even mentioning it was more to contrast how wonderful his son is. I remembered a serious boy from when I had him in school, but after talking to him during my interview, it was easy to see how that quiet belied a man whose thoughts run deep."

Jackie's assessment was a match for his own. And while Marty had always felt guilty for the misgivings he'd initially harbored over Harper and Gray's relationship, the young man Gray had been had never given him any reason for those concerns. "Gray dated my daughter."

"Hadley?" Jackie asked, obviously surprised.

"No, my younger daughter, Harper. She and Gray were very intense and then things just ended. Harper's never said a lot about the breakup, but I always got a sense that Gray ended things because of his father." Marty reconsidered, the limited things Harper had said over the years forming a sort of patchwork of understanding. "Or if not because of Burt, certainly in mind of the outsized influence a man like that would play in someone's life."

"That must be hard."

"For Gray?"

"Yes, of course. For Gray and for Harper." Jackie ran her index finger around the base of her wineglass before adding, "But for you, too. Watching your child go through something like that. Worrying about them and knowing all the potential challenges she faced. Knowing how much it hurts and knowing there's nothing you can do about it."

It *had* been difficult to watch.

They'd all grieved so much with Maria's passing, and Gray had been a bright spot in Harper's life. More, Marty had come to understand in time, Gray's friendship had been key to helping Harper work through her grief.

"I'm a parent so I worry about both my daughters. But Harper has always been different from Hadley."

"How so?"

"They're both amazing women. Smart, kind and thoughtful of others." Marty laughed and reached for his own wine. "And about a million other things I could say, since I'm wildly proud of both of them."

"But?" Jackie pressed gently.

"But Harper is quiet. Not reserved so much as she doesn't wear her emotions as clearly as Hadley. It's easier to think she's doing fine before you realize there's a lot more going on below the surface."

"It doesn't ever go away, does it?"

Her question was quiet—soft-spoken—and in it he heard both question and affirmation. "Being a parent?"

"Yes, that. And the worry."

"No, it doesn't. It changes in some ways. I mean, I do acknowledge my girls are adults. But," he laughed, "since I just called them both *girls*, clearly it doesn't change all that much, either."

"It's nice you care so much. It's special." That pretty brown gaze captured his again. "I had the opposite experience with my mother and it leaves marks. Even after all these years."

Their phone calls hadn't dwelled much on Jackie's life before coming to Montana, but he had gotten the distinct sense she had a challenging relationship with her family.

"You want to talk about it?"

"There's surprisingly little to say. But—" She stilled as neatly as her words, before seeming to come to a decision. "I was married, before I came to Montana."

As principal of the high school he had access to teacher records, so he knew her age, even without doing the math to count just how many years they'd known one another. Which meant this marriage she spoke of had to have happened when she was quite young.

As if sensing the calculations he was already doing in his head, she added, "I was just twenty-one. And I was divorced before twenty-two."

He'd also married young, so it wasn't her age at the wedding that was the surprise so much as the divorce. "What happened?"

"Thankfully something I hope happens a lot less nowadays. Thornton was gay and tried to hide who he really was. From his family and obviously, from me, too."

"I'm sorry you had to go through that."

"I am, too. For both of us. It took me a lot of years to get to that point until I realized one day he was as wrapped up and manipulated in our life as I was."

"Manipulated?"

"From a very young age I was raised as 'the right kind of girl.' The sort who has an impeccable society record of cotillions and genteel interests and some additional personal interest that others could ask me about."

Jackie smiled, and Marty got the distinct sense she was surfacing from memories that weighed a lot more than she perhaps even realized.

"For me that was being an equestrian."

"And Olympian, too."

"Yes, that, too." A dim smile hovered around the edges of her lips. "In the end, it was my travels and involvement with my horses that kept me out of the house. Thornton was always so encouraging and supportive of my time away and it wasn't until . . . *after* that I realized I'd inadvertently given him the space he so desperately needed."

Marty set his glass on the counter before he leaned forward and laid a hand over hers. "I'm still sorry you had to go through that."

Her gaze lifted to his, and in her eyes he saw each reason he'd been nervous.

And every reason he didn't have to be.

There were memories behind that gaze. Life experiences. Interests and thoughts and knowledge that intrigued him and pulled at him in some elemental way.

He'd always believed he and Maria would have grown old so well together. That they'd have weathered the storms of life and found their way through each decade's challenges and joys.

But they hadn't been given that chance.

And in all the years since she'd died, he'd never found a woman who he could remotely conceive of wanting to make the attempt with.

Until now.

It was unsettling and seemed far too quick, yet at the same time it felt like a lifetime in the making.

He *knew* her.

Not with the level of depth that came with time, but she also wasn't a stranger to him. And in the past few weeks he'd come to realize that on a very elemental level, he'd always been aware of her. Had always valued her presence in his life.

Maybe that's what made it so easy to reach over and take her glass from her hand and lay it on the counter. And then it was even easier to move closer and bend his head to press his lips against hers.

Something soft and warm and electric and wildly powerful filled him as she laid a hand on his shoulder, moving a few inches closer so their bodies touched.

She was tall, nearly his height, and it was so

easy to wrap his arms around that fit frame and
cradle her against himself. So easy to deepen the
kiss, their breaths mingling and merging as their
tongues met and did the same.

So easy to simply take, reveling in the joy of
being together.

Of finding each other.

It had been so long since he'd felt that spark of
the new and exciting, but as the kiss wove a spell
around them both, he had to admit there was
something different here. As if life's experiences—
everything good and wonderful as well as the
challenging and the devastating—arced between
the two of them.

As if kissing Jackie and being with her was
some sort of perfect blend of all they'd both experienced.

Of all they'd both survived.

It was heady and tempting and comfortable all
at once. And it made a special sort of sense he
could never have imagined.

One hand drifted over her spine as the other
settled at her waist, the material of her thin blouse
bunching in his fingers.

"Martin," she whispered against his lips.

"Yes?"

"I'm not opposed to kitchen sex, but admittedly
I'm not quite as young as I used to be. Perhaps we
can try the bed for our first time together?"

He laughed at that, the sound spilling from his
chest in a happy wave. A happiness that didn't
dim as he made his next admission. "It's been a

while since I've done this, I think I'd better not lose my head and get too cocky attempting it standing up, too."

Her smile was bright and vivid, radiating joy as she pressed her lips to his for a quick kiss. "Consider me smitten with a wise man who knows how to present his assets in the very best light."

Marty reached for her hand, linking their fingers. And as he led her to his bedroom, he had to admit that perhaps age and wisdom had a lot more going for it than he'd ever imagined.

Chapter 9

ᛒᏔᏔ

Harper drove over to her father's house, careful to navigate the endless rivers of slush as she went. Although she had to be mindful of icy patches that hadn't yet thawed, it felt good to get out of the house. Off the ranch and driving somewhere.

Anywhere.

More than anywhere. She smiled. *To see her dad.*

And to have an honest, adult conversation about how happy she was for him if he wanted to date. No, she amended as she drove through downtown, that he *did* date. He didn't need her permission or approval, but hopefully he'd be happy that she was happy for him.

Plus, it would be nice to spend some time together. She'd forgotten how busy his schedule always got in the spring. With upcoming graduations as well as all the things the seniors were doing that led up to it—college applications and prom at the top of the list—she hadn't seen him much since coming back to Rustlers Creek.

Although the snow was melting, she'd heard through one of the married ranch hands that the kids had gotten one more day off school. So it would be fun to spend some of it together. He hadn't answered when she'd called to say she was coming, so hopefully he wasn't outside overtaxing himself with shoveling snow. But she was already wearing some snow boots borrowed from Hadley, so she could help him if he needed it.

It was only as she hit the stoplight at the end of the main thoroughfare through town that Harper saw Gray, unlocking his truck where it was parked along the sidewalk. She considered waving and going on, but the temptation to stop and say hi was too great.

Especially when her pulse slammed against her chest at the way his jeans molded to his slim hips and his shoulders looked extra broad in the long-sleeved, faded gray T-shirt with UC Davis printed across the front.

She wanted to ignore the hard shot of attraction, but in that moment, helpless to look away, she couldn't deny the thoughts that swirled in the back of her mind, offering a tempting alternative to her current situation.

Although she'd been in Rustlers Creek for a longer stretch than any other time in her adult life, she wasn't staying. What would be the harm in spending time with him? The kiss they'd shared a few weeks before had proven they still had chemistry.

Blindingly good chemistry.

Harper quickly steamrolled over the thought, trying to keep what limited objectivity she still had on the matter well in hand. Even as another thought, even craftier than the first, whispered through her mind.

Are you willing to give him a pass that easily?

She hadn't spent a lot of time dwelling on that aspect of things, seeing him again more emotionally overwhelming than she'd wanted to admit. But it was a consideration.

An important one, she reminded herself.

Whatever his reasons—and she did give him the slightest pass that no matter how misguided, he'd believed he was doing her a favor *and* the right thing—he'd broken them apart all those years ago. Gray had been the one to walk away, telling her he didn't want to be in a relationship any longer.

He'd done that.

And even after all the work to get past the pain of their breakup, somewhere in her mind, hadn't she still lived with the lingering idea that he was the one who got away? An antiquated and, if she were honest, dangerous notion that suggested all the years that had passed were some sort of lull.

An emotional way station until they could be together again.

And that wasn't just dangerous, it was some sort of weird, magical thinking that gave no account to real, honest feelings.

Abandonment.

Anger.

Grief.

She'd felt them all, and pretending she hadn't lived through each and every one of those emotions wasn't what she wanted for herself, either.

Even if, damn it all, she *wanted* him.

The man who still looked like a dream come true standing there in that T-shirt and jeans. Oblivious to every thought pinwheeling through her mind.

Since those thoughts were just as unsettling as every other emotion that had surfaced in recent weeks, Harper opted to get out of her head and into the moment and slowed as she pulled up alongside Gray.

"Is that an actual doctor's bag in your hands?"

She couldn't deny how cute he looked as he surfaced from whatever thoughts were occupying his mind. It was funny how similar he looked to Hadley's earlier absentminded professor expression when she'd worked on her baking. And if she were fair, Harper knew she regularly wore that same look when in the middle of a deep coding session.

Flow, various articles called it.

She just thought it was a lovely place to disappear for a while.

But it was the slow grin that spread across his face that pulled her up short.

Vivid proof that no matter how much armor she wanted to wrap around her heart, Gray McClain had the frustrating ability to sneak through all of it.

HE HAD NO right thinking about her.

Thinking about her. Fantasizing about her. Reimagining the kiss they'd shared a few weeks ago.

None of it.

But God help him, he hadn't been able to stop.

And now here she was. Smiling at him, bright and shiny and vibrantly, brilliantly Harper.

Although he'd gotten surprisingly comfortable through the years with the reality that Harper Allen would never fully vanish from his thoughts, Gray had come to a certain sort of equilibrium. He had to see her family in and around town. That was even more pronounced when he'd become the main vet for Wayne and Sons ranch, coming into contact with Hadley on a regular basis. So he'd come up with a system where he asked after her casually every third or fourth time.

He hadn't missed the sympathy in Hadley's eyes the first few times he asked, but they'd gotten into an unspoken rhythm over the years.

Hadley shared the surface details of Harper's life, and he hoarded them like precious scraps.

All while pretending that he was just being polite and friendly, of course.

It rubbed something raw in his heart, even as he knew he didn't even have the right to ask as often as he did since he'd sent her away.

He'd been resolute, too.

Once he'd made the decision—after a particularly ugly fight with his father—he hadn't wavered.

But he could still picture her, those hazel eyes shimmering with tears as she pressed him.

"What is this about, Gray?"

"It's about you needing a life. Something well beyond here."

"I have a life, Gray. We both do. Especially since we've spent a lot of time these past six months talking about our future. I can code anywhere and you're graduating in six more months."

"No, Harper, we don't."

"What's wrong with you? We've talked about this. Agreed on what our future looked like."

"Your future, Harper. Yours. Mine is here."

"My future is with you."

He'd shaken his head at her words, a physical denial, even as everything inside of him broke in half. He set his features so he projected nothing that she could latch on to as a way to press her point. So he could show no weakness as he did this.

Whatever anger and pain he'd suffered over the

years from his father   the random backhands or the yelling or the hunger-fueled nights—none of them compared to this. This agonizing pain of sending her away.

Even as he knew he had to.

"We have no future."

How many times through the years had those words echoed in his head? From the flat, robotic way he'd said them to the sharp stabs of pain that lit him up, head to toe, as he watched something die in her eyes.

We have no future.

It was a grief too big for words and he'd felt it. He was twenty-four years old and his body felt like he'd lived a hundred years, he ached so badly.

"Gray?" Her smile wavered ever so slightly. "You in there?"

"Yeah. Of course." He made a show of lifting his medical bag high. "And this is, in fact, a doctor's bag. Just because my patients aren't human doesn't mean they don't require a heck of a lot of instruments to check them out."

It was inane, silly conversation, but it was enough to give him some of his equilibrium back.

Back from that awful memory that never failed to drag at him like the heaviest of weights.

"Where are you headed?"

"Out to see my dad. He wasn't answering his phone but I know he's home today. The kids got one more snow day out of this mess. Knowing him, he's probably taking advantage of the lull to shovel."

Although Marty was still pretty hale and hearty, it bothered Gray to think of the man shoveling his property of all this wet, heavy snow. "Why don't we run into the diner and pick up some lunch and I'll go with you. I can give him a hand."

"You don't have to do that."

"You and your father just solved all my challenges with the horse rescue and have ensured I can get started in June like I planned. Buying you both lunch and shoveling the driveway is the least I can do."

And it was.

He'd thought more than a few times over the past few weeks how neatly that accidental meeting with Harper at Parkers' Ice Cream Parlor had given him the access he needed to Jackie Delaney. They'd had their initial meeting as well as a few calls over the past few weeks, and he couldn't be happier with having her join him in this endeavor.

Her ideas on training and supporting blind horses, as well as the additional therapy opportunities they could create at the rescue, were cutting-edge. She'd obviously kept up with her equestrian interests through the years, even though she no longer rode professionally.

"Pull around to the diner and I'll meet you there."

Harper moved on past him, turning into the diner parking lot. He stowed his medical bag, a lightness settling over him. It always amazed him how easily she steadied him. The edgy, roiling thoughts that were his near-constant companions lost their teeth when she was near.

He'd made some time for therapy when he was in college, the constant encouragement around campus to talk to someone and seek support far more prevalent in California than he'd ever experienced in Montana. Although he'd hesitated at first, when he'd realized after the breakup that he had no life beyond his graduate studies and his sadness over Harper, he'd recognized he needed to do something.

The time he'd spent with a therapist had helped him realize the ceaseless trauma his father's behavior had caused. It had been as far as he'd emotionally been willing to go—he never once discussed his relationship with Harper in his sessions—but he had learned how to better cope with that persistent anxiety. And he'd come to learn that while his thoughts still had teeth, they rarely bit anymore.

He'd done the work. The hard work of finding himself and understanding who he was, and he'd always been proud of that. Maybe if his father had been a bit more broad-minded on that front, he'd have found a better path as well.

Despite that pride, Gray had never known quite how to make it all up to Harper.

And maybe the real reason was that he

couldn't. He'd broken up with her, with minimal reason, and that was his to own. There was simply moving on. Being who they were now and finding a way forward.

As he swung into the diner—full of people who were obviously out after some serious cabin fever—he had to admit that it was a place to start.

He couldn't erase all that had come before. But he could sink back into the friendship they'd always had, especially since she seemed determined to make the effort. Could find a way to know the woman she was now and respect the boundaries that needed to remain in place.

He'd broken all the fences. And while he could mend some of them, there were others that he had to live with.

A reality that struck particularly hard as he caught sight of her, ordering at the long bar counter. The bright sun that was rapidly melting the snow outside haloed over her through the wide windows that fronted the diner, her features standing out in sharp relief.

Where her sister was famous for her red hair, Harper's was more of a deep auburn. The sun glinted off the red strands, bringing out their richness and adding a sense of glamour to the woman dressed in a sweatshirt, rolled-up sweatpants and thick fuzzy boots. Truth be told, she looked like an elf, on vacation from the North Pole, with her small, slim shoulders and pointed chin.

It was silly and fanciful, but in Harper's animated conversation with Penny at the counter, the idea took root and held.

And along with it, he remembered what she'd looked like the first day he'd seen her at their high school vet job. She'd dressed casually, obviously told to wear something old to work with the animals as they were bathed and groomed. She'd worn a pair of Rustlers Creek High School sweatpants, also rolled at the ankle, and a T-shirt that was three sizes too big. All her hair was pulled up in a high ponytail and she didn't wear any makeup.

And he'd been enchanted.

Utterly gobsmacked and blindsided so hard by the look of her he'd made Mark Jefferson's springer spaniel, Monty, squeak out a bark when Gray had held him too tight. Doc Andrews had laid a hand on Gray's arm, gentling his hold, before offering him a small wink.

"She's awfully pretty."

Gray felt the heat crawling up his neck and had refocused on Monty. "You think he's going to be okay?"

"*He* will be."

Gray had glanced up at Doc Andrews at the man's strange emphasis on the dog being okay. The lingering insinuation that Gray might not be had stuck with him for days.

And, how oddly prescient, Gray thought as he moved up to the counter to give Penny his order, that Doc Andrews had keyed in so quickly on far more than Gray could have ever imagined.

"You want your usual burger, Gray?" Penny asked.

"Sounds great, Pen. And the sweet potato fries."

"As if we'd give you any other kind."

Penny took off down the counter, but it was hard to miss the curious look she'd given him and Harper before heading off to put in their order.

"She's wondering what we're doing here together." Harper kept her voice low but he didn't miss the amusement there.

"I'm sure ordering three meals added to the confusion."

"Why?"

"A lover's tryst is one thing. A lover's tryst for three really gets the gossips going."

Harper stared up at him, her eyes going wide. "Gray! I'm sure she doesn't think that."

"Probably not." He shrugged. "But people have always thought a lot of things about me, very little of it true. I stopped worrying about it a long time ago. Especially with her."

"With her?"

He waved it off, aware they had a possible audience in the diner beyond Penny's prying gaze, and as he did, Harper nodded, remembrance filling her gaze.

Voice low, she said, "She used to date your father."

"Off and on."

As with most of Burt's relationships, women

drifted in and out of his life, but a few drifted back in on some sort of dysfunctional loop. Penny had been one of those. Gray had been able to see past it into adulthood, the two of them capable of being cordial to each other when he saw her around town or when he came into the diner.

But that cordiality had never fully erased the fact that Penny was the adult in the odd tableau with his father when he was in high school. And as the adult, she could have helped him and she hadn't. He'd always figured her stilted behavior with him was more about her not acting when she could have than anything that had come since.

Or she could just be curious.

One of the many funny things about living in a small town. You might know everyone, but you really didn't know anybody.

"I'm sorry."

Again, her voice was low and meant only for him, but he heard the underlying sentiment with all the force of a gunshot. Odd how that only reinforced his decision so many years ago to break up.

"Let me make a prediction that you don't run into your past each and every time you buy lunch out in Seattle."

"I can't say that I do. Although I did run into Bill Gates once. Oh, and the guy who plays a bartender on Grey's Anatomy."

"Really?"

"Yep. Both at the same place, actually."

"But not at the same time?"

She grinned at his dumb question, and the silly conversation was enough to pull them out of that subtle malaise that had descended after the mention of his father.

"No, the sightings were about three years apart."

"Who knew people who founded tech companies would become celebrities."

"Or my sister."

"That's for sure." Gray looked around the inside of the diner. "This place got a face-lift because of Hadley."

"Seriously?"

"Oh yeah. Their business boomed with all the crew in town. And then when all the tourists started coming, I guess they had enough to remodel. Hadley's work has lifted all the businesses in Rustlers Creek."

Harper shook her head, those slim shoulders suddenly shaking with laughter.

"What's so funny?"

"My sister. Every time I think I have a handle on the idea that she's a famous person, there's another aspect I never considered. Who knew all those meals she tried out on my dad and I would pay off like it has."

"Does it bother you?"

"Hadley?" Her tone was so crisp—so absolute—that it was clear she was far from bothered. "I'm insanely proud of her. What she's done and built? It's amazing, I mean, holy shit, she's responsible for the town's face-lift. If that's not crazy-awesome, I don't know what is."

"But does it ever make you feel left out?"

Gray had no idea why he was pressing this, but now that he was thinking about it, he realized he was curious. Because he knew Harper and Hadley, before. And then he'd watched Hadley's star rise along with the rest of the town, marveling at what she'd created.

Wasn't it odd to see your family's life change so monumentally?

"I don't feel left out at all. That sort of attention isn't something I'd find easy to handle. And it's not that I think Hadley is an attention hog, but the idea of that many people noticing me?" Harper shuddered, shrugging her shoulders so they nearly touched her ears before dropping them back into place. "Absolutely not.

"Hadley seems way better adjusted to it than most Hollywood tell-alls would have people believe. She's the same girl I grew up knowing.

"Not to take anything at all away from her, because Hadley is awesome, but I also think that's a testament to my dad and how he raised us." Her gaze unfocused a bit before she continued. "It struck me recently, actually, when I was thinking about quitting my job and buying Coffee 2.0. I'm only five or six years younger than he was when we lost my mom. And back then, he seemed so grown-up. I mean, he *was* grown-up. He was the adult."

"That's the weird perspective of children for adults."

"True, but it's still so odd to think that he got married, had kids and had a life in that time. I still feel a bit like Peter Pan, sometimes, you know? Still footloose and fancy-free without a few children to chase after."

"I think you look like a cute Tinker Bell." Without even realizing his intention, he bent forward and dropped a quick kiss on her nose.

It was odd and unexpected and something he used to do when they were dating. Those unanticipated little kisses they'd both give one another on impulse.

Penny was already walking back with their carryout so Gray didn't have time to say anything else about the kiss. Which was probably a good idea, he thought, as he dug his wallet out to pay for lunch.

Because Harper still wore a dazed expression on her face, memories in her eyes that he knew well because he shared them, too.

JACKIE STRETCHED LAZILY in bed before turning to stare at Martin. She couldn't hold back the smile or the way it seemed to ignite this happy glow throughout her body.

Or maybe that was the power of the man's clever hands, which had made quick work of her clothing, among other things, on the trek to his bedroom.

She hadn't come over here to have sex.

She'd *hoped*, she admitted to herself, that smile only growing bigger, but she hadn't planned. Though she had made sure everything was buffed and polished and she'd also diligently hit her Peloton every day for the past two weeks.

But that was still hope, right? Not overt planning.

Martin rolled onto his side, his gaze locking on hers as he took her hand. "I'm glad you came over today."

"I am, too."

"Not just because we had sex."

"Can I be glad to come over *and* glad we had sex?" She pressed a quick kiss to his lips, in awe that she could do that so easily. How the gesture was responded to in-kind.

He lingered a moment over the kiss, and Jackie felt the answering response gathering, building inside of her. Goodness, she felt insatiable. And she wasn't sure she could say she'd ever felt that before.

As if she could stay right here, locked in his arms for a week, and it wouldn't be enough.

Since thoughts of a week-long sex fest brought on a sense of permanence she wasn't sure they'd gotten to yet, she forced herself to slow down.

Hoping was one thing.

Planning another entirely.

"That works for me," Martin said as he lifted his head. "Although, you could equally accuse me of starving you. Are you hungry?"

"I am."

She was tempted to stay right where they were, lunch be damned, but he was being a sweet host. And, well, those thoughts of something more permanent had churned up emotions better left still.

Nothing that had happened today, or over the past few weeks as they'd talked and gotten to know each other better, could change the fact that she'd had unrequited feelings for him for a long time. It felt imbalanced. And a little shameful, she admitted to herself.

With that dour thought clouding her mind, she sat up, suddenly feeling more exposed than she was in her nakedness. Here she was, making up fantasies about something *more* between them, and they'd barely spent any time together.

"Jackie?" The deep blue of his eyes, so recently twinkling, had turned more serious. "Is everything okay?"

"Yes. Better than okay, actually." She stilled her roiling thoughts and turned to him to press a kiss to his lips, lingering just long enough to impress her point that things were okay. "But you've inspired me with talk of lunch."

He didn't seem entirely convinced, but he did smile before getting out of bed. "How do you feel about steak stir-fry?"

"Like I'm a very lucky woman."

She reached for her discarded blouse and slacks, surprised to feel his attention on her.

"What?" she asked, turning around.

"Nothing. It's just that—" He stopped, scrubbing a hand over his jaw. "I'm sorry. I'm terribly out of practice at this. It's just that . . ."

"What, Martin?"

"When I suggested we get some lunch, it wasn't to make you think I wanted you to leave. In fact, that wasn't my intention at all."

Those concerns that had felt so heavy and weighted while she was still in bed lifted at his sweet remarks. "I'd like to stay for a while. For lunch and to spend more time with you."

"I'm glad." Relief etched his features before he turned to the dresser and dug into a drawer. When he turned back it was to toss a Rustlers Creek High School T-shirt her way. Navy blue with gold letters, which were a match for the school's colors. "Here's a T-shirt. It'll be easier. Later."

"I like easier."

He came around the bed, leaning down to kiss her. As his lips met hers, she wrapped her arms around his waist. The bare skin of his chest met her breasts and once more, all those swaying, swirling, whirling feelings swamped her, robbing her ability to think clearly.

Rationally.

Or with any of her normal good sense to keep her feelings veiled and well in check.

She didn't do big sprawling, sweeping emotion. She wasn't raised that way, and she obviously had never inspired that in others. So it wouldn't do to lose her head over a sweet little romance with a man she'd had a long-standing crush on.

But when he stepped back and smiled down at her, she really couldn't hold back that shot of hope that danced through her chest before moving out to flood her bloodstream.

"I thought you promised me steak stir-fry."

"So I did."

In moments they were back in the kitchen. She poured wine and set the table while he worked his magic at the stove. A few times she caught his gaze on her, warming under the steady attention and grinning at his lopsided smile.

Besotted.

She'd heard the word her entire life, Jackie thought, but had really never understood it. Only now she knew, because that was exactly how she felt. Besotted and tipsy, as if they'd shared the entire bottle of wine and started in on a second, even though they'd only taken a few sips.

Martin turned off the stove with a flourish, the pan in his hand as he walked to the table and their waiting plates. He distributed their lunch before setting the pan back on the stove. "I hope you're hungry."

"I worked up quite an appetite."

"Me, too."

And then he did the most magnificent thing, pulling her into his arms and wrapping her close. "I think I might have mentioned this, but I'm so glad you're here."

All those doubts she'd struggled against up-

stairs in the bedroom vanished on swift feet as
Jackie turned into him fully. She lifted her head
for another kiss, that thought about insatiability
striking her once more.

She was insatiable for him. She *felt* ravenous,
as if the rest of her world had spun down to very
little and all she could see or feel or hear was
Martin Allen.

It was wondrous.

And amazing.

And beyond mortifying when a loud voice interrupted them, the echo of "Dad!" spilling into
the kitchen.

Chapter 10

Harper came to an abrupt halt in the doorway of her father's kitchen—nay, *her* kitchen since she'd been a small child—and hadn't been able to hold back the shock. Or the squeaked "Dad!" that had spilled out before she could stop it.

Gray nearly bumped into her from behind, the swinging bag of lunch hitting her in the ass before he stilled the motion. And his forward progress.

But it was Gray's eloquent words that came next that shocked Harper even more. "Mart Jackie. I'm sorry we interrupted you. We'll just see ourselves out."

Gray's hand was already on her forearm, trying to dislodge her from where she stood, and Harper had the twin sensations of wanting to be led away and wanting to shake him off like a fly at a picnic.

When she only stood still like a garden gnome stuck in the front yard, she knew she was in trouble.

And before either of them could move, her father and Jackie were both in motion. If she hadn't been still so shocked, she might have found it funny the way they leaped apart like two cats who'd been unceremoniously tossed into water.

It was Jackie's quiet "excuse me" that finally got Harper moving, after the woman had left the kitchen to, presumably, put on some clothes, since all she wore was a T-shirt that was a few sizes too big.

A Rustlers Creek High School T-shirt Harper was pretty sure was her dad's.

Eeew.

Even as she thought it, she knew the reaction was monumentally unfair. And juvenile. But oh my God! Her father had just had sex. In her house.

His house.

Their house.

Oh hell. She spotted a glass of wine on the counter and headed for it, taking a large sip before checking the impulse.

She's not the first woman he's dated, you know.

Hadley's earlier statement—had it really only been that morning when they'd spoken?—filtered through Harper's panic.

Wasn't that why she was coming over? To tell her dad how happy she was for him.

"Harper, honey. I'm sorry you—" Her father seemed to catch himself. "No, that's not right. I'm not sorry. But I do recognize this is awkward."

"It is." She pointed toward Gray, who still stood in the doorway to the kitchen. "We were bringing you lunch. I saw Gray when I was heading through downtown on my way over. And I told him where I was going and he wanted to buy you lunch since you'd been so great about recommending Jackie for the job at his ranch. And so we decided to drive over. With lunch. And to see you."

She'd grown inane, overexplaining what was likely obvious by the name of the diner printed on the side of the takeout bag and the scents of burgers wafting toward all of them.

"That was sweet of you. Thank you."

"Look, I'm going to go." She'd already turned for the door when her father's hand snaked out and grabbed hers. She stopped, turning back to him and meeting his gaze, even though it was a bit of a struggle.

"Give it a bit of time. To settle. Then text me? I'd like to talk to you."

"Okay." She nodded, surprised when, once again that day, tears tightened her throat.

Unsure she could hold them back this time, she only nodded once more and headed for the door.

Since she and Gray had driven over separately, she'd expected they'd leave that way, but he reached for her arm once more, steering her toward his truck. "Why don't you let me drive for a bit?"

"I can't just leave my car. I'll have to come back."

"You'll come back eventually. Let's not worry about it right now."

Gray escorted her around to the passenger side of his truck, and Harper allowed him to help her into the cab. He settled the food back at her feet on the floor before closing the door. In moments, he had them out of the neighborhood and back on the road toward downtown.

"Would you like me to take you back to Hadley and Zack's?"

"Not really."

"Okay, I'll just drive around for a bit."

"Look, I know I'm being ridiculous." They passed the diner now in the opposite direction, and Harper wondered how everything had gone from seemingly okay to wildly upside-down in what was only a six-mile round trip.

"You got a bit of a jarring surprise. I wouldn't be so hard on yourself."

"No, actually, I should be. I've been laboring under the delusion everyone else's life has sat still while mine moved ahead. It's not right and it's not fair. Not to anyone."

And it wasn't fair.

She could be upset or she could treat this entire situation with the open mind it required.

Her father had been a widower for twenty years. And while it pained her to think about him having lived that long without her mother, it pained her even more to think about him being alone.

It wasn't the idea of him moving on. It was the idea that he had to.

Wasn't that what hurt so much?

He should have had the opportunity to grow old with her mother. She and Hadley should have had all the years since with their mother. And she should have had her mother when she went through the pain of breaking up with Gray.

Which brought Harper right back to the other thought that had pulled at her earlier. For all her protests that she'd moved on with her life, she'd been wildly unsuccessful in holding down a long-term relationship. She'd had a few, but none that had even come close to a whisper of marriage.

Neither had Gray.

Those earlier thoughts of the two of them being stuck in some sort of emotional limbo, despite being apart, seemed even sharper now that she'd admitted to how poorly she'd handled her father.

Which made her next question inevitable.

"Why haven't you gotten married?"

GRAY WAS GRATEFUL no one was traveling nearby as he headed out of downtown in the direction of the highway. He'd gripped the steering wheel so hard it was a wonder he hadn't run off the road.

Why haven't you gotten married?

She'd asked the question several moments ago, and he was still trying to figure out how to answer.

Or how to answer in a way that didn't make him sound like a pining tool who hadn't moved on.

He *had* moved on, damn it. He'd had to.

Who you trying to convince there, cowboy?

It was a question without answers. Because no matter how long he'd been hung up on Harper, moving on from what they'd shared wasn't equal to finding someone new to marry.

Falling in love wasn't that simple.

"I haven't gotten married because I haven't found the right person."

"Have you been in love?" She wasn't quite as forceful with this question, her voice softening in a way that made him think she was afraid to hear the answer.

"Not since you."

If Harper was going to ask the hard questions, he was going to give the hard answers.

He hadn't been in love with anyone else. Not before her and not since.

That didn't mean he was incapable. Nor did the fact that he hadn't moved on mean it wouldn't happen eventually. It just hadn't happened for him yet.

"Have you tried?"

What did he do with that question?

Had he tried what?

Moving on from her? Yes, every day since they broke up.

Had he tried falling in love with someone else? Did you try to fall in love with other people or did it just happen?

And why did it feel like he was defending himself from a series of questions he couldn't win?

"I date, Harper. I go out with women. I've even slept with a few of them. Is that what you're asking?"

Once again, silence stretched out between them, filled with a decade of hurts.

"Maybe I am."

"To what end?"

"Because I'd like to understand why this is so hard, Gray. Why it feels so insanely *present*. Why two seemingly healthy, vibrant people who are no longer together haven't seemed able to move the fuck on!"

Her words hung there between them, an outburst that had been brewing since she'd come home to Rustlers Creek. Hell, if he were honest, it was an outpouring of anger and confusion that was a decade in the making.

"I don't know."

It briefly crossed his mind as he navigated onto the interstate that he should be angry, too. That by this point he should have built up a head of steam that needed an outlet. Yet all he could muster was an overwhelming sort of sad for both of them.

He might have carried the guilt for breaking their relationship, but he'd also lived with that decision. No matter how "right" he'd believed himself to be, it hadn't done a damn thing to make him feel better in all those months after she'd moved to Washington.

It hadn't made him feel any better in all the years since.

And damn it to hell, it hadn't made him feel better when he'd dated those other women he'd spoken of, or when he'd taken them to bed.

So yeah, he should be angry. But he couldn't seem to find a single bit of it.

"Where are we going?"

"I thought you might want to see the horse I'm taking over the weekend."

"The rescue?"

"Yep. Cabernet will be mine in a few days."

He kept his gaze focused on the road but didn't miss the way she kept moving in his peripheral vision. He'd obviously caught her off guard with the decision to head to see the horse.

Even if it was on the heels of the decision to share his past.

A past she likely shared, even if he had no desire to ask the question of whether or not she'd dated and slept with other men. He wasn't big on questions he didn't want the answers to. And he'd worked through the reality a long time ago that giving her up meant she'd become someone else's.

"I didn't realize you were ready to do an intake."

He considered how to respond but some Band-Aids were meant to be ripped off. "With Jackie starting, it made sense to get going. We'll move slow, but it's time to get Cabernet into his new home."

"I'm sorry for before. For my reaction to Jackie and my dad."

"There's nothing to apologize for."

"There is. Maybe not to you, but consider this me practicing right now."

"Practice away."

Since they'd delved into challenging territory, he was tempted to keep it light, but the fact they'd gone deeper also felt like he had a bit of leeway to get a few more details. "Did you mean what you said before? About feeling like Peter Pan?"

"Yes and no. It's not so much that I haven't embraced adulthood. I have a job and responsibilities and I prefer it that way. But the world does see you as a bit carefree when you aren't settled down and raising children."

"Does it bother you that you're not?"

"That's another yes and no."

Gray sensed there was a whole lot wrapped up in both those answers but was surprised to realize just how much he wanted to know them.

"I do want children. I always have and would like that to be a part of my future. But I also want children with the right person. So until that part of my life is figured out, children are on hold."

"I'm sorry."

"For what?"

Although it felt presumptuous now to think she'd have had that family with him, it was the way their relationship had been going. He had little doubt that if he hadn't broken off their relationship, things would have progressed to marriage and a family.

"I'm sorry you've had to spend the last decade looking for that answer."

"Thank you."

As they continued the drive in silence, Gray had to admit his earlier assessment held. The anger still hadn't come.

But that persistent realization that he'd given up far more than he ever could have imagined was shockingly clear.

HARPER STAYED AROUND the edge of the paddock, watching several horses in various stages of exercise, while she waited for Gray. He'd gone in to talk to the owner of the stables, and she'd opted to stay outside and enjoy the warm afternoon.

And take the time to gather her thoughts.

The car ride had been . . . intense. And revealing. And full of all the things she always avoided talking about.

Maybe because they're things that needed to be said.

It was truth, even if it was stark and raw and uncomfortable.

"And the ongoing theme of Harper's trip home to Big Sky Country." She muttered the words, surprised when she felt a hard butt against her shoulder.

Delighted by the equine intruder, she turned to face the interior of the paddock and her new visitor, a gorgeous chestnut-colored horse with a white star on its foreleg. "Hello, beautiful boy. How are you?"

When the horse seemed content to stand there with her, Harper reached up to pet his nose, even more delighted when her new friend bent his head closer against her.

"Aren't you handsome. And so sweet."

She continued to pet the horse, breathing the fresh afternoon air deep into her lungs and willing her thoughts—a frustrating mix of past and future—into the back of her mind. It was time to enjoy the present. Concentrating on the warm spring breeze wafting over her skin and the soft feel of the horse's coat beneath her fingers.

I'm sorry you've had to spend the last decade looking for that answer.

Gray's apology lingered in her thoughts, despite her desire to remain firmly in the moment. And then a young rider was striding toward her across the paddock, and Harper pulled herself firmly back to the present.

"Looks like you've met Cooper." The young girl smiled as she reached for Cooper's lead. "I'm Macy. My dad, Rick Pruett, owns the ranch."

"I'm Harper."

Cooper continued to nuzzle her hand, and Macy smiled at the horse indulgently before she pulled out some sugar cubes from her pocket and handed them over. "Here. He already loves you but this will seal the deal."

Harper settled the cubes on her palm, enjoying the tickle of Cooper's nose as he greedily lapped up the cubes.

"You're the ones here to take Cabernet, right?"

"My friend is. He's taking Cabernet to his rescue."

"That's amazing. He's a good horse. He's been sad, but I'm really happy he's getting a new home."

"Sad?" Harper asked, intrigued.

"He was one of our best racers and had an accident last year."

Although Gray had mentioned Cabernet's past when he'd told her about the rescue, Macy intrigued her. The child was obviously in love with horses, but her clear-eyed statements ensured she understood what she was doing around horses, too.

More evidence Rick Pruett ran a good stable.

"What happened?"

"He had a bad turn around the track and

hit the fence." Tears filled Macy's eyes and she brushed at them. "We've all been really sad about it, and I think Cabernet can feel that."

"I'm sorry."

"When my dad heard about your friend's program, he thought it was the perfect home."

"Your dad's right. I can promise you Gray will give Cabernet a really great life."

Before she could ask any more questions, Gray and the man she assumed was Macy's father came out of the stable leading a horse. Both men remained close, guiding the animal as Harper watched, fascinated, as the two of them maneuvered Cabernet out of the stable and into the wider ring of the paddock.

"Does Cabernet spend a lot of time out here? Since his accident?"

"Only when he's got two people leading him. He's really skittish if there isn't someone on either side of him."

Harper considered the horse, a pretty bay with a long dark mane. Just as she'd been enamored with Cooper, she immediately saw the strength and power that was still evident in Cabernet's bearing. He'd thinned out and was edging toward gaunt, but there was obvious strength there, too.

Cabernet had been a racer. That didn't simply vanish because he'd been hurt and lost one of his senses. There was a pride in his stance that his injury hadn't fully erased. An elegance, too.

With a stark moment of clarity, she thought of

her father and her reaction earlier. And had to admit that she'd found it far easier to see a future for an injured horse than she had for her own father.

That needed to stop, right now.

Pulling her phone out of her pocket, she shot him a quick text.

Sorry about earlier. I'm near Bozeman looking at Gray's new rescue horse. Call you later? Love you.

Feeling lighter with the text sent, she refocused on Gray and Cabernet. She could hear Gray's low, steady voice, encouraging the horse as they walked farther into the paddock. She'd always marveled at his gift with animals, his love for them innately entwined with his ability to care for them. She'd always believed that an animal sensed that quality in him and responded to the inherent safety they felt in his presence.

It was a gift.

One he'd only honed and refined over the years. One that would serve him well as he brought animals into his rescue.

As if sensing her scrutiny, Gray looked up, their gazes locking. She waved, suddenly nervous without knowing why.

This was Gray.

And for all the emotional territory they'd covered over the past few weeks—today's revelations by far the biggest—she'd have thought she would feel more comfortable.

So why had nerves taken up residence in her stomach with all the finesse of a stampede?

"Would you like to come meet Cabernet?"

Gray kept his tone modulated, his hold firm on Cabernet's halter as they continued their forward movement. It was only as they got closer that Harper heard the softer, murmured words Gray spoke to the horse.

"Cabernet, I have someone I'd like you to meet. Her name's Harper and she's a friend. You're safe with her, just like you are with me."

That gentle crooning tugged at her heart, and she watched and waited from where she stood at the paddock rail as Gray, Cabernet and Macy's father, Rick, came closer.

"Macy, honey," her father called out. "Lead Cooper over to the far side of the paddock. We're going to give Cabernet a bit of space."

The girl did as she was asked, taking Cooper's halter. She started leading the horse when she seemed to remember herself. With her hand in her riding jacket, she dug out some extra sugar cubes and ran them back to Harper.

"A nice way to sweeten the introduction."

Harper's hand closed over the cubes. "Thank you."

With Cooper off to the farther reaches of the paddock, Gray waved a hand, gesturing Harper over. "Why don't you come on in here? Bring some of that sugar I know you now have in your pocket."

Harper considered going to the gate but opted

to climb through the fence rails instead, such was her impatience to meet the horse.

Whatever feelings she had for Gray—and she was increasingly torn on what to do about them—she could focus on this horse and what it meant to Gray's future.

Because whether or not she belonged with Gray, she knew he didn't deserve to live a life alone. And part of finding that future was building a life for himself that made him happy.

She moved cautiously toward the horse, Gray continuing to talk to him softly. She'd nearly reached them when she heard a heavy shout from the opposite end of the paddock.

Macy screamed as Cooper reared, the large horse too much for her to handle as he spooked over something. Her father dropped his hold on Cabernet, racing for his daughter. The shouts and the sudden abandonment of a second person he trusted by his side had Cabernet rearing, too. It was all she could do to get out of the way when Gray took firm hold of the horse, grabbing his halter and lead, that steady voice never wavering as he got the horse into order.

"Whoa! Whoa. You're safe, boy. You're safe."

Harper took her first easy breath as Cabernet stilled under the firm hand, but waited until Gray waved her forward. "It's okay. Let's keep to the plan and get you on his other side. That sugar will be his reward and a second person beside him will ease his anxiety."

Gray's attention was fully focused on the

horse as Harper closed the rest of the distance to the duo. She already had the sugar in hand, ready to meet Cabernet, when the heavy ping of her phone went off with the incoming text.

Cabernet's ears perked and he stamped his foreleg, close enough to Harper to sidestep into her.

She struggled to hold her ground, but with the confusion of losing his second handler he wasn't to be calmed. Cabernet reared once more and Gray fought to hold his halter and lead, just as he'd done before.

It was only as his hand slipped, just missing the leather of the halter, that Cabernet took advantage of the quick feeling of freedom.

Harper watched the horse rear again, everything slowing down as Cabernet's powerful body slammed into Gray. The horse struggled against all the new sensations while Gray fought to recapture his hold. No matter where he tried to get a firm grip, the panicked animal evaded, impervious to Gray's ability to calm him down.

They were closer to the fence rails than Harper realized, and it was only when Cabernet bucked yet again that Gray lost his tentative grip entirely. That large reddish-brown body slammed into Gray once more, the two of them locked in a physical hold as Gray fought again to still the horse by any means possible. Harper moved in to try and help but Gray's shout to stay back only added to the confusion.

With one final bucking motion, Cabernet reared up, the move enough to send Gray tumbling backward. Cabernet continued his frenzied movements and Gray took another solid hit from the horse, the motion forcing him against the paddock rail.

As he hit his head solidly on the metal rails, Harper screamed and raced toward Gray, oblivious to the thousand pounds of horseflesh that took off in a panicked run.

Harper sank to the ground beside Gray and reached for his heavy form as he lay limp on the ground, doing her best to drag him onto her lap. She got his head pillowed on her thighs, but when his eyes remained firmly closed, despite her frantic calling of his name, a panic to rival the horse's settled deep into her bones.

Chapter 11

Gray drifted in and out of dreams, his thoughts fuzzy and full of weird images of Harper and a horse and hammering nails into a stall. Over and over, he hammered those nails, like a dream that seemed to run on repeat. Then he'd lose consciousness again and fall asleep, with no idea how long he was out.

When he did wake up, with odd moments of lucidity, Harper would smile at him and smooth a hand over his cheek before allowing the medical staff to work. One of those times he'd even held on long enough to sign all the papers the hospital administration foisted off on him that affirmed he would, in fact, pay all his medical bills.

But he felt best when Harper returned to his side, that hand caressing his cheek. He turned into that warm palm each time, welcoming the comfort of her touch.

Had her hair looked like that before? The light swing around her chin was shorter than he remembered. Hadn't he smoothed those strands and toyed with them, wrapping them around his finger the other night when they'd made love? Why were they shorter now?

It was an abstract thought, and he'd forget about it when he drifted back to sleep and into dreams filled with more of those wood boards and nails. And just when he thought he couldn't hammer one more nail, the world would shift and a big horse pressed its withers against his palm.

"Gray." Harper's soft voice filtered through the dream, and he tried to open his eyes, pleased when the feeling of having them stuck together faded and he was able to look at her.

Why did it feel like he hadn't seen her in so long? Like they'd been apart for a long time, but that didn't make any sense because she was here.

"How are you feeling? How's your head?"

Her smile was gentle, and for the first time he realized that the room was dimly lit and it was dark outside. "Where am I?"

"You had an accident."

"Where?"

"With a horse you were leading around a paddock. One of the horses for your rescue. He got startled and pushed you into the fence rails."

"Cabernet, right?"

She smiled at that, and he felt some small shot of triumph flow through him. "That's right. He got a little spooked and reared. That's what caused the accident."

"Is he alright?"

That smile softened, and he had no idea why, but something sad flitted through Harper's gaze. He knew that look and knew when she was trying to hold back her feelings.

But why was she sad?

It wasn't like he was dying or anything. He'd had a little accident. He'd be fine.

With that foremost in his thoughts, he lifted a hand to her cheek. "Don't look so worried. I'll be fine."

"You have a concussion."

"I also have a hard head. I'll be okay."

"You seem very sure about that."

"It's not my first run-in with a large animal."

Something deeply sad still hovered in her eyes, and Gray struggled to answer the questions that filled his mind. Why did she look sad?

And why did it feel like it had been so long since he'd seen her? Or touched her? Especially because they spent all their free time together. Every moment they could get.

Before he could dwell too long on any of them or even consider asking her, a doctor came into the room.

"How are you feeling, Gray?"

He glanced up at the young woman in the

long white coat, the badge on her chest reading Dr. Oakes, and gave her his most sincere smile. "Like I was kicked in the head?"

"Since that's a rather close description, I won't correct you."

Harper moved away from the bed, giving the woman room to do a series of tests. Gray submitted to having his pupils checked and followed the doctor's finger as she moved it in various directions in front of his face. He also answered a few questions about what he'd been doing yesterday, his date of birth and his profession.

"All the tests are back and you do have a concussion. I'm going to need you to take it easy for the next week. I'd like you to avoid the computer and your cell phone as much as you can. The screens might aggravate the headaches, especially these next few days."

Since he basically tolerated his phone as a necessary evil, being given leave of it for a week sounded like heaven. "Okay. What about my work?"

Doctor Oakes glanced down at her clipboard. "You're a vet."

"Large animal, mostly."

"Do you have others at your practice who can take over in your absence?"

"I partner with a vet in Three Forks, and I usually have a rotating crop of interns."

"Lean on all of them for the next week if you can. Two weeks would be my preference, but I understand it's spring and your practice is likely very busy. We'll plan for a checkup in a week and can go from there."

Harper spoke up from where she stood near the small built-in desk that was there for patient items. "He's ready to be checked out?"

"I see no reason he has to stay. Let me get this paperwork wrapped up and we'll get you checked out."

Harper just nodded, and again, Gray couldn't quite shake the feeling that he was missing something. The accident with Cabernet was upsetting but he'd be fine. A few days down wasn't ideal, especially because, as the doctor accurately assessed, it was spring, but he'd figure it out.

He always did.

"Come over here." He waved Harper closer, reaching for her hand when she approached the bed.

Something flitted through her gaze once again, opening something raw in his gut as his hand closed over hers, their fingers linking.

What was she hiding?

First the sadness and now this strange sort of reticence that wasn't Harper.

"What aren't you telling me? Did something else happen in the paddock?"

"No." She shook her head, seemingly aligned with her denial, but her hand was so stiff in his.

"Is Cabernet okay?"

"He is. Rick was able to get him under control

pretty quickly. I think Cabernet scared himself more than anything."

"It's hard. He's lost one of his senses and he's confused. We'll help him adjust."

"We?"

"You and me. Jackie and the interns who are going to join us this summer." He stroked his thumb over her palm where their hands met, still unable to understand what had her so spooked. When her hand was still stiff beneath his, Gray gave it a small tug, pleased when he caught her off-balance.

With his free hand at her nape, he pulled her close for a kiss. As their lips met, he whispered against her lips, "I really am okay."

That stiff fit of her hand against his was a match for her lips, and Gray registered her subtle resistance mere moments before she sighed hard against him. Whether acquiescence or relief he had no idea, but her mouth opened beneath his, warm, welcoming and familiar.

His Harper.

God, he loved her.

That deep-seated comfort that always flowed so easily between them gave way to something more intense. More powerful. And the passion that wove effortlessly with that easy contentment rose up to swamp him in hard waves of desire.

Again, those strange thoughts about not seeing her in a while intruded on the moment even as he tried to ignore all of them in favor of the kiss. Her lips were so sweet, soft and plump, with the lingering taste of coffee and that flavor that was so uniquely her.

His Harper.

Whatever resistance he'd felt had faded as she nestled her hip against him. The angle of their bodies—him in the bed and her seated next to him—gave her an advantage over the kiss, and he felt the moment she relinquished whatever lingering worry dogged her.

A soft moan escaped the back of her throat as her mouth came down on his once more. Sexy and sensual, her lips played over his with a hunger that caught him off guard. The heady flare of sexual arousal was quick, sky-high in its intensity. And without warning, he was ravenous for her.

The hand still in his squeezed, gripping his fingers, and Gray held on just as tight. What was this sudden madness? Because while he always wanted Harper, the headache pounding through his temples should have put sex off the table.

Hell, lying in a hospital bed should have put sex off the table.

Yet he wanted her with a hunger that scared him.

What had happened?

And why was he unable to remove that lingering feeling of having been away from her?

The light cough from the doorway was enough

to have her pulling her mouth from his, leaping off the bed. "Hello, Dr. Oakes."

The doctor kept her features flat, but it was hard to miss the twinkle in her gaze. "I probably should have been more specific. You've just had a concussion so any sort of amorous activities are off the table for about a week."

"I can't kiss her?"

That twinkle finally reached her lips. "Some kissing will probably be okay. But I do mean it. Give your body a chance to rest. While I realize it's not our first thought, we use our brains during sex, too. And yours needs rest right now."

He caught Harper's eye where she'd resumed her place against the small built-in desk. Even in the muted lights of the room he could see the flush of embarrassment on her cheeks.

And the puzzled confusion that wrinkled her forehead.

He knew her expressions, and for the life of him he had no idea why she was acting so strange. He had no idea how he could reassure her he was going to be fine.

And like the doctor's advice, maybe he just needed to give it a few days.

"Okay, I promise to take it easy, Doc. No screens. No work. And no sex with my girlfriend."

The audible gasp from across the room brought Gray right back to Harper. But she moved before he could say anything, slipping from the room before he could ask why she was upset.

His girlfriend?

Harper paced the small area in front of the nurses' station, replaying the past half hour in her mind.

Gray woke up. He was extra touchy-feely and sweet, which she chalked up to being still loopy from the accident. Then he kissed her, the reminder of which still coursed through her body with all the sexual power of an oncoming freight train.

And not a regular old everyday train, no ma'am, but a high-speed, superpowered train that could puncture through a mountainside.

Good God, what was wrong with her? Who wanted to have sex with a concussed man?

Pushing that aside when a resounding "I do!" echoed in her thoughts, Harper went back to the last piece. He called her his girlfriend to the doctor.

Why would he do that?

What happened to him in that paddock?

She caught sight of Dr. Oakes leaving Gray's room and rushed down to the woman, trying to keep her voice low so it didn't filter back in to Gray.

"Dr. Oakes. Would you have a minute?"

"Of course."

"Maybe somewhere down the hall?"

Harper didn't miss the subtle confusion at the request, but the doctor did follow her back down the hallway.

"Your boyfriend will be okay, Miss—" She stopped and Harper extended her hand.

"I'm Harper. Harper Allen."

"He'll be okay, Harper."

"I don't think he is."

"Concussion is a common outcome of an accident like you described. He needs to take the proper care, especially this week as his body's healing, but he should be fine. He's young and healthy and his MRI didn't turn up anything serious like a bleed."

"Yes, I know, but he clearly thought we were together."

The lightly teasing smile the doctor had worn when she caught them kissing was back. "He seems crazy about you."

"I mean, I was his girlfriend once, but we haven't dated in ten years."

"But you were together today." The doctor tilted her head back toward the room. "There in the bed."

That same flush that had flooded her neck and upper chest when she and Gray were caught like two teenagers kissing was back, but Harper pressed on. "Yes, but that was him. Who initiated it. I mean, he pulled me close before I realized. And I'm not . . . I mean, we don't kiss in beds anymore."

"Ms. Allen, it's really none of my business."

Damn it, she was a grown woman. She could do this.

"Gray and I had a very bad breakup about ten years ago. I left Montana and have been gone ever since. I just happened to be with him, to see this horse he's rescuing. Yet he—" Even as the thought floated in, oddly enticing, she wanted to deny it. "He doesn't seem to remember any of that. Since he woke up, he's been acting like those ten years never happened."

Whatever soothing words the doctor had been using to get out of the hallway conversation abruptly changed, her gaze growing sharp.

"Did he say anything else that seemed off?"

"That's what's so strange. He knew the name of the horse we were seeing and seemed very clear that he was rescuing the animal to bring him home. But he then said that *we* were going to take care of the horse, like it was something *we'd* planned. But we're so not a we."

"Confusion is extremely common with concussion, Ms. Allen. If you and Gray have a past history, it's possible he's just a bit confused in light of the accident. It should clear up as he heals."

"But he kissed me."

"You kissed him, too." The doctor's gentle smile was back.

"It's not like that between us. We don't see each other. I don't live in Montana any longer and, well, he called me his girlfriend."

The doctor frowned at that, before staring down at the electronic tablet in her hands. "He did do that. Quite matter-of-factly." She tapped a few times on the screen, and Harper could see where Gray's brain scans popped back up on the screen.

"Why don't you give me a few minutes to talk to him again, Ms. Allen. Would you mind staying out here?"

"Of course."

Dr. Oakes left her, and Harper saw an overhead sign for a small waiting room about halfway down the hall. It was only when she got to the small alcove that she turned to look back down the hall.

And saw Dr. Oakes in deep conversation with another doctor outside Gray's room.

JACKIE PULLED A tray of cookies out of the oven and stared down at the various shapes she'd cut out before baking. She had a flowerpot, a sun and a cloud that, sadly, with the brown dough she'd baked, looked like the poop emoji her students had been so fond of.

"Not like the horse will know or care. You could have just made long strips," she muttered to herself, and she transferred the cookies from the hot tray to a rack to cool.

The treats had been on her list of things to do for her new job, the wholesome bars made of oats and molasses, an equine favorite. She'd made them regularly for her own horse when she'd been actively riding, and it seemed like the right thing to do to welcome the new horse to Gray's ranch and help him settle.

While her stoic, still rail-thin mother would be appalled to hear her say this, Jackie had learned over the years that food was love and the sense of welcome others felt when offered a meal went a long way toward building bonds.

A truth with animals, too.

Besides, who didn't enjoy a sweet treat?

And now baking those treats seemed like the exact right thing to do to keep her mind off the complete debacle of a day she'd had.

She'd had a lunch date.

She'd slept with a man.

She'd been discovered in his T-shirt and nothing else by his adult daughter.

Was it possible to be more mortified?

Unbidden, her memory of the day she'd come home to find Thornton and his friend in bed filled her mind. It wasn't something she thought about, the memory having grown rather fuzzy and hazy in the ensuing decades.

But one thing had stuck, leaving a lingering feeling she'd never quite gotten past.

For all Thornton's infidelity had brought some elements of their relationship into sharp relief—no matter how much he cared for her, he fundamentally didn't want to be *in* the marriage—that experience had left something else behind.

A sense of inadequacy that she'd never been able to shake.

Even as she knew her husband's infidelity

wasn't her fault. Hell, on a deeper level she'd always believed it wasn't even Thornton's fault. He was pretending to be someone he wasn't, and she got caught in the cross fire, his choices an expression of the trap he was caught in.

A fact that she could rationally understand and still not process on a personal level as meaning something other than inadequacy.

Was that why she'd been unable to find a lasting relationship? Or why she'd pined so long for Martin, unwilling to either put herself out there or walk away from that safe crush and go find someone else.

That had been the real mortification, she acknowledged, as she cut out the remaining cookies on her counter.

Those thoughts that had swirled in her mind as she lay in his bed—the realization that she'd wanted him for a very long time—had forced her to look at the reality of her personal life. The man was a widower. And while it would have been inappropriate twenty years ago to hit on him, in all the years that had come since she'd never found a way to act on her feelings.

Nor had she given him the slightest inclination that she might be interested in entertaining his.

She might have excused her actions in saying she didn't want to hit on a fellow educator in a leadership role, but what she'd really been was a coward. She'd locked her heart up tight and hadn't risked anything.

Not a damn thing.

She did the last cutout—one of those stupid clouds—and laid it on the pan as her doorbell rang. Her heart leaped in spite of her deeply unpeppy talk with herself that it might be Martin.

Even if he hadn't called or texted all afternoon. Which probably meant it was just her neighbor.

But if it was him . . .

Jackie stared down at her flour-dusted sweatshirt and the frumpiest pair of sweatpants she owned that made her ass look like the broad side of a Mack truck and put the cookies in the oven.

Since there was nothing to be done for it, she headed for the door as the doorbell rang again.

And opened it to find him standing on the other side.

"Can I come in?"

He was dressed in slacks and a button-down shirt, and Jackie had the uncomfortable—yet tempting—thought that it would be preferable to slam the door in his face and go hide in her bedroom. But that would prove she was a coward and, besides, he looked good.

Really good.

Like some sort of cosmically unfair counterpoint to her dirty sweatshirt and Mack-ass sweats.

When he stepped in anyway, she added a "Sure, come in," to punctuate her irritation.

He moved in beyond her small foyer, his gaze roaming around her living room before it landed squarely on her. "It smells great in here."

"I'm baking. For the horses."

"Oh."

"People can eat them, too. It's just some oats and molasses and a few other items. But they're horse cookies. I mean, they're for the horses."

A small smile twitched at the edges of his lips. "I wasn't asking for one, but now that you've made them sound so enticing . . ."

"Look, Martin—" She stared down at her wrist, absently brushing away some flour that clung to her forearm. "You didn't need to come over. And we don't need to talk."

"I think we do."

She'd heard that voice several times through the years. He didn't pull it out often, but in his own way, deeply gentle and kind Martin Allen knew how to be forceful. To make his point so others would listen.

It had been one of the things that had always impressed her in the way he led the school. His job had far more facets than most realized, the biggest of which was that he dealt with people all day, with all their human faults, foibles and general wackiness. And whether they were happy or sad, petulant and hormonal or scared and frustrated, he dealt with it all.

In their students and in their faculty.

So with no small measure of surprise she realized that he'd used his stern "let-me-make-my-point" voice on her.

"I know it was uncomfortable that we were interrupted today."

"Is that what we're calling it?"

"Awkward as ass, perhaps?" His eyebrows shot

up along with one side of his mouth that quirked just high enough to show the shallow dent of a dimple.

"Your daughter discovered me half-naked in your kitchen after we'd had sex."

"We sure did." That lopsided grin morphed into a full one, and he moved closer, his hand going to her waist. "And you didn't need to leave."

She stepped back, and the hand he'd laid at her waist fell to his side, along with the smile. "We're adults, Jackie. And I'm not going to feel ashamed or be embarrassed that I'm seeing you or sleeping with you. My kids have had long enough to forget the fact that I'm a healthy, adult male. I don't need to coddle them."

"I'm sure they haven't forgotten."

"No, I think they have. I haven't dated a lot, and I sure as hell didn't do it when they were young and still in my home. But in the years since?" He held up his hands. "I haven't been all that successful at any long-term relationship I've attempted. It's time they realized I'm as entitled to one as they are."

"Why do you think that is? That you haven't had many long-term relationships?"

She didn't want to be drawn in to his words. Nor was she all that convinced they had "long-term" written all over whatever this was between them.

But she was still curious to know the answer.

"I don't know. I told myself it was my lifestyle. I realize it's never going to make the top ten sexiest jobs in the world, but a high school principal has very little free time when all's said and done. And between evening and weekend commitments to the students, the school and the school board, I'm probably not as available as a prospective long-term partner would like."

"You think that's the reason?"

"I did. It's the excuse I told myself. And then I started talking with this woman that I've always had something of a tendre for."

His sweet words hit her so squarely in the chest she was surprised she didn't actually stumble backward from the force of them. "You like me?"

That small quirk of his lips was back, tugging at something deep inside of her. "You somehow thought this was about *not* liking you?"

When she didn't say anything, he simply continued on.

"Well, I've come to realize that I do like you and have for a lot longer than I realized. I always considered you a valued colleague. And it's only been in the last few months that you've been gone from the school that I understood just how much I missed you. How much I've missed seeing you every day."

They were the right words.

Each and every one of them.

Yet with them came more of that overwhelming fear and inadequacy.

And shame.

She'd wanted him for so long, even when his wife was alive. And no, she hadn't done anything.

Wouldn't have dared. But it hadn't changed how she felt.

Or how attractive she'd always found him.

How did you explain that to someone?

Gee, Martin, thanks for telling me. As a funny point of comparison, I've wanted you, too. I even wanted you when you were married.

She'd lived with the realities of infidelity. And whether intentional or not, she'd allowed herself to feel attraction for someone she couldn't have. A man who was *only* available because his wife's death now made that attraction possible.

It hadn't sat well with her then, and it was tragic to realize how much worse it felt now. Like she'd lied, hiding her feelings and allowing her desire for him to lie in wait. A stealthy sort of infidelity that dragged at her soul and made her feel dirty.

And unworthy.

Which was exactly how she'd felt when Harper walked into the kitchen today and saw her standing there in Martin's T-shirt.

She'd felt sleazy and sordid.

And that was one thing she'd vowed never to be.

Because she'd been the person on the other side of the door. And she knew what it did to you.

"I've really enjoyed spending time with you, Martin. These past few weeks and today—" She broke off, catching her breath and willing herself to get through it.

Each and every word that needed to be said.

"But I don't think we should see each other. Because as it turns out, I'm not particularly good at long-term relationships. I'm not made for them. And I think it would be better if we ended things now."

"Jackie, don't do this. Don't say that."

The timer for the cookies went off in the kitchen and she used it as a lifeline. "I'd better go get those. You can see yourself out."

She gave herself one last moment to stare into that gorgeous blue gaze, now full of swirling emotion.

Then she turned away, knowing she'd see that unmistakable regret endlessly in her mind. Was well aware she'd feel the same in return.

Chapter 12

Harper stared at Dr. Oakes, shocked when the swirling, mysterious thoughts she'd had earlier were reinforced by the doctor's diagnosis.

"I believe Gray is suffering from some aspects of amnesia."

"Some aspects?"

"It's not particularly well understood and, despite pop culture's fascination with memory loss, it's not all that common."

The doctor had already walked her through the basics of Gray's injury. He did have a concussion and his scans were reassuring in that there was no bleeding or any reason to think he'd sustained permanent damage.

All details she'd gotten before.

And details, she suspected, the doctor felt in-

creasingly guilty about sharing, even though Gray
had assigned Harper as eligible to receive his medical information.

Who else would receive it?

That thought had become increasingly clear as
they'd spent the afternoon and evening and now,
a good portion of the night, in the hospital. Who
was going to take care of him? Because potential
amnesia aside, he couldn't stay by himself.

Nor could she leave him if he wasn't in full
control of his faculties.

But could she actually stay with him? Especially as the power of his kiss—from a freaking
hospital bed, no less—still packed such a punch.

But not nearly as big a punch as his words.

*Okay, I promise to take it easy, Doc. No screens. No
work. And no sex with my girlfriend.*

In what world was this real?

A world, she forced herself to acknowledge,
where Gray McClain lay in a hospital bed with no
one else on earth to care for him.

It was a humbling thought and a soul-quaking
match to some of the thoughts she'd had herself
through the years. What would she do if she was
ever really injured? Who would help her? Care
for her?

Yes, she had her father and her sister, and she
lived in the very sure knowledge they would
move heaven and earth for her.

But it hadn't stopped the fact that she had no
idea what she would have done if something

happened to her all by herself in Seattle. Even with those concerns, she knew she had her dad and Hadley.

Who did Gray have?

While he'd always been deeply determined to keep her away from his father, she knew who Burt McClain was. She supposed she could call him, but something held her back there. Gray's relationship with him was bad, bordering on non-existent. Even with a head injury, her instincts screamed at her that calling Gray's dad would only upset him and make the situation worse.

Which left her.

"You said some amnesia? What is *some*?"

"For all we've learned about the brain, there's so much we don't know. But we do know amnesia comes from three main causes. An accident, as Gray has sustained. A trauma that the mind deliberately forgets so as to protect itself from the shock. Or degenerative disease in the brain from illness or chronic behavior like excessive drug and alcohol use."

"So if it's from his concussion, it should be alleviated as his brain heals?"

"Yes, but what isn't clear is why Dr. McClain is able to remember the injury and not that you and he are no longer together. Especially since you mentioned that you'd been apart for ten years. In cases of trauma, a person is usually able to remember longer term memories versus shorter term ones."

That trauma explanation briefly flitted through her thoughts before Harper tamped it down. While it was tempting to think breaking up with her was so traumatic Gray would have to find a way to forget it, she wasn't that vain.

Or deluded.

"Whatever the reason is, it'll be temporary. He'll heal, and then we'll be back to where we were."

Dr. Oakes folded her hands over the desk where she sat. "Miss Allen. I don't want to mislead you here. This is something we simply don't know or understand enough to give you a time frame. Based on all existing medical understanding, Gray should get his memory back. But how long that will take is not something I can accurately tell you."

"Okay. I understand."

"He will be able to go back to his regular activities once he heals from the concussion. And while I am not well versed in veterinary medicine, he did mention his fellow doctor who he works with. I'd be comfortable saying Gray can go back to work if that doctor feels his practice on animals is back to professional standards."

"That's good." And necessary, Harper thought, as a key step to getting back to his normal life. To *remembering* his life by getting immersed back in the day-to-day.

"Is there someone I can call for you? Someone you'd like to call to come and pick you both up."

"You're releasing him?"

"I have no reason to keep him. I would like to see him again next week as I'd mentioned."

"Of course." Harper nodded, keying back into the other questions. "And no, I'm fine driving us home."

Dr. Oakes seemed to consider her next words, before finally speaking. "As I said earlier, amnesia isn't as common as TV would like us to think, which means there's not a lot of practical, clinical knowledge I've got as a doctor. I have worked extensively, though, with patients with diminished memory from dementia or Alzheimer's."

At the mention of those conditions, Dr. Oakes must have seen Harper's horror because she rushed on.

"Which I'm not at all suggesting he has. But I have learned from those patients that giving them the mental space to have their thoughts is important."

"So I should let Gray have his del—" Harper nearly said *delusions* before catching herself. "Misplaced memories?"

"I think you should give him the space to heal. If that means thinking a few things that he'll naturally come to understand aren't true, what harm is there? Give him that space."

Give him space.

She'd seen Cabernet rear and knew the absolute horror at seeing the horse slam Gray into the paddock rails. Of course she wanted him to heal.

And even with all the water under their personal bridge, she cared for him still. She'd never wish him ill or not want the very best for him.

But doing what the doctor asked?

Pretending they were a couple for a week or two? Could she do that?

How could she not?

As if sensing Harper's mental gymnastics, the doctor finally nodded and stood. "I'll get his discharge papers ready, then. You can go see him whenever you'd like."

"Thank you."

Dr. Oakes picked up the tablet that never seemed out of range of her hands. It was only as she came around the desk that she stopped beside Harper.

"I can see you care for him. Just use that compassion to help him through this. He's healthy and his injury is something he should recover from in one to two weeks."

Harper said thank you again, even as she tried to process the mixed messages and the doctor's continued unwillingness to set a timeline for when Gray would get his memory fully back. He would physically heal, but they had no idea what his mind was doing to protect itself. From the injury.

Or from something else?

Nor did they understand how long that healing would take, even if his injury got better along normal timelines.

Again, the tempting thought that his amnesia was tied to her flitted through her mind, and she pushed it away with more force.

Allowing those magical fantasies of hers any space to breathe was not productive, nor was it going to help Gray.

Even if there was a part of her that was clamoring in joy. Great, lapping waves of it that felt decidedly like a second chance.

Because whether she should be happy about it or scared down to the tips of her toes, she was going to take care of Gray McClain for the next two weeks.

God help them both.

GRAY FELT THE light nudge on his shoulder just as a husky, tired voice pulled him awake.

"Gray."

"Hmmm?"

He'd closed his eyes when he and Harper got in the truck to leave the hospital, the bright lights of the oncoming cars bothering his vision and taking the slamming in his head up about six notches.

The basic equivalent of shoving a fire alarm inside his skull.

The headache had quieted its clamoring to something more manageable as they drove, and he'd tried to have a conversation, only to feel himself drifting off.

And where were they now?

He opened his eyes and saw the cabin through the windshield of his truck.

"You're home." Harper's voice was still gentle, those husky tones floating over him and tightening his chest in a fist.

Why did it feel like it had been ages since he'd heard it? Her sleepy sex voice, he'd always called it in his head. Those husky tones that came on when she was tired, after they'd stayed up way past their bedtime to make love.

She had it when she stayed up late studying, too, or working on one of her coding projects, but his baser nature enjoyed equating it to sex.

Which was never too big a stretch when Harper was near.

"I'll come around to help you."

He'd felt silly leaning on her but had been surprised to realize how tired he was just walking out of the hospital. The nurse helping them to the car had assured him that this was normal with head injuries and that he'd be okay in a few days. In the meantime, he needed to give his body the rest it needed.

Since he felt like he could sleep for days, Gray figured that wasn't too big an ask.

The door beside him opened, and Harper's scent filled him as she reached over him to undo his seat belt.

"Hey, baby."

The words felt oddly slurred but he didn't miss the humor in her voice. "Easy there, cowboy. You're not as steady on your feet as you think you are."

Much as it embarrassed him, he had to admit
that she was right. So he opted to take comfort
from the arm that snaked around his waist as she
gently encouraged him to pull his legs out of the
truck.

Their positions were awkward as he slowly
moved his legs, bumping into her waist with his
knee, and it made him think about that moment
in his hospital bed when their bodies were tan-
gled at a strange angle as she sat beside him.

"I think there's a reason people kiss facing each
other."

"What?"

"This." He gestured between their still-twisted
bodies, but his hand snaked out wildly and hit
the doorframe.

"Gray!" Her voice was soft but he heard the
stern tones, like a kindergarten teacher reeling in
her unruly charges. "Be careful."

"I'm careful."

"No, sweetie, you're loopy and there's a difference. Here. Let's try this a different way."

She kept a hand on his shoulder—to hold him
still as he hung halfway out the truck door?—
before repositioning herself so she faced him.
"Let me help you down."

Since he had about eight inches of height on
her and at least eighty pounds, it was a laughable
suggestion. One he nearly did laugh at when a
spike of pain lasered through his skull.

"Gray!"

The kindergarten teacher had vanished and

distinct notes of panic flared in her voice when he half fell, half tumbled out of the truck.

He felt her arms lock around his waist but her frantic movements grew more pronounced as she fought to hold them both upright. Gray's legs scrabbled beneath him for a few more steps before he caught his balance. He locked an arm around her shoulders, stilling them both.

After they both stood there for a second, Harper finally spoke. "Why does it feel like some weird drunken stumble home from the Branded Mark?"

"Because I've got the equivalent of about twelve hangovers?"

"That might have something to do with it."

Her arm never left his waist, but she did lay a hand on his chest as she looked up at him. "Are you okay? Do you have your balance?"

As he stared down at her, he was forced to ask himself that very question.

Did he?

"I'm good."

He was pretty sure he didn't have her fully convinced, but she did leave him standing still just long enough to get the truck door closed and locked up for the night, before she returned to his side.

"Be careful where you walk. It was warm today and a lot of the snow melted, but a few patches have probably refrozen." They slowly navigated the walk from the truck to the house. By the time they got to the door, his head was pounding again, and he reached for the doorjamb to hold himself upright as she fumbled with the keys.

"Damn it." She muttered under her breath as she tried a key, jiggling the lock but not getting the door open.

Didn't she know which key it was?

Gray extended a hand. "Here, babe. I'll get it."

Something he couldn't describe glittered in her gaze under the porch lights that had come on with their motions. He could barely keep his eyes open under the assault of light, but he didn't miss that look.

It was just like the heavy glances she'd given him in the hospital.

He'd thought them sad at the time, but now that he caught sight of them under the fresh glow of the lights, he realized there was something more.

Grief.

He really was going to be alright. Why couldn't he assure her of that? Even if his head did feel like it was being slammed repeatedly between the two walls of a squeeze chute, it was a temporary condition. One that he'd heal from.

He'd learned early on, back in those days they'd worked together in high school, that Harper was a person who needed to work through her troubles. Only when she worked through them herself could she share them.

With that—and the furious headache—he decided it was time to leave it alone and give her space. It had been a tough day for both of them and they could talk about it tomorrow.

He barely registered the rest of the house as she helped him to bed. Nor did he notice when she slipped away from him a few minutes after they lay down, fully clothed.

But he felt it, when he rolled over and drew the other pillow in the bed under his arm. It was oddly familiar, he thought as he drifted off to sleep.

Even if he had no idea why.

"AMNESIA?" HADLEY'S EYES were wide as she stared at Harper across Gray's small kitchen table. "Like nighttime soap amnesia?"

Harper smiled fondly at the memories of the nighttime soaps she and Hadley snarfed in large quantities as teenagers. "The same."

"No way."

"Apparently it's very *yes way*, according to the doctor. She really hasn't seen it before but she does know the symptoms and causes."

"Maybe not here but I bet doctors in New York have seen it. Do you want me to call Bea and see if she knows anyone?"

At the mention of Hadley's show producer and friend, Harper waved a hand. "It's his personal business. I can't ask someone else about it. Plus, she's focused on her pregnancy."

"She'll be careful."

"I know. It's just—" Harper toyed with the handle of her coffee mug. She'd fixed coffee to go with the tray of sticky buns her sister had brought over, spoils from the kitchen testing the day before

And since she'd already inhaled two of the sinful buns and was contemplating a third as a way to deal with the sexual awareness that had hit with full force that morning as she lay on Gray's couch, she needed to take it easy. Not make rash decisions.

"It's just what?"

"He's alone. And I don't want to overstep, you know?"

"I can see that. But Bea will be careful and discreet if you decide you'd like her help. Between her contacts and the power of the network, she can probably get you some answers if you need them or Gray decides he wants them."

"He doesn't know."

"Excuse me?"

"He doesn't know. About the amnesia part. I mean, he knows he has a concussion and that he was run into by a horse."

"Harper, what do you mean he doesn't know?"

"The doctor said people with memory issues often do better when they're placated in their memories. That's what she finds with her dementia and Alzheimer's patients."

"People who are no doubt fifty years older than Gray." Hadley frowned. "This seems like some seriously shitty medical advice."

"She didn't tell me to lie to him."

"But omitting telling the man he has amnesia is being all honest and up-front?"

"You want to dial back the judgy tone?"

"Sorry." Hadley toyed with the edge of her cuticle. "Really, I'm sorry."

"And it did seem like strange advice. Strange advice with a layer of common sense, though."

"What did the doctor say, exactly?"

"That he should heal in one to two weeks from the concussion. And that it's not lying, but I should give him some 'space to heal,' she called it." Harper ran through the doctor's list again. "She said that if he was talking in a confused way about things that he'll naturally figure it out on his own."

"That doesn't sound so bad." Hadley tore off a small piece of her sticky bun—her first—before landing on the one point Harper would have preferred to avoid.

"What can't he remember? How to be a doctor?"

"He seems okay there. I mean, he knew we were at the ranch to look at a rescue horse. And he knew he was a vet."

"That's great news."

"It is."

"Okay, so maybe the doctor's advice makes sense. So he doesn't remember how to treat a cow for a few days or how to treat laminitis in a horse. I can see where pushing him about it will only make him feel bad or frustrated. It'll come back."

"I think he does know those things."

Hadley's sharp gaze never lost its focus, and Harper knew that was the exact reason she'd called her sister over. Because as she had lain

on the couch this morning, she'd indulged in a
few more of those magical thinking fantasies
that were the increasing proof she could not be
trusted.

She'd thought about the fact that she had to
spend time with Gray. Forced time to make sure
he healed. And that if he thought they were
dating—and she couldn't exactly tell him they
weren't—then she could enjoy the week with him
in guilt-free bliss.

Because all the telling herself that she was over
Gray McClain was a pile of steaming bullshit, and
fate had just stepped in and handed her a lovely
opportunity to forget for a little while that they
weren't a couple.

"What doesn't he know, Harper?"

"It's silly. Really silly. I mean, I wouldn't be surprised if he woke up this morning and realized
how hard he'd hit his head yesterday."

"Harper?"

Before she could answer, Gray's bedroom door
opened and he padded into the kitchen. Even
with his hair sticking up at odd angles and the
night's growth of beard, he looked a lot better
than the night before. And his steps were definitely straighter as he walked toward the kitchen.

"Hadley." Gray smiled before walking to the
counter. "It's good to see you. And really awesome that you brought sustenance."

"How are you feeling?" Hadley's question was
careful, her tones measured. "Harper said you
had a nasty fall yesterday."

"My head is still pounding but I feel like I can think a lot clearer than yesterday."

That was *good*, Harper thought, as she shot Hadley a triumphant look. One that only grew stronger as she watched him pour himself a cup of coffee with a steady hand.

More good news.

"Come on over here and sit down," Harper finally said. "I'll get you a plate."

"It feels good to stand." Gray turned, resting his butt against the countertop, his long legs stretched out before him. "Zack doing okay with the new calves?"

"He's good. He was out with the herd when I left this morning to head over."

"I'm under orders to give my patients to Shep Rodgers for the next week but tell him to call me if he needs anything. I can at least keep notes and pass them on to Shep if he needs to come out to the ranch."

"I'll let him know." Hadley took a sip of her coffee. "It's great that you won't be down too long. And you seem pretty up on your caseload for a man who got hit in the head yesterday."

"It's like I told Harper. I'm made of sterner stuff." He took a sip of his coffee, his grin easy. "And my head's pretty damn hard."

"A trait you and my sister share in spades."

"Thanks, Had." Harper got up, suddenly needing something to do. She wanted to ask Gray how he was feeling, and she was suddenly sorry she had an audience. Even if she had needed Hadley's support that morning, both the emotional sup-port and the solid dose of common sense.

"Here, Gray. Let me get you that plate." She opened a cabinet a few feet down from where he stood, turning her back to him where the counter cornered. It was the only reason she didn't see him coming.

Or so she'd tell herself later.

In the moment, it was all she could do to hold back the half squeak/half scream as two big arms came around her and a set of very delectable lips nuzzled her neck.

Chapter 13

Harper turned down the pot of soup she was cooking to a simmer and crossed back over to her laptop at the kitchen table. Hadley had brought the ingredients earlier along with a small bag of Harper's things. Between the boredom from the snowstorm and Gray's accident, Harper hadn't done a bit of work in more than forty-eight hours and was now trying diligently to catch up on work for Coffee 2.0 in between dodging Gray's hands and convincing him to take a nap.

Oh, and dodging her sister's meaningful glares as Harper unceremoniously shoved her out of the house that morning under the guise that Gray needed more rest.

Even if his hands and his lips felt *very* wide-awake every time he came near her. Or maybe that was just the erection he'd pressed against her lower back when he'd kissed her.

An imprint she could still feel several hours later.

It hadn't taken a lecture out by the car from her sister to reinforce all the reasons why staying here with Gray was a bad idea, but no matter how she twisted it in her mind, Harper knew she couldn't leave him.

And he was under doctor's orders not to have sex, so they'd be fine.

The timer on her phone went off, reminding her to get the dough she had rising under a towel out for another round of kneading and Harper jumped at the task like a lifeline, the opportunity to punch something welcome.

Deeply welcome, she thought a few minutes later, as she slammed a fist into the rising dough.

Although cooking was her sister's domain, Harper had become proficient on a few key dishes through the years. Her chicken soup was one of her best meals, and when it was paired with homemade bread, she considered herself sufficiently capable to feed someone. The soup would do Gray good and it would give them leftovers for the week, too.

Them.

When had they become a them? Or better said, when had they become a them *again*?

An answer that was wrapped up in all the things she'd avoided thinking about for too long, including that question she'd lobbed at him the day before like a grenade.

Why haven't you gotten married?

Had she really asked that? And why was she still modestly—okay, *really*—put out that he hadn't asked the question in return.

"Hey. What did that bread ever do to you?"

Gray stood at the entry to the kitchen. He'd showered and shaved, his hair still wet. She could see the strain around his eyes but other than that, he looked good.

Better than good.

And healthy, she quickly reminded herself, cutting off any thoughts of how appealing he was. His healing had to be her focus.

"It's been a tough couple of days. And the dough can handle it."

"So you say." He crossed the small space, coming up behind her and wrapping his arms around her.

Again. Just like when Hadley was there, sitting in the kitchen.

Then they'd had an audience. And now—

Harper ignored the lingering admonishments of her sister and the even louder ones that clamored in her head and gave herself a moment.

Just one moment to take something she'd long missed.

It had been one of their favorite poses when they'd been together. The natural way he'd seek her out, whatever she was doing. He'd wrap her in one of those big hugs and she'd nestle back into his strong arms and just . . . be. They'd stand like that, holding each other and reveling in the beauty of being with one another.

Hadn't that been one of the things she'd missed most after they'd broken up? The complete lack of touching someone and of being touched?

She'd moved within a few months of their breakup, which had only exacerbated the situation. Where she did still hug her father and sister, her brother-in-law and several friends while in and around Rustlers Creek, she'd moved to Seattle and started from scratch.

And had no one.

Over time she'd learned to live without it. That physical ease and intimacy had been a part of her life once, but now she had a new life. A different life. And dwelling on all the things she no longer had instead of the ones she did was pointless.

And now . . .

His fingers drifted over her stomach, making lazy circles beneath her breastbone, and she leaned back into his chest, that tender caress so lovely, so intoxicating, so . . .

"Gray!"

She shimmied out of his hold and crossed to the sink, washing her hands after kneading the dough. "The doctor said no fooling around."

"She said no sex."

"There's a lot of sex before sex that's off the table."

"I'd say there's a lot of sex before sex that's most

definitely on the table. She did say I could kiss you."

His grin was unrepentant and she got caught up in it, unable to resist him. "You got railroaded yesterday by a horse. Maybe you can take it down a notch."

"I know." That quick smile faded, his face drawing up in stark lines. "I don't know why I feel this way, but I can't seem to hold back this awareness of you. I mean, I'm always aware of you. Always." He moved closer and reached for her hand. "But it's like I can't stop thinking about you. Like some floodgate's opened and I can't stop thinking about touching you."

I think you should give him the space to heal. If that means thinking a few things that he'll naturally come to understand aren't true, what harm is there?

The doctor's words echoed over and over in her mind, but this was going to be a hell of a long week if she didn't get some details figured out. And while there might not be harm to Gray now as he healed, what would he experience after he remembered? Especially if she didn't make a few gentle attempts to help him understand.

To help make this right.

"What do you remember before the accident with Cabernet?" When he seemed caught off guard by the question, she added, "The doctor said that it's normal to lose some memories with a head trauma. I'd like to see what you remember."

The answer seemed to placate him, and he was quick to answer, his words sure. "We drove over

to Rick Pruett's ranch. We went there after we
were at your dad's for lunch."

"Do you remember that part?"

"Oh wow, Harper!" Memory stamped itself in
his blue gaze and Gray moved in closer, pulling
her in for a hug. "You had quite an experience yesterday. Your dad and Jackie. How are you doing?"

"Good. I'm good with it. And he and I spoke
for a bit last night while you were getting some
of those tests run. I'm okay with his relationship.
Really I am."

Funny enough, whatever horror she'd felt seeing a woman standing in the kitchen in nothing
but a T-shirt had been nearly forgotten in the mo-
mentous events with Gray. She and her father had
talked, and he'd spoken so glowingly of Jackie
Delaney it made Harper wish they'd gotten reac-
quainted under less embarrassing circumstances.

For all of them.

Which was why, when he said he was going
over to see her after they finished their call, that
Harper gave specific instructions to plan a dinner
for all of them.

"I'm glad."

"I am, too. It's good to think of my dad with
someone. He's been alone for a long time." She
thought of all those years of her own, not touching anyone. "Too long."

It was amazing, she marveled to herself, how
much brighter the world looked when someone
kept pulling you into their arms. She felt like
one of the barn cats she had petted at Hadley's

while walking around the ranch a few weeks ago. The cat had preened and purred in her arms while they sat on a haystack in one of the barns, a shaft of sunlight bathing them from the upper windows.

Somehow, in the space of a few full body hugs from Gray, she was nearly purring herself. A thought that registered as she laid her head against his chest. "Do you remember anything else? About us, I mean?"

"I know you've been working really hard on your coffee company. You've been practicing at the Trading Post."

She let the words drift over her, surprised by just how sad it made her that he seemed to remember everything except the reality of their relationship.

Or who they no longer were to each other.

"I have been."

He twisted slightly so he could bend his head to look down at her, and she used the moment to look up and really study him. "What are you trying to say, Harper?"

"We've spent time apart, Gray. Quite a bit of time, actually."

"Apart?"

"I've been in Seattle. For a while. To work." She avoided mentioning that it had been ten years, curious to see if the lack of details would help or hurt his memory.

"Okay."

"Do you remember that?"

"No. But it does explain why I feel like I haven't seen you for a while."

Her heart crumpled a bit at the admission, and Harper wondered if it was good to keep going. Especially when she noticed the dark circles under his eyes, a match for the strain at the edges.

She needed to be strong. Realistically, she knew that. But images of Cabernet forcing him into the fence and the confusion lacing his gaze and the feel of his hands on her arms kept her from pressing him anymore.

She wouldn't take this too far. And she wasn't going to do anything to hurt him. But continuing to push wasn't something he was ready for, either.

With gentle motions, she laid a hand on his cheek. "We were apart for a bit. But I'm here now."

Without checking herself, Harper met his lips when he bent his head to kiss her. She wrapped her arms around his neck and held him cradled against her body when he pressed against her, her back against the counter. And when his hands drifted lower, his fingers brushing over her breasts, she leaned into his touch.

And simply took the beauty of a few moments of connection as the sun bathed them in the afternoon light.

GRAY WALKED AROUND the nearly completed stable and evaluated what still needed to be done before he could bring Cabernet to his ranch. He knew he could call Zack Wayne and employ the services of any one of Zack's ranch hands for a bit of extra work. He could likely do the same with any number of clients.

But whether it was pride or his own stubborn hard head, it bugged him that he couldn't do it himself.

He was on day five of the healing process. The headaches hadn't subsided yet, but they weren't as nasty as they had been and they'd dulled to a subtle throb instead of the pounding jackhammers of the first few days.

What had been frustrating were the threads of memory that seemed to wave at him, like something flashing in his peripheral vision. He knew something was there but couldn't get a read on it.

Couldn't quite see it clearly enough.

Like Harper.

He'd tried to better understand her time away, as she called it, but each time he brought it up she'd tell him just enough to answer the question and not nearly enough to help him actually understand what was going on.

But they were together.

He knew that. She was his girlfriend and he loved her. Wasn't that the way it always had been?

When those odd wisps of memory swirled once more, he tried to snatch one but came up with nothing except a kick up in the pain of his headache.

So he'd try later.

He'd taken it easy in terms of looking at his computer or his phone, but he had read the discharge papers from the doctor as well as some materials she'd sent him on concussion. And while he didn't regularly worry about brain injury in his animal patients, he knew the medical basics of his condition.

Rest and recuperation were the name of the game. While necessary, after five days of it he was out of his mind with boredom.

And increasingly frustrated at those stray wisps that never seemed to land.

"Hello?"

Gray turned at the sound, pleased to see Jackie Delaney at the opposite end of the stable, and waved her back. "Come on in."

He gestured her to a small picnic table he'd set up in the back area of the stable.

"Gray." Jackie laid a hand on his shoulder, her gaze seeking. "I heard what happened last week. How are you?"

"Fine."

"Fine?" Her warm smile fell. "Why don't I believe you?"

"Had a concussion before, have you?"

"No, but close. I have been thrown a few times from the back of a horse. It shakes you up."

"Then you know a polite lie when you hear one." He waited until she took a seat at the small table, then took one of his own. "If I could get rid of the headache, I'd say I was fine."

"You need time and rest."

"So I hear. Harper's been saying the same thing."

"Harper's right."

She was also a traitorous ally to the damned doctor, Gray thought with no small measure of frustration. He still hadn't persuaded her that he was healthy enough for more than kissing. An outcome he'd likely have been more successful at if he hadn't fallen asleep by eight every night.

"Look, I know you might not be focused on the rescue right now until you're feeling better, but I did want to talk about my employment."

"I got your W-9 paperwork taken care of before the accident so I'm ready for you to start. I'd like to get Cabernet in this week. I spoke with Rick Pruett, and since I have to go back to the doctor on Thursday, we're going to make the exchange then, too. I'd like to have you along to do that."

"Gray, I—"

He'd always considered himself a much better judge of animals than people, but for the past few days, his senses about others seemed to be heightened. Whether it was everyone walking on eggshells over his injury or some strange outgrowth of getting coshed in the head, Gray had no idea, but it didn't take a lot of insight to see that Jackie was upset. "What's wrong?"

"I don't think it's a good idea for me to work here. Not with what happened with Harper and Marty and, well, it just isn't a good idea."

"Why not? Harper's happy you and her dad are dating."

"That's the problem. We're not."

The headache might still be wreaking havoc with his focus, but it wasn't hard to see Jackie's unhappiness, grooving across her face in sad lines. "It's none of my business, but didn't you just start dating?"

"Yes, we did. But it's not going to work out."

Gray much preferred staying out of other people's relationships—it was a policy he'd employed most of his life and it worked for him—but something in Jackie's misery caught him up short.

Especially because Gray had seen a light, happy expression on Marty Allen's face, even in that exceptionally awkward moment in the kitchen, that he'd never seen before.

"The guy's pretty smitten with you."

"Smitten?"

"An old-fashioned word for a feeling that never goes out of style." *And something I know a bit about,* he thought as his arms itched to pull Harper close against his chest. She might have limited his additional activities, but she'd been more than willing to snuggle with him. It had been sweet and surprisingly intoxicating.

"That's nice of you to say, but things aren't going to work out."

Gray sensed that his role in this conversation was to listen so he simply pressed on. "I'm sorry to hear that, but it doesn't have anything to do with you working for me."

"It seems awkward."

"For who? Me?"

She glanced down at her hands, folded on the table, before seeming to come to some conclusion. "Martin gave you my name for the job."

"And he's saved my bacon because of it. Look, Jackie. I am sorry that things haven't worked out with you and Marty. But my rescue is really important to me. And having someone I can trust and who knows horses is invaluable. I'd like you to still join me on this."

Since he wasn't sure he'd convinced her, Gray went for broke. With a tap to his forehead, he added, "It's obvious I'm not equipped to handle the horse myself."

Although he got a faint smile, his comment was enough to get her leaning forward, which Gray took as a very good sign.

"What did happen?"

"I should have known better. Rick Pruett's daughter had another horse in the paddock. Although we'd put considerable distance between the horses, she's young and her horse bucked, scaring her. In the ensuing commotion, Rick left Cabernet to go help her and Cabernet was unsettled by the situation."

"It's unfortunate."

"Unfortunate, but more proof of why I need to do this."

"How so?"

"Cabernet needs support. He needs an environment that's more conducive to his needs. I'm going to create that. Animals aren't disposable."

People weren't, either.

He wasn't sure where that came from or why he felt so convinced about it, but the thought settled in deep, one of those stray wisps of memory that he managed to hold on to.

"No, they're not. It's what I'm most excited about with this job."

"Then you'll stay on?"

Jackie glanced around the stable, her gaze seemingly faraway, before she nodded. "I'll stay."

"And you'll come with us on Thursday to get Cabernet?"

He knew seeing Harper was likely a pain point when it came to whatever had happened with Jackie and Marty, but there wasn't any help for it. Harper was a part of his life, and the two women would need to be around one another.

Harper was part of his life.

One of those wisps drifted through his mind with all the substance of the dust motes catching the light through the barn door. She *was* a part of his life and had been since high school.

We've spent time apart, Gray.

Quite a bit of time, actually.

I've been in Seattle. For a while. To work.

Her work was important to her, just as the rescue mattered to him. She'd worked so hard in school, and they had the right commitment between the two of them to share their lives and still work toward their goals.

He was certain of it.

HARPER HAD WAITED long enough. She'd given Jackie time to leave and figured Gray would be back inside by now, but she still hadn't seen him. The reprieve had been welcome at first, since she'd needed to get some work done today and had encouraged Gray when he'd claimed he wanted to get outside a bit and that the fresh air would do him good.

And maybe help jog that stubborn lapse of memory that didn't seem in any hurry to return.

All in all, the reprieve had been good. She and Gray had spent a lot of time in close proximity and she needed the break. From the increasingly challenging feelings that refused to settle when she was around him and from the man himself. She'd been able to keep the physical aspects between them to nothing more than kissing and cuddling, but God, it was a challenge.

All she wanted to do was rip Gray's clothes off, and that was the last thing either of them needed. Her, because her head was already upside-down about her feelings, and him, because his head was just upside-down. Each day she'd found some way to ask him about the things he remembered, encouraged when he seemed to fully know something, including complicated medical procedures and diagnoses. But his continued belief that they were a couple?

That synaptic lapse simply didn't seem to be reconnecting.

What she couldn't understand was how he

didn't seem to have any questions about their time apart or where she lived. It was like however his mind was processing what they were to each other, it just omitted the details it didn't want to deal with and ignored all other ambiguities.

Shrugging into her coat, she headed out to the stables. And as she came upon him, sitting at a small table in the back of the barn, his eyes closed and his face turned up to the sun, she had another realization.

She'd known this man half her life. Had loved him for all that time, too.

While the actual amount of time they'd spent together had been limited, what they had shared had been some of the most powerful moments of her life.

The things she'd discussed with him about her mother. Her grief and sadness and her deep need to have someone listen to her.

The sharing of food when she'd realized that he often had none and how she'd needed to both take care of him and protect his pride.

And the time when they actually had a relationship, learning each other, loving each other and understanding how to make one another feel good. How to touch and tease, how to draw out pleasure and how to give it as well as accept it.

How to be vulnerable.

Hadn't that been the real truth of her relationship with Gray? Its foundation and the reason that bond meant so much to her. He wasn't just the first man she'd loved or the man she'd lost her virginity to.

He was the man she'd bared her soul to and had known she had the safest of places to be that exposed.

His eyes popped open as if he was suddenly aware of her gaze on him. "Hey."

She thought about all those moments. All those hours they'd spent, sharing experiences not typical for people so young.

It was because of that shared vulnerability that she needed to walk away. He was confused and recovering from an injury right now. He didn't understand what had actually happened between them, and if she pressed a physical advantage, she was taking emotional advantage.

Even as she knew it—knew that she needed to stay strong—she couldn't stay away from him.

Could no longer stand apart.

"I should go."

It was the only thing she knew to say. And maybe if she said it loud enough or with enough conviction, she'd believe it.

Turning on her heel, the words tore out of her before she ran from the barn.

"I need to go."

Chapter 14

Gray moved before he even realized the impulse, racing after Harper as she ran from the barn. He'd seen the look in her eyes—and the sadness that seemed to radiate from her, all focused in his direction—and could only follow.

He had to get to the bottom of this. This sadness he kept seeing, shimmering in her eyes and cloaking her so that it choked the air around her.

What wasn't she telling him?

Because this sure as hell wasn't about his injury.

The front door had nearly slammed in her wake before he stopped it with his palm. Pushing through the door, he came to a halt in the entryway and watched as she ran to a kitchen chair, her grip on the back so tight her knuckles were nearly white.

"What's going on?"

"I can't—" She heaved a hard sob before her face broke, her shoulders crumpling as tears filled her eyes.

"Harper. What is it?" He moved toward her, shocked when she evaded him, moving around the table. "What is wrong?"

"It's not right. And I can't—"

There were those words again. "You can't what?"

"I can't. I mean we can't." She dashed at the tears, keeping a wary eye on him across the table.

He'd finally stilled because each time he moved, she moved too, determined to keep the table between them.

"We can't what?"

"We can't be together, Gray. I can't want you like this. I can't want you when you don't know who we are or what we've become. I can't pretend and make love with you and know that you don't know. That you don't understand."

He'd struggled through the headaches since the accident more than he'd wanted to let on, and because of it Gray knew there were areas he wasn't paying full attention to. The way she kept questioning him about what he knew. The strange discussion they'd had about spending time apart. Even the misery that seemed to swamp her and scare her, all at the same time.

It wasn't a surprise, per se, but he still couldn't wrap his mind around *why*.

Like he knew there was an answer—one he

knew somewhere in his own mind—but he couldn't conjure up the right mix of memories to bring it fully to life.

"Please stop moving."

"Please don't come closer."

Although it pained him to hear those words, he pointed toward the living room. "Come sit down and talk to me. You on the couch and me on the chair."

They might have spent each night cuddling on the couch before he inevitably dropped off to sleep early, but that didn't mean he couldn't talk to her without touching her.

That he couldn't listen to her without wanting more.

When she didn't move from her spot in the kitchen, he walked into the living room, taking the chair as he'd promised. When she finally followed him, it was to take the spot farthest away on the couch.

What was this?

"First, please tell me I haven't hurt you or done something to make you afraid."

Harper shook her head, her gaze dropping to the floor before returning to his. "No, nothing like that."

"Then let's talk about what is bothering you. Why every time we talk or you sit with me, I see this deep sadness in you that never really goes away."

"I'm not sad."

"Yeah, you are. It's like this bone-deep weariness, and I can only believe I'm the one who put it there."

"Do you remember when we first met?"

"At Dr. Andrews's practice. Of course."

"What did you think of me?"

"I thought you were the most beautiful girl I'd ever seen."

"Is that all?"

"You're still the most beautiful girl I've ever seen."

He got a small smile for that, breaking through the serious for a minute.

"A sweet thing to say. But what else do you remember? After that?"

"I knew that I couldn't date you. Not then. You were too young at fifteen."

"And?"

"So I waited until you were a hottie college student, and then pursued you for all I was worth."

He wiggled his eyebrows at that, pleased when he finally got a laugh out of her.

"Will you be serious?"

"You're serious enough for the both of us."

"I have to be. You're injured."

"A fact you've reminded me of repeatedly."

"And while you seem to recall most things, you don't seem to remember anything about us."

Don't remember?

Was that what she'd been angling around for these past few days?

"What am I forgetting that has you so concerned?"

It felt like a simple question, yet as the words filled the space between them, Gray couldn't dismiss the sudden swirl of anxiety and near panic that lodged in his chest.

"I'm struggling to understand how you can remember most aspects of your life, yet don't seem to recall anything about our history."

"But I do remember. How we met at Doc Andrews's practice. Dating each other all through college. Remember that first Christmas when you were home on break?"

He saw the moment his point registered, the sly smile that broke across her face sparking hope beneath the panic. "I remember."

"You were so insistent we couldn't find a private place on the town square during the Christmas tree lighting."

"And you proved me wrong."

"With your full support and that jingling set of keys."

That secretive smile of hers took him back, the moment so clear it could have happened the week prior he saw it so vividly in his mind's eye.

"Gray! We can't leave the square. My father's the grand master of the ceremony. We need to stay and watch the tree lighting."

"It looks the same every year. A twenty-foot spruce that they decorate in white lights."

"I heard there's a new star for the top this year."

"Oooh." He wiggled his eyebrows at her, even as he wrapped his arms around her waist and pulled her close. "We can come back and look at it before I take

you home. You can wax rhapsodic about how gorgeous the new star looks. All five points of it."

He knew the moment he had her. The mock-stern look on her face softened as she lifted a hand to brush his hair over his forehead. "You're incorrigible."

"For you, I am. And I've missed you." He rested his forehead against hers. "God, Harper, I've missed you so much."

"We're each where we need to be. And you've got that large animal program locked up. They've got to be incredibly impressed with the credit load you're taking. Enough to graduate in three years with your undergrad degree."

"It's just more time away from you. Because the faster I get it done the faster we can be together."

She smiled at that, one of those secretive smiles they shared that made him feel a hundred feet tall. "More time becoming who you're meant to be."

They'd had the conversation before. How important it was to get their educations. Her continued support of him, even on the days when he was convinced he'd never pay off his school loans and what was the point of it all anyway.

The gentle reminders from her that he wasn't his father and that the opportunity to live his dream would be worth it.

That it was worth it already.

She made him better, Gray realized as he stared down into those hazel eyes, sparkling under the lights of the town square. She always had.

And God, how he loved her.

He couldn't remember a moment since he'd met her

where he didn't think of her through a love of wild attraction and this goopy sort of love that filled him up.

He didn't know what to do with it.

And he'd never have imagined he could feel it, based
on how he'd grown up.

His mother had left when he was young. Despite his
role in that decision, he'd blamed her for a long time,
but it was only over the past few years, when he'd begun to see his father through the eyes of a man instead
of as a child, that he'd begun to understand her, too.

And as he'd come to comprehend what he had with
Harper—the mutual respect and affection they had for
each other—his mother's choices had begun to make
more sense, too.

The child inside would never stop missing her. But
the man was happy she got out.

Which made being away from Harper that much
worse. They did have something good. Something real
and lasting and sort of perfect.

When he was away from her it was agony. He'd had
more than a few friends at college who'd told him to live
a little, flirt with the coeds and stop worrying about his
girlfriend back home.

But he hadn't been able to do it.

Harper was the one he wanted. She'd been the one
from the first.

And now that he had her in his arms, he knew he
was right. There was no one better than her and there
was no one else that he wanted.

He bent his head to kiss her, happy in the moment
that he finally could. All those hours spent thinking of

her and dreaming about finally having her in his arms when they both got back to Rustlers Creek were finally here.

Gray lifted his head, determined to move them off the town square, when he caught sight of the butt end of a cigarette, lit up in the cold December air. His father's leering grin as he exhaled a stream of smoke, directed at Gray from the opposite side of the square, shot something through him. An ugly, roiling mix of nauseous oil and lingering anger broke through the carefree happiness of having Harper in his arms.

He hadn't seen the old man since he'd been home, choosing instead to bunk on Chance's couch in the small cabin Chance had on the Beaumont Farms property. It had been hard-won independence from his own father, but Chance had ultimately lobbied for some personal space, and his father had relented with the agreement of letting him renovate the foreman's cabin. They'd let their foreman go the prior spring and the cabin had sat empty. Since Chance was basically doing the work of foreman and three hands, Gray figured he'd earned the space in spades, but the negotiation with Trevor Beaumont hadn't been smooth.

It never was when you negotiated with someone who wanted to screw you instead of support you, he thought bitterly.

A point that seemed extra sharp in the cold December air, the end of that cigarette flaring an angry orange in the dark.

"Let's get out of here."

Harper sensed his mood change immediately. To her

credit, she didn't turn in Burt's direction, but she did tilt her head ever so slightly in acknowledgment of the direction Gray had been staring. "Your dad's here?"

"He is."

"Have you seen him yet? Since you've been home."

"No. And I wasn't planning on it, either."

"You can't ignore him forever."

"Sure I can."

It was old ground, one they'd trod each time they'd been reunited in Rustlers Creek while home from school. Although Harper was firmly on his side, she seemed insistent that a few solid outreaches would soften the relationship Gray had with his father, and he knew all too well that wasn't possible.

A lifetime spent with the man had proven over and over Burt wasn't wired in a way that would support a positive father-son relationship. Nor was that suddenly going to change since Gray had aged out of Burt's house.

But he didn't want to think about that now. Nor did he want Burt's presence or any mention of his father to mar the evening.

"I have a much better idea of how we can spend our time."

Linking arms, they moved swiftly through the town square, smiling for people they knew, but never stopping long enough to stand still.

The need for each other was too great.

The stolen moments they'd each waited months for, finally theirs.

Harper jingled the key ring in her hand. "Hadley will kill me if she finds out."

"No one will know we were in there."

"We'll know."

He caught nothing but agreement in her tone and smiled to himself as they snuck down the last block. Gray knew it would collectively embarrass them beyond measure, if he and Harper were caught in the small bakery Harper's sister worked at near the edge of town. But when Harper had borrowed her sister's car earlier, the key Hadley used for her early morning arrivals jingled along with her car and house keys. It had seemed like fate and the universe giving them an extra boon to their evening.

Because no matter how grateful he was to Chance for the space on the man's couch, there was no way he could bring Harper back to the cabin. And her own home was out of the question. Which had left them to their own creativity to figure out ways to be together.

Harper had the back door of the bakery open, and in a matter of moments they were both wrapped up in each other, the scents of vanilla and sugar enveloping them as they moved through the shop to the small storeroom off the kitchen.

"I don't believe we're doing this." Harper's voice was low, whispered against his lips even as her hands worked his heavy winter jacket off his shoulders.

"I can't believe I finally have you in my arms."

The urgency that carried them off the town square changed the moment they hit the privacy of the bakery's storeroom. The light filtering in through the front windows had faded to a small sliver, the space not visible from the street. It gave them the privacy they needed, and despite the desperate urgency for her *coursing through every cell in his body, Gray found himself stilling in the moment.*

One of those small slivers filtered over her face, high-lighting the soft blush on her cheeks and the desire clear in her large pupils.

But it was the sexy, knowing smile she gave him that nearly dropped him to his knees.

Here.

Right here was everything he needed in the entire world. It stole his breath, all while humbling him be-yond measure.

He loved her.

But even more than that, he liked her. He was a dif-ferent person when he was with her—a person he also liked and wanted to be. He'd spent so long working so hard not to be Burt McClain's son that it was awe-inspiring to realize that with Harper he was himself. Gray McClain. A man worth knowing.

A man he wanted to be.

It was so much more than simply wanting to be bet-ter. When he was with her, he liked who he was. All the possibility she saw in him he could see, too.

And it filled him with hope.

It was a commodity that had been in short supply until Harper Allen had walked into his life.

They stripped each other of their clothes, their movements strangely calm for all the need that coiled through him in whip-quick snaps. As he pulled her close, his hands roaming over the now-naked skin of her back, her breasts pressed to his bare chest, he found her mouth once more.

And sank into the woman who'd made him realize he could be enough.

HARPER'S SMILE FELL as she took in Gray, sitting opposite her across the small living room. How could he remember that night they'd spent in the storeroom at Hadley's bakery and not remember what had come only a few short years later?

Harper wanted to scream with the frustration of it all and had to fight the urge to question if he was deliberately being obtuse, using his head injury to his advantage. Even if that would be the very last thing she'd expect of Gray McClain.

The man was honest *and* honorable to a fault.

But she still wanted to ask him because it would be a damn bit easier to understand if he were just playing at this weird amnesia thing. It would make sense, unlike the past five days where he seemed to have awakened in this strange state of limbo, remembering his entire life except for the break between the two of them.

A break he'd instigated all those years ago.

Harper would own the fact that, from time to time, she'd imagined a different life for them than the one they'd lived for the past decade. In her quiet moments, the ones that snuck up on her and reminded her that losing Gray had left a tear in her soul that had never fully mended, she could picture them with a happy life and likely two or three kids by now. In those fantasies she'd never really considered what their life actually looked like day-to-day which, she supposed, was the beauty of a fantasy.

In dreams, the world just looked a certain way and you accepted it.

How odd, then, that Gray's memories seemed to have done the same. Those fuzzy edges a person had in dreams had become his reality. At least with respect to the two of them.

"Harper. What aren't you telling me?"

That same earnestness she'd always associated with him pulled her from her strange reverie. More, she couldn't ignore the realization that the past decade meant more to her than she'd ever given credit. The past ten years hadn't been a fantasy, fuzzy-edged or not. It had been her life.

Somewhere down deep, she had to admit, there'd been a part she'd held back, as if finding joy in her life in Seattle seemed like giving up. On her and Gray. On the life she'd envisioned for herself. Even on the idea of true love.

Only it wasn't.

She'd found a life. And it had been just as real as her relationship with Gray. And it had meant something, too.

But how much could she really tell him about all that time apart? The truth mattered, even if she needed to tread carefully and not push his mind too hard.

So in the end, she opted for honesty and the details she was able to share and hoped like hell it was enough for now.

"I'm not afraid of you, Gray. I'd never be afraid of you. But I can't fall straight into this."

"Into the physical?"

"Into anything that resembles a relationship. I shared with you that we'd spent time apart. And while I'm happy I'm here and committed to helping you while you heal, I need a little distance."

He'd always been a man who held his emotions close to his chest, but there was no hiding the mix of disappointment and frustration that filled that sky-blue gaze.

"I respect your wishes, Harper. Always. But I can't help but feel I've hurt you deeply, and I can only say I'm sorry."

He had hurt her. On every level she could have ever imagined. But with that new reality resting on her shoulders—the vivid realization that she also liked who she'd become—she needed time to process what it all meant.

Which made it as easy as breathing to reach across the small space between them to take his hand, certainty filling her voice when she spoke.

"This isn't about anger or pain or even emotional hurt. It's about healing, Gray. Your physical healing and some work I've needed to do on myself, too. I think I'm finally beginning to understand it."

"Do you want to help me understand it?"

The earnest question caught her up short. For all her agony over how to tell him which end was up for the past week, it was easy to forget that Gray's lack of awareness of what had happened between them was a hardship unto itself. She had the benefit of working through it, while he was left sitting in an emotional dark room, his entire life on some sort of dramatic pause.

"You and I've known each other since we were young. And there's something special in that knowledge, but there's a shared history, too. It's—" She broke off, wondering how to put all of her jumbled thoughts into some sort of coherent logic. Because the past week had given her some new perspective she'd lacked for so long.

And whatever this time together was meant to be, shouldn't she take that new perspective as a gift all unto itself?

She and Gray had spent time together, without all the baggage they'd carried for the past decade. Yes, there was the pain of her own memories, but there was the carefree weight of pretending it hadn't happened, either. A gentle acknowledgment of his reality that gave her a reprieve from her own.

"Just because we were young doesn't negate our feelings," he insisted. "It doesn't mean our experiences meant less. Or were less."

"No, it doesn't. And I don't think that."

"Then what do you think?"

"I think age and experience opens the world to us in ways we don't expect or anticipate or ever imagine."

His brow furrowed, dark eyebrows slashing over those vivid pools of blue that never failed to draw her in. "Which brings me back to my bigger concern. I'm so incredibly sorry if I've hurt you."

It was a risk, but for the first time she finally felt like she had the runway to get underneath what had happened all those years ago.

Why he'd ended things.

"Do you ever wonder if you were hurt, too?"

"By you?"

"By me, maybe. Or by something else. Something that had the power to come between us."

His eyebrows drew even harder over his eyes, a tug of remembrance playing in his gaze as surely as she churned up the memories his mind was determined to keep buried.

"I'm not sure I—" He stopped, those swirling memories doing battle somewhere deep in his mind. "I'm sorry, but I just don't know."

"No, Gray, I'm sorry. You're still healing and I'm pushing more at you than is fair."

"I want to know."

"And I want you to know." She squeezed his hand, that firm press of palms still one of the most reassuring feelings in the entire world. "When it's time, you will."

Chapter 15

Gray wasn't afraid of much in life. Or he didn't think he was. So it struck him with both surprise and an odd twinge of regret that he was questioning his decision to start the horse rescue.

It was an important project—one he'd wanted to create for longer than he could remember—but what if he was taking on too much? And what if he wasn't able to create the sort of home for the horses he envisioned in his mind?

Or what he *believed* he'd always envisioned in his mind.

Because after Harper's words the night before, he finally had to admit to himself that his life wasn't entirely what he believed it to be.

Even if he had no fucking clue what parts of his life he had wrong.

It galled him, he thought as he hammered a large hook into a pegboard, set up to hold various pieces of tack equipment in the stables.

He *felt* confident.

More than that, he did know things. His headache had dulled enough that he'd finally felt up to reading a bit. He'd walked himself through several of his veterinary school texts, easily able to recall instances where he'd treated the noted condition or knew what key elements were required to consider for an animal's care.

So why was he so blocked with Harper?

I'm not afraid of you, Gray. I'd never be afraid of you. But I can't fall straight into this . . . I need a little distance.

What did she have to fall into? Or what circumstance required distance?

Because no matter how softly she'd spoken or how well-intentioned her words, that low-grade panic hadn't left his gut. Nor had he found any equilibrium in her words. Yet each time he tried to process what she actually meant, he came up blank.

He *loved* Harper.

He was *with* Harper.

So what sort of distance was she seeking?

Had his accident come at a bad time? Were they having challenges as a couple and he'd somehow blocked it all out with his injuries?

He finished hammering and stood back to consider his work and the spacing of the various hooks on the oversized board.

And admitted the truth, even if only to himself.

Whatever the reason was, he'd have no cause to block anything out if it wasn't bad.

"How you feeling, Hardhead?"

Gray turned to find Zack Wayne standing at the opposite end of the stable. If he hadn't been worried up to now, facing Zack midafternoon on a workday was a surprise. "You're usually working this time of day. What brings you out here?"

Zack moved farther into the barn, coming over to shake Gray's hand. "I had some business with Chance and figured it would give me an opportunity to also check in on my friend. How're you feeling?"

"The headaches have faded to the dull, monotonous roar of a train over metal tracks."

Zack's brows shot up. "That good, huh?"

"Since it's an improvement over the screaming drill bit that was driving into my skull for the first few days, yeah, I'd say so."

"You took quite a hit. Hadley told me about it when she got home the other day."

The temptation to ask Zack about the details of his own life was great, but Gray tamped down the impulse. Aside from feeling like an ass, how did one actually open that conversation?

So, Zack, am I in a healthy, happy relationship with your sister-in-law?

No fucking way was he asking that. Even as something sly worked its way through the back of his mind. It was an abstract thought, really, one more of those damn wisps of memory that he seemed stuck with in place of real, genuine recall of his life.

Even if this one took slightly more form and shape than what had come before it.

"How is Harper doing?"

"Good, good," Zack said, his gaze darting toward the horse he'd called Gray out to the ranch to look at. *"She's staying busy and doing really good."*

The thought winked out, along with the odd memory of Zack Wayne at a clear loss for words that didn't involve the use of the word *good*. But it did strike Gray as strange that he had a memory of asking the man about Harper.

Had he and Harper gone through rough patches before? Something so bad he'd needed to ask Zack about her?

Before he could dwell on it, Zack rolled on through the current conversation. "I've taken a few hits myself through the years. Nothing that sounds as bad as what you're dealing with, but a thousand pounds of animal has a lot of power behind them. Are you still moving ahead with the plans to rescue the horse?"

"I was just thinking about that."

Zack's gaze grew sharp. "Thinking about what, exactly?"

"If it's the right time to do this. I'm feeling better every day, but it's a lot to take on and it's struck me that I might have bitten off a bit too much here. The stable's not even done yet."

"I can give you a hand, and I have a ranch full of men who'd be equally happy to do the same."

"Your staff's not coming here to do my chores."

"I've got a group of hands who think the world of you and would be happy to pitch in a few hours to help you get this wrapped up." Zack turned to stare at the structure that stood around them. "You've made a ton of progress already."

It was a lot to ask but he knew Zack spoke from the heart. And he couldn't deny that the extra support to get the stable done and finished for Cabernet's arrival would go a long way toward making him feel better about the operations of the horse rescue.

"Only if I can return the favor. Next few visits out to the ranch are free of charge."

Zack looked about to argue when he stopped and held up a hand. "I'd be grateful."

"Then so am I."

Zack shot him a quick grin. "Hadley's going to be beside herself."

"For what?"

"My wife is at her happiest when she's feeding people. She's going to consider tomorrow a good old-fashioned barn raising."

"Does she know the barn's mostly raised?"

Zack waved a hand. "I don't think she'll be deterred."

An image of Hadley cooking him something stuck a hard landing in his thoughts, and Gray had a memory of nuking something in his microwave. "She loves to feed people. Me, especially, as I recall."

Zack's smile dropped, his gaze careful as he stood opposite Gray in the sunlight filtering through the barn. "Harper mentioned that the memories come and go. You doing okay with that?"

"I'm not sure I'd give them enough credit to say they arrive fully formed, but I keep getting snatches of certain things. Hadley giving me leftovers is rock-solid in my mind."

"Anything else?"

"No, damn it. And I feel like I'm forgetting something important, even if I have no clue what it is or why I forgot it in the first place."

"Give yourself time, Gray. You took a solid hit to the head. It'll come back."

Harper was convinced of the same. So was the doctor and all of the literature she'd given him to read.

So why wasn't he?

He remembered so much. Nearly everything, assuming his mind wasn't playing tricks on him.

Everything except for his relationship with Harper.

There was a reason he was blocking it. He was increasingly convinced of that truth.

The real reason was why.

And what the hell was he going to do with that truth when his memory finally came back?

MARTY STARED DOWN at the sandwich on his desk and marveled at the fact that he'd eaten most of it and hadn't tasted a bite. The week had moved swiftly, a series of student events taking up his time, yet he could barely remember doing any of it.

He missed Jackie.

A fact that was ridiculous in the extreme since the two of them had barely been dating, let alone a part of each other's lives.

Only you are a part of each other's lives, a small voice whispered as he took another tasteless bite of his ham and cheese. *You have been for thirty years.*

And wasn't that the rub?

What had taken him so damn long to realize he cared for her?

He'd been living a lonely life for decades now. And he had no one to blame but himself.

Maria's death had hit him hard, cutting him off at the knees. But he had survived. He'd raised his girls. He'd made a career for himself. Yet all the while, he'd somehow convinced himself that no one was lucky enough to get what he and Maria had twice.

More, that if you were lucky enough to find that sort of love, you needed to preserve it in some way. Hold tight to it and use it as a shield to hold your heart safely away from getting hurt again.

Fat fucking lot of good that did him.

He'd still managed to have his broken *and* he'd likely pissed his late wife off in the process.

Despite feeling like deviled crap, he smiled to himself as he heard Maria's voice echoing in his head.

Marty, my love. You are the man of my dreams and were from the day we met. And you've been a stupid, ridiculous ass for far too many years now. How could you not know I've wanted this for you for so very long?

It was a conversation in his own mind—one likely designed to make himself feel better—yet on some level he knew Maria was there, too. She'd been beside him always. Through their marriage she'd been his partner and even after they'd lost her, he knew she'd watched over them. Knew that she was cheering him on and helping him to find the strength he needed each day to keep putting one foot in front of the other.

Quietly encouraging him that he had *exactly* what it took to raise two teenage girls.

Steadfastly pushing him on as season morphed into season and year into year, showing him that he could—and *would*—move on without her.

He'd resisted, but in her own gentle way, she'd still pushed. And on the days when it was too hard—when he'd walked his daughter down the aisle alone or when he celebrated yet another anniversary without her—he'd remember what she'd said those last few days in the hospital.

"I can't be there with you but I will never leave you. I hope you know that, my love."

"I don't know if I can do this without you."

"I know you can. And I wish with everything I am that you didn't have to. But I can't give you that."

He'd held her hand then and said nothing fur-ther. He hated that she was in pain. Hated the endless diagnoses that confirmed what they both already knew. There wasn't a bright end to her illness that somehow promised a cure.

But he'd be damned if he was going to add to her burdens by complaining about his own.

"Marty?" The knock on his door pulled him from his thoughts and his conversations with Maria, both imagined and remembered. His assistant, Georgia, stood in the doorway, her stern face set in concerned lines. "I'm sorry to disturb your lunch, but I have some paperwork I need you to sign."

"Sure, come on in."

They'd worked together for so long they practically shared a brain, so it surprised him when she waved to the outer office before turning back to him, her brisk efficiency on full display. "I've got some paperwork for Cole Dunning's college application and Leticia Bain's scholarship recommendation. And Ms. Delaney's here to see you as well."

"Jackie's here?"

Georgia's expression never changed, but he'd swear he saw a mischievous smile light up the corners of her eyes. Which was ridiculous, because while he might not be an English teacher by trade, waxing rhapsodic in similes or metaphors—he never remembered which—he did damn well know eyes didn't smile.

Even though the look on Georgia's face suggested otherwise.

And then she laid the paperwork down on his desk—all neatly printed and tabbed for his signature—and his efficient wraith of an administrative assistant vanished as if she'd never been.

And Jackie stood in her place in the doorway.

"Martin. Hello. I'm sorry to bother you."

"You're not bothering me." He realized that he was still sitting and quickly scrambled to stand. "Please. Come on in."

"I won't stay long but I have a few details on my retirement paperwork Georgia said I needed to come in to sign."

"What details?"

Even as the words left his lips an image of those smiling eyes filled him once more, and he crossed around his desk to take the papers Jackie extended toward him.

"I'm afraid I don't know. But she said something needed to be signed."

Marty glanced down at the sheaf of papers in his hand and only saw the details he'd signed off on several months ago when her retirement was first put through. He nearly said as much when it dawned on him that he had a captive audience for a few minutes and he might as well put it to good use.

"Come on in and I'll pull the details up on my computer."

He glanced outside the door of his office into

the area where Georgia normally sat, her seat suspiciously empty, considering she was waiting on him to sign paperwork.

And then he closed the door, a common occurrence for a principal handling private matters, and turned to face Jackie.

God, she looked gorgeous.

It felt like forever since he'd seen her, even though it had been less than a week. That lithe, elegant frame that spoke of energy and vitality looked as it always did, standing straight and tall in the middle of his office, but there were telltale circles under her eyes that were a surprising match for the ones he'd seen beneath his own eyes that morning.

"Please. Take a seat."

Jackie took the chair opposite his desk, even as her back remained stiff and straight. Marty made his way around his desk and after sitting, pulled up the required fields on his computer. Although he had his suspicions on whether or not this visit was needed, he still wanted to make sure all of Jackie's details had processed properly.

"I'm sorry to bother you during your lunch. I'd assumed this would be a good time to come but—" She broke off, whatever else she was about to say fading away.

"You thought it would be a good time to avoid me?"

"I assumed I could take care of whatever was missing from my paperwork with Georgia. I thought it might be easier that way."

"Easier? Or more convenient for you?"

Although he wasn't confrontational by nature, he'd learned early on in his career how to get the upper hand with teenagers. And while he had no interest in treating Jackie like a child, he wasn't about to let her off the hook, either.

"Come on, Martin."

"No, you come on, Jackie. I thought we were getting to know each other. Quite well, in fact. Then we slept together and we got to know each other a whole lot better. And then you dumped me over a plate of horse cookies. Or just before them. Or after them. I can't quite remember since it felt like I'd been kicked in the chest by a horse."

He kept his stare level and direct. "But now that I've gotten my breath back, I realized I should have stayed and argued with you."

"About what?"

"About the fact that I think I deserved better from you. And that frankly, you do, too."

"Martin, can we please not do this? I told you how I felt about us and I told you why I felt that way. Let's just get this paperwork issue taken care of and I'll get out of your hair."

"What if I don't want you out of my hair?"

"I believe I have some say in that."

He saw the first sparks of anger, blazing up beneath the sadness and the empty gaze, and it gave him hope. It meant that she wasn't unaffected by him or by what had happened between them.

And if she wasn't unaffected, he might have a chance to salvage this relationship.

"Do you know what I was doing before you walked in here?"

Confusion creased her brow before she pointed toward his desk. "Eating your lunch, apparently."

"Yes, I was. And I was talking to my late wife."

"Oh."

Whatever possible confusion had been there at his abrupt subject change vanished, replaced by something that looked suspiciously like remorse. And of all the feelings Jackie Delaney should feel, that one wasn't on the list.

So why did she?

"We talk often. Or I talk, and I imagine what she'd say back. It's oddly effective, even if it's mostly a conversation with myself. For some reason, though, I tend to listen better when it's in Maria's voice."

"You loved your wife very much. It's only natural you'd want to keep her memory alive."

"True." He nodded, blazing clarity filling him up and electrifying every nerve ending.

How could you not know I've wanted this for you for so very long?

"But I also realize I've been using my wife as an excuse."

"What sort of excuse? You loved her."

"Yes, I did. I still do. But I'm alive and she isn't."

"Martin, please don't—"

He interrupted her because now that he understood—truly, deeply understood—he needed to say the words. "And for a long time it hurt to say that. To even think it. But it's true. And part of the pain was that way down deep inside I wanted to deny it. If I simply didn't utter the words or think them at all, then they couldn't possibly reflect what my life had become.

"But they do."

"Martin, I'm sorry if I've churned up memories that hurt you and give you pain."

He had no idea if it was the right move or not, but in that moment Marty knew he couldn't sit there any longer, staring at her across a desk. He got up and moved around beside her, taking her hand as he dropped to his knee beside the chair.

"I didn't cheat on my wife with you, Jackie. And you didn't cheat, either. And the only pain is continuing to live in a relationship that doesn't exist any longer."

"Martin." She took a deep breath. "I've had feelings for you for far longer than I should have."

If she meant the words as a confession, Marty suspected she'd be woefully disappointed in his response. Guilt and regret—either real or imagined—had no place between them. But all he could do was hold tight to that voice in his head that wanted him to move forward and try to make her see reason.

"You didn't act on them. You never even gave me any reason to think you had them, nor did you ever make any untoward advances or attempts to violate my marriage. How is an attraction you never acted on cheating?"

"You don't understand. I lived through that. Lived with the pain of betrayal. And while I might have come to understand all the reasons why, it doesn't change the feeling. It doesn't change the way you see yourself."

"I can't change what came before. Your experiences are yours, and your feelings and emotions on that experience are yours, too. But I refuse to accept you taking blame for something in my life you didn't do or act on."

"It's not that simple, Martin."

"Maybe it is." He stood back up and allowed his hand to brush over her shoulder before pulling away. "Maybe it's as simple and as easy as taking the beauty of what's in front of us."

"I don't think I can."

"I know. And that's the real sadness here. I've grieved my wife's death, and I will mourn her passing every day for the rest of my life. I loved her and I continue to love her. Always. But I love you, too. And we're both alive to make something of that."

Tears shimmered in her deep brown eyes before she seemed to catch herself. That spine stiffened even further and she swiped her fingertips beneath her eyes, highlighting those deep grooves of sadness beneath. "Martin, I'm sorry. Truly I am. But I just can't."

Before he could stop her, Jackie was up and out of her chair and out his office door. He wanted to go after her, but the knowledge that his staff obviously already knew about his personal business had him staying put.

Whatever came of this relationship—and he

still wasn't ready to give up on her—it didn't need an audience on school grounds. And somewhere, in that small corner of his heart that still knew how to hope, he had to believe that he'd planted the notion that she was wrong in thinking her feelings for him were tainted or misguided.

God, he hoped so.

It was only as he sat down and scanned the paperwork once more, confirming that it was, in fact, all completed correctly the first time, that Maria's voice drifted through his mind once more.

Oh Marty, she's lovely. But however did you manage to find someone more stubborn than you? You know, my love, once she gets her head out of her ass, you two might just have a shot at something worth hanging on to.

As he took the last bite of his sandwich, he was surprised to realize it had a bit more flavor than he thought.

And, maybe, if his equally stubborn wife had her way, he might just have a shot at giving her exactly what she'd wanted for him all along.

"HAVE YOU GIVEN in and jumped the man yet?"

Harper stared at the matched, expectant gazes of Hadley and Charlotte and wondered where she could run and hide. Except Rustlers Creek was small and Gray's cabin was even smaller.

And her sister would hunt her down until she gave in anyway.

"I think that's an inappropriate and crass question, Hadley Allen Wayne."

"We're all thinking it." Charlotte popped a small appetizer into her mouth and chewed thoughtfully. "She just gets a pass to ask because she's your sister."

"What do you mean you're all thinking it?" Harper frowned at the high, squeaky pitch of her own voice. "What does that even mean?"

"I know Mom's interested in what's happening. Mamma Wayne, too," Charlotte said, referring to her wily grandmother. "And hell, Harper, we're only human. You and Gray make a great pair. Is it so wrong to want to see those sparks flare up a bit?"

"We're not a couple."

Charlotte wagged a finger in Harper's direction before snagging another appetizer off the plate Hadley had prepared. "Which I might have understood if you were still twenty. But you're a healthy, mature woman with mature appetites and a brain that can process the difference between a good time and forever. And it's not like you and Gray got to spend all that much time together years ago when you were a couple. How much sexy time did the two of you really get?"

It was a harsh truth, but also an accurate one.

And it was strangely matched to the thoughts that had increasingly troubled Harper all week.

Hell, those tantalizing thoughts of throwing caution to the wind and jumping back into bed with the man had even lured her when she was still in Seattle, contemplating coming back to Rustlers Creek for a few months.

But now? After spending days on end in the same house with him?

Oh, they weren't just throwing lures, they damn well had a big old hook firmly locked in her jaw.

And while she desperately wanted to be casual about the decision, it *did* all matter, Harper thought miserably. She was stuck between her hormones and her heart and that was a shitty place to be since her head had very little say in the tug-of-war.

But oh, the imagined sexy times . . .

She and Gray hadn't had a lot of privacy when they were younger, their college schedules and limited access to private spaces—or the money to spend on one—had also limited their sexual encounters. They made do when they could—and she fought the blush that crept up her neck at the memories of their night in the bakery—but they hadn't exactly been burning up the sheets.

Which had seemed unfair at the time but a fact of life while still living under her father's roof.

And then it had seemed even more unfair when their relationship had gone to hell and she didn't have an endless treasure trove of sexual memories to keep her warm at night.

"We had our good times. And besides," Harper added lamely, even as she suspected her nose might be growing, "I don't think that really matters all that much."

"You're right. You could have had endless monkey sex a decade ago and you'd still want more.

He's hot. You're both healthy." Charlotte screwed up her mouth before adding, "Mostly healthy, as soon as his head injury heals. Why not go for it?"

"You know, you're very good at dispensing all this advice, and I'm so not touching the monkey sex comment. But if you were really serious, you could put your money where your mouth is and march your cute, sassy, jean-clad ass across the yard to the barn and offer the same to Chance Beaumont."

"We hate each other."

"You're a mature woman." Harper tossed Charlotte's words back at her. "I think you're more than capable of processing the difference between a good time and forever."

Charlotte grinned at that, her even white teeth flashing beneath the lights of the kitchen. "I'd never tell him since he's such a raging ass, but that man is fine." Charlotte shook her head. "And if you ever tell him I said that, I will personally hunt you down with my daddy's shotgun and bury you so far in the woods they won't find you for centuries."

"You're sort of scary." Harper mock shuddered. "Especially when you're protesting the inevitable so much."

Harper meant it as a joke, but she didn't miss the shot of longing that filled Charlotte's eyes before Charlotte seemed to catch herself. "I'm a woman who knows my own mind. And despite a raging case of hotness, Chance Beaumont is not the one for me."

It seemed a shame to waste all that chemistry on a decades-long grudge that started in grade school, and Harper almost said as much when the front door of the cabin opened, and Zack, Chance and Gray trooped inside. If she were scripting a movie, she couldn't have planned a shot any better. Like a tableau straight out of the canon of the American West, that impressive line of men captured immediate attention. All three sported broad shoulders, but where Zack was solidly built, a seeming wall of muscle, Gray had a longer, leaner contour to his frame. And Chance was a mix of the two, part linebacker, part cowboy in his tall frame and slim hips.

Harper could have sworn she heard a light sigh escape Charlotte's lips, and she *knew* she heard one escape her sister before Hadley leaped out of her chair and marched across the room to kiss her husband.

It was only when her own breath caught in her chest that Harper knew she was in real trouble. For all her big talk about staying strong and knowing her own mind and attempting to lob the conversational football straight back onto Charlotte, she was the one in real danger.

Because there might be a sizable distance between a good time and forever, but it was damnably hard to separate the two when Gray McClain leveled that vivid blue gaze right at you.

Chapter 16

There was a moment in every intricate medical procedure when the world seemed to soften around him and his full focus lasered onto his patient. Gray had discovered that in his earliest days with Doc Andrews, and the feeling had only grown stronger through his years of practicing veterinary medicine.

The only other place he'd ever experienced that same sense of the world fading around him was when he was with Harper. There was something about the woman that made his vision sharper so that all he could see was her.

All he knew was her.

And all he wanted was her.

Gray wasn't sure what had changed from the point he'd left the cabin earlier to meet Zack,

Chance and the Wayne ranch hands, but he knew something had.

More than that, he knew Harper had changed. That sense of sadness and reticence he'd felt all week had vanished and in its place was a warmth that rivaled the sun on a perfect Montana day.

And it was all directed at him.

Although he wanted nothing more than to go over to her and pull her into his arms, he held back. This was between them. The heated glances and the tenuous connection that had bonded them the moment he walked in the door wasn't for public consumption. And while Hadley and Charlotte were some of the closest women he had to family in his life, their interest in whatever was between him and Harper was abundantly clear.

Even as Gray knew whatever was between him and Harper was theirs.

Suddenly aware of the quiet, he tilted his head toward the door. "Hadley, your husband is a man of his word. Fifteen ranch hands in addition to these two and the stable is done."

"Zack and his crew don't mess around." Hadley's adoring smile for Zack fell, her expression going distracted as something obviously caught her fancy. "Bea's going to be so mad she didn't get a camera crew out here to cover this."

"Carter would have a fit if she was around all the construction dust we kicked up." Zack's voice was reasonable, but it was hard to miss the

rolled eyes as he referred to his foreman's cluck-
ing hen behavior as his wife finished the last few
months of her pregnancy.

"I love him, but God, he's turned into such a
worrywart," Hadley said, before smiling. "It's as
sweet as it is maddening. Especially since Bea's
totally healthy and she'd have loved covering all
this."

"Cover what exactly?" Gray couldn't imagine
what Hadley's show producer would want with
his small stable.

"The camaraderie and small-town aspect of fin-
ishing up your stables. She loves showing off our
relationships here in Rustlers Creek." Hadley's
eyes grew wide. "Maybe you could add on to the
barn for the next season. It'd be great publicity for
the horse rescue, too! Oh, and I could make something for the animals like that time I did homemade dog biscuits. People went nuts for those."

Harper's and Charlotte's knowing looks arced
across the room, despite the distance between
the two of them before Charlotte finally spoke.
"Look out, Gray, she's on a roll."

"On a roll of what?" He was still a little confused, the references to cameras and dog biscuits
seemingly unrelated.

"She wants to make a *Cowgirl Gourmet* episode
around you," Harper said. "And don't worry. I
had to hear all about the unphotogenic qualities
of brown doughballs last week. She'll come back
to us in a few minutes once she's worked it all
out in her head."

He'd managed to avoid any time on Hadley's show since they'd begun filming it, content to watch episodes as they aired. While he'd heard enough chatter to know the Wayne ranch hands enjoyed their light brush with fame, Gray had been perfectly happy to steer clear of Hollywood's influence over Rustlers Creek.

"Why would anyone be interested in that?"

Hadley shrugged, coming back to the collective conversation. "Because people are. And what you're doing is really special."

Gray couldn't see the appeal, nor could he imagine anyone wanting to watch him walk a blind horse around a corral, but he kept that thought to himself. When Hadley Wayne got going there was little to get in her way. And she seemed so excited by the idea that it felt ungrateful to burst her bubble.

In the end, he was prevented from having to say anything more when Harper neatly redirected her sister. "Why don't we get these platters outside and get that hardworking crew fed?"

The subject change had its desired effect, and Hadley was already moving toward the kitchen. "Let me just do one final check on the meat in the slow cooker."

Harper and Charlotte followed Hadley into his small kitchen, and Gray watched the three women line up at the counter, each working in tandem over platters full of potato salad, coleslaw and rolls. Then Chance and Zack moved into action, Zack taking the heavy slow cooker from his wife's hands and Chance hefting a cooler that had been set up near the door.

It was only as everyone headed back out his front door toward the newly completed stable and the folding tables Chance had brought over in his truck that Gray realized he'd been staring.

In bemusement, but even more, in a sort of shocked awe.

His friends had all come to help him. They'd worked on his barn and brought food to eat and had made sure he could bring Cabernet back to the ranch.

That he could make his dreams come true.

It was a humbling realization, one that shot hard waves of gratitude through his chest.

But it was Harper's small smile, as she headed out the door last, that nearly cut him off at the knees. Those memories of so long ago, standing on the town square at Christmas, came back to him in a rush. That feeling that he mattered. That the things he cared about mattered.

It was a gift.

One she'd brought into his life, along with all these amazing people.

He might have found some of it on his own. He and Chance were friends, after all. And he hoped he'd have found his way to veterinary medicine, even without her continued pushing for him to go to college, but knowing his childhood, he recognized that hadn't been a given, either.

As he followed out the door behind her, he sent up a silent prayer of thanks for this woman. The one who saw him when no one else did.

The one who'd believed in him when no one else did.

And the one who made sure he'd come around to the idea of believing in himself.

HARPER WATCHED THE sun slip behind the barn, leaving the sky with a wash of gold as the afternoon slowly faded away.

It had been a good day.

Better than good, she had to admit. She'd felt a part of something. Sure, it had been a bit uncomfortable to be on display with her sister and Charlotte as they'd grilled her about Gray, but it had also been a lot of fun.

The mix of feminine ritual and good-natured teasing often were.

But there had been other things, too. Preparing all the food, even though it looked like her sister was feeding fifty instead of their party size of about twenty. The easy conversation about people they grew up with and knew in town. Charlotte's sweet story about a shopping trip to Bozeman with her grandmother. Hadley's funny story about the day Bea recounted telling her that Carter had read up on the subject of mucus plugs and had refused to have sex for a week for fear of dislodging Bea's during her pregnancy.

It had all been easy. And fun. And silly at times, though she wasn't sure she could face Bea and Carter for a while after *that* story.

But it was life.

Living it, experiencing it, laughing about it.

For all her realization about how she'd built a life for herself in Seattle—one she was proud of—she'd forgotten how good it felt to laugh with the people who'd known you the longest and who knew you best.

The forgotten memory of the way her dress had torn at the homecoming dance junior year and Charlotte had whipped out a sewing kit out of her tiny purse to rival something on a New York runway. Hadley's first failed attempt at making bread that had clogged the kitchen sink as her starter grew and grew. And the night of Hadley's bachelorette party when Harper, Hadley and Charlotte had gotten drunk on cheap wine behind the house and her father had come out to cover all of them in blankets where they lay sprawled on various lawn chairs.

She'd left Rustlers Creek and believed herself free of the town that she'd grown up calling home, but the more time she spent here, the more she had to admit that she never really shook it off.

Or not entirely, anyway.

Just like she'd never truly shaken Gray.

She had moved on and if she'd never quit her job, never started her coffee company, never come back to Rustlers Creek, she could have gone on forgetting.

But she had done those things.

And now she was at a crossroads.

Between choosing to forget and choosing to remember.

Gray's gaze caught hers, something that had happened throughout the meal as the afternoon wound down. She didn't miss the knowing smile or the way his attention seemed so focused—so deliberately attentive—to her.

He'd been that way all afternoon, ever since that moment when he'd walked into the house.

And in that knowing she recognized the truth.

Everything had been leading the two of them to this moment. Her return to town. The choices she'd made over her job. Even her purchase of Coffee 2.0, which had freed her to come home.

All of it had led her straight back to where she'd left.

She'd seen a quote once, scrolling through one of those endless streams on social media, when she'd stopped short. She never remembered the exact phrasing, but the gist was that you were still allowed to be sad over something you'd believed you'd healed from.

She'd spent a lot of time the past month thinking about healing and all the sadness that had come with the end of her relationship with Gray. But she hadn't spent a hell of a lot of time remembering the joy. Or maybe more specifically, remembering it through a happy lens instead of the morass of memories that usually overshadowed the good.

Maybe she'd done them both a disservice.

Although Hadley and Charlotte had only been teasing her earlier, in that silly way of friends, it was deeply tempting to see her current situation with Gray only through the veil of sexual attraction.

But what she felt for him was so much more. What she'd discovered about the two of them since returning home was so much more.

It had been equally tempting to continue seeing him through the memories she had of a man in his early twenties. But he'd had life experiences, too. He was a competent vet and a landowner and a man on the verge of creating his second business with the horse rescue. He had *employees*, she thought with no small measure of pride.

Hell, she thought with surprise, so did she!

And what it all came down to was that they weren't the same people they each remembered. It was why the idea of jumping into bed with him carried so much more weight than simply acting on the "mature appetites" Charlotte had teased her about earlier.

"Back me up, Harper." Chance caught her attention from across the table. "Coffee is a religion."

Grateful for the escape from her thoughts—even if they were strangely lighter than any she'd had in a month—Harper grinned at that. "It certainly is in Seattle. A fact I'm banking on with my shop corner temples to coffee scattered all around the city as well as a cutting-edge website you can peruse at your leisure."

Chance laughed at that. "The Allen girls do know how to sell a good thing."

"Which is oddly humorous," Hadley added, "since our father is the most down-to-earth, solid man you'd ever want to meet."

"Oh, I don't know." Gray looked thoughtful. "He did a pretty great sales job on me in high school when we talked about applying to college."

"He's done the same to me when he's encouraged several of our staff to take some night classes to get their GED," Zack added.

At the mention of the hands, Harper glanced around to find that the last of them had left. Several had talked about heading back to the ranch and their own plans for the evening, but it was interesting to realize their party had dwindled to the six of them.

And how comfortable it was to simply sit and share the evening with old friends.

"Maybe we did get our sales blood from Dad," Harper said with a fond smile at the thought of her father. "We certainly didn't get his innate patience."

"Or his ability to put up with the crazy bullshit teenagers are famous for." Hadley laid a hand on Zack's arm. "What was that story he told us a few months back at dinner? The one about the kid who was obsessed with singing in class."

"He was practicing for his tryout for one of those reality singing shows." Zack picked up the conversational thread. "Apparently the kid even sang the answers to his algebra quiz."

"God, were we ever that stupid?" Chance asked.

"We were entirely that stupid," Charlotte answered him, clear in her conviction. "Or have you forgotten how you and I have paid for our stupidity since grade school? I gave you an unrequited Valentine and the town has never let me forget it."

It was an odd moment, potentially fraught with serious danger or wild possibility, and Harper didn't miss how the air seemed to quiet and still.

But it was Zack who broke it, bumping his sister with his shoulder. "The fact that you two have had a few legendary tussles in front of half the damn town has nothing to do with it?"

"People are just nosy. It doesn't mean it's anyone's business," Charlotte huffed.

Zack kept pressing, in that way only older brothers could. "Then you shouldn't have made it everyone's business."

Chance had been quiet up to then, an odd observer of a subject that included him, before murmuring, "Small-town life at its finest."

That stillness hovered between Charlotte and

Chance once more where they sat on opposite
sides of the table, and Harper knew her sister's
question earlier fit this situation just as easily.

Have you given in and jumped the man yet?

Why did sex always seem like the right *and*
wrong answer, all at the same time?

"Well, small-town life just got me my finished stables"—Gray shot Harper the subtlest of
winks—"so who am I to complain?"

It was just the right thing to defuse the moment, and Charlotte and Chance both seemed to
shrink a little, each backing down.

And, in the dying light, Harper saw how they
didn't just back away from the moment, but from
each other, too.

Was that a good thing?

Even if it was exactly what she'd been doing
for the past month with Gray.

She might still carry scars from the first time
they were together, but she also wasn't that same
girl any longer. She'd lived a lifetime in the past
ten years. One far away from here and, because
of the distance, one she'd forged solely on her
own.

That meant something. Something that mattered.

And in the dying light of a very good day,
Harper knew she'd made her decision.

About Gray.

About herself.

And about the fact that the woman she was
today wanted to make love with him.

CHARLOTTE WAYNE HAD always been adept at getting under his skin, but the past month had exacerbated that state exponentially, Chance thought with a level of moroseness that made him want to go bang his own head into a row of fence posts.

What was it with this one woman? Was she his friend? His enemy? His nemesis for life? Increasingly, it seemed like all of the above. This tall, elegant bombshell of a woman that pissed him off and turned him on all at the same time.

His father would have dubbed her a cock tease. It wasn't an apt description—for Charlotte or for any woman—but Trevor Beaumont had been a major asshole and had only seen women in one way: that they were disposable.

Charlotte didn't fit that bill; she never had. And while she was a determined person who knew her own mind better than anyone he'd ever met in his life, she had the unique ability to make him want to scream all while trying to be a better person.

And it had all started with that damn Valentine's card in the fourth grade.

The one she'd sprung on him as a surprise and with all the advanced maturity a ten-year-old girl managed to have over a ten-year-old boy. She'd determined she was interested in him and had bought him the biggest, prettiest card delivered in any of the carefully crafted boxes made by their class.

She'd put her heart into that card and he'd

crushed it in his embarrassment and shame, feelings he could still conjure all these years later. Charlotte Wayne was the prettiest girl in school and pretty much the wealthiest, too. And while no one really knew his circumstances at home, he did. His dad was a loser, and at ten, he was convinced he was on the same path.

Despite the innately poor way he handled her card, the hurt he saw in her eyes was worth it to make sure she didn't look at him that way again.

It should have worked. Only she somehow doubled down after that and the two of them had morphed into the town joke as they fought— rather publicly—each time they were together. Each time it happened he swore he wouldn't do it again.

And then he'd try his best to remain calm and detached in a conversation or discussion with her and it would happen all over again. Charlotte Wayne had known her own mind twenty-two years ago and she still did.

It was all he could do to keep up.

That's what it had felt like all night as they'd enjoyed dinner with their friends, just sitting out in the cooling evening, shooting the breeze on any number of topics.

That casual conversation and easy camaraderie and the reality that, somehow, he had landed in Charlotte's orbit once again. It had happened more often than usual of late, and now because of it he had to figure out what end was up and what was down.

He never had an issue talking to women or flirting with them or asking them out on dates. But the strange thing with Charlotte Wayne was that they did a hell of a lot of talking and a hell of a lot of bickering that felt the same way flirting did. Yet he never managed to quite screw up the courage to ask her out.

Because you know you'll get a no.

An especially troubling fact because he didn't usually use that excuse to deter him from asking a woman out.

No, what bothered him more was the fact that he felt like he was dancing on eggshells, trying to hide the depths of his business problems from her.

From all of them, really.

Zack Wayne knew the beef industry from one end to the other and likely had the best understanding of Chance's issues. And *fuck*, had his father run this place into the ground. It was bad. He'd known it was bad. But the level of debt, poor business practices and shitty quality that he'd finally understood in the past two years since his old man died had been startling.

Even as he still cursed himself for the very fact that he shouldn't have been surprised.

Trevor Beaumont used whatever he could— women, his land, hell, his son—to meet his own ends, and he'd done it with Beaumont Farms.

It wasn't bad enough his father had screwed him while he was alive, but it increasingly seemed like he'd plotted it in death, too.

"I really appreciate the help here today, Chance," Gray said, meeting him at the edge of the corral several of Zack's hands had framed out. "It means a lot to me that you guys would do this."

"That's what friends do, man."

It was what friends did, and Gray had been his closest one longer than anyone else. Chance valued the man's place in his life.

He was also worried about him. Both the head injury and the likely injury to more sensitive parts if this thing with Harper continued on too long.

He didn't know the full details, but Zack had given him the basics on Gray's head injury and the risk of startling him with too much information too soon, especially on the things he was struggling to remember.

But Harper?

How could Gray possibly have forgotten the realities of that relationship? Especially because he seemed like his usual sharp self on every other topic.

"How are you doing?"

"Good. Feeling better every day. I still have a dull, persistent headache." Gray smiled as he tapped his forehead. "But it's getting better, too."

"Are you and Harper on each other's last nerve yet?"

As questions went it was a gamble, but he was curious what was going on between his friend and his old flame. Gray had always kept his own counsel on what had gone down between the two of them years ago, before Harper had moved away, but Chance had pieced together some of it through the years.

The constant problem that was Burt McClain.

Harper's extraordinary talents, and Gray's concern that she would be cheated of fulfilling their promise if she stayed in Rustlers Creek.

Even the reality of just trying to make a go of a relationship so young.

It was hard. And it was even harder when you carried the hulking weight and presence of your old man on your shoulders.

"You think she's sick of me?"

"I think a week cooped up in the same house would make anyone stir-crazy. And that's coming off the snowstorm we had that made half the town nuts."

"I don't think we have anything to worry about." Gray's confidence on the subject was clear, and Chance figured he'd said enough. Whatever the man was facing was ultimately his business and he'd figure out how to handle it. And then the opportunity to mention anything passed when Harper and Charlotte chose that moment to walk up to them, their laughter and a shared joke preceding them.

"I think I'm going to get going."

Chance wasn't sure why, but the urge to get away had suddenly become overwhelming. Maybe it was Charlotte's light laughter, or those dumb memories of when they were kids, or that heartbreaking beauty that never failed to grab him by the throat.

All he knew was that he had to leave. Now.

"Chance"—Charlotte waved him down before he could quietly escape—"would you mind giving me a ride back to your driveway? Hadley parked there and I need to borrow her car tomorrow."

Of course the answer was yes, Chance thought, pushing against that continued urge to escape as Charlotte dangled the borrowed keys in her hand. They might easily fall into ten-year-old combat mode with minimal provocation, but he wasn't a total dick. And despite his father's poor example, Chance considered himself a gentleman.

Which was how he found himself locked in the cab of his truck, bumping along over the interior roads that crisscrossed his ranch, Charlotte's throaty voice and light scent washing over him in waves.

"Can I ask you a question?"

"Shoot."

"I know tonight was sort of weird, but it was nice, too, right?"

It was nice. The unpleasant side effect of unrequited attraction and sexual frustration were simply the price he would have to pay for it. More proof he needed to get his damn head on straight.

But even with his internal battle, he couldn't disagree with her. Other than his friendly concern over Gray and Harper, he couldn't deny how nice it had been to sit and talk with everyone. Age appropriate conversation with people who had dreams and goals.

Who had a focus on their future.

Hell, who *believed* they could have one if they did the work and strived hard enough.

He'd mostly moved past that young boy who'd expected he'd end up like Trevor Beaumont. But he didn't always have the opportunity to see that truth reflected so clearly in his social life.

Only here, tonight, looking at what Gray was building, and hearing Harper and Charlotte and Hadley talking about their businesses and getting Zack's promise to connect him to one of the buyers at Total Foods, Wayne's newest grocery partner, Chance couldn't deny his excitement that maybe there was a way past the fear of losing his ranch and his business.

That maybe the future he'd always envisioned was possible.

"It was nice."

"I've been so focused on getting my business off the ground, tonight was a reminder that I've let a lot of other things slide. I don't want to do that anymore."

He slowed as he pulled down the driveway, glancing over at her profile. "Starting a business is hard work and it doesn't fit neatly into the nine-to-five routine."

"Definitely not." She laid her head back on the

rest. "I never thought I'd be this tired at thirty-two."

"Amen to that. I haven't slept more than six hours a night for damn near a decade. And that's a good night."

It was nice, that quiet camaraderie and mutual understanding of what it took to prosper. Even if, by all accounts, she was doing far more prospering than him.

Did it really matter? It wasn't a contest, after all.

Especially when given the opportunity to quietly share the day and discuss the tremendous weight on your shoulders.

He pulled up beside Hadley's SUV, intending to come around and let Charlotte out, only to find her standing beside his truck when he got there. "I could have opened the door for you."

"I know how to open the door, Chance."

Where a situation like this—something so silly and dumb—could often set off their bickering, nothing flared between them as they stared at each other under the lights of the garage.

Nothing except attraction, Chance admitted, as he allowed his gaze to roam over Charlotte as she stood before him.

It was heady, that opportunity to simply gaze on her, he acknowledged to himself. Normally he had to keep the urge to look at her on lockdown, holding himself back because looking inevitably led to the deep urge to touch.

But God, she was beautiful.

And strong.

And *interesting*.

Damn it, wasn't that part of what made all of this so difficult? He genuinely liked her. She had grit and tenacity, both evident in the way she spoke of her business, the PR firm she'd started a few years ago. She wasn't depending on the Wayne name to make her way, but instead was focused on making something strong and solid and hers.

All of it swirled in his head, drawing him to her like a magnet, even as he knew all the forces that had repelled them from each other for so long.

More, he recognized his own role in allowing those forces to drive outcomes.

The childish behavior that had started them down a path where the only communication they managed rested in underlying anger and a hurt that, despite being sustained so young, still had power.

It was his last conscious thought as Charlotte moved into him. He thought he was ready for it. Hell, he'd even toyed with the fantasy on the ride to his driveway that something like this would happen.

But none of it compared to the woman that wrapped her arms around him and pressed her body to his.

And then Chance gave up all of it—the endlessly roiling thoughts, the lingering belief he wasn't enough and the hopeless frustration— and sank into this amazing woman he'd wanted long before he understood what those feelings meant.

What had begun on impulse quickly transitioned to glorious purpose, their bodies blending in the sweetest torture. Male to female matched only by a need that had gone far too long unsated.

He tightened his hold on her, wrapping her snug in his arms both to draw her closer and to ward off the increasing chill of the evening. Her slim figure pressed against him, the curves of her breasts pressed to his chest.

Had he ever felt anything sweeter? Chance marveled as their mouths met again, the kiss lingering, then urgent, then back to a teasing sort of torture that seemed fitting between him and Charlotte.

Was anything easy between them?

As the kiss continued, he realized he didn't really want it to be. Not if just a kiss could be this hot.

He was still considering that when Charlotte broke off the contact, staring up at him. Her eyes were wide, her pupils dilated with the drugging effects of their kiss.

It was only as a frown turned down her passion-ripened lips that Chance got his first inkling the road that had seemingly smoothed out between them was anything but straight.

"I can't do this." She said the words like they could ward off the intense pleasure the two of them had just shared.

Like they could go back to the way they were.

And no matter how badly he wanted to fight the instinct, he fell right back into the patterns that had defined their life.

"Can't? Or won't?"

"Chance, please don't—"

"Just leave, Charlotte. There's nothing more to say, but we both know that never stops us."

He expected that small flag of battle would be more than she could resist, but Charlotte only nodded, touching the tips of her fingers to her lips before she marched to the car.

It was a long while later, as he still stared at the place where she'd stood, that Chance finally turned to enter the house, the phantom taste of her lingering on his lips.

Chapter 17

Harper stared at the empty sink and oddly wished for a pile of dishes. Although one of her least favorite tasks, the mindless effort of scrubbing braised meat off the bottom of her sister's slow cooker would have at least given her a chance to weigh her decision to sleep with Gray.

Dirty dishes, after all, had a way of grounding a person.

And after the heated glances she and Gray had shared all evening, she was floating near the stars.

Her head—the one part of her that had kept those feet firmly planted for the past month—had even abandoned her, souped up on enough hormones to put its more calming, practical urges to sleep.

So here she was. Horny and dishless, since her ever efficient sister had piled the cooker into the back of Zack's truck to take home, claiming that she'd brought dinner and could handle the cleanup in her own kitchen. And Hadley had already been superefficient by bringing disposable plates for the meal so cleanup had been a breeze.

Harper's environment-loving self had chafed a bit at the plates, but she knew a good thing when she saw one. And no cleanup detail for twenty people was as much a part of Hadley's dinner gift as the barn raising had been from Zack.

So here they were.

Or here she was.

Gray had stepped into the bedroom to take a call on one of the animals at a nearby ranch he provided care for, and she had been pleased to hear his calm, confident voice as he walked one of his graduate students through a few of the tests they needed to run on a horse's bloodwork.

While great to hear him focused on his work again, it was one more check in the plus column that kept adding up to sleeping together.

Nearly a week since his accident. Check.

Clear memories of his work. Check again.

An ability to recall their history?

That's where she kept coming up short—the doctor's unwillingness the week before to commit to the time frame Gray's memories would return was an ongoing concern.

Why did his mind stubbornly continue to block that time out? Because their evening had suggested he was well and whole in every other way.

The details he'd given to his intern, the funny an-
ecdotes he and Chance had told during dinner
about things they'd gotten into as kids, even the
way he'd told the hands about his plans for the
horse rescue.

All of it smacked of a man who remembered
his life.

And all of it continued to reinforce the voice
in her head that kept telling her to give him the
truth. He was healed—or close enough—and it
was time he understood what was really between
them.

Because maybe if he did, they could come to
this place between them on even ground.

That had been the best part of tonight. When
she'd sat at that picnic table with Gray, talking
with everyone, she'd seen the two people they'd
become. But in those new, more interesting personalities, she also saw their history.

Their shared interests and perspectives.

Their easy chemistry and ability to talk to one
another.

And their solid friendship, forged in those
years when learning who you were was an essen-
tial piece of building relationships.

She'd spent so long bearing up under the
weight of their earlier relationship that it was a
brand-new sensation to be free of it.

"You look happy."

Gray snuck up behind her, his arms wrapping
around her midsection as he pulled her back

against him. Even the cuddling—a throwback to their relationship—had taken on new meaning over the past week.

Where she'd remembered the embraces of years past with a tall, slim young man who'd grown taller faster than he'd filled out, she now knew the form and feel of a fully muscled man. His chest felt different against her back. The strength in his biceps felt different where they lay against her arms. And the husky timbre of his voice had deepened a few more degrees, only adding to his ability to elicit shivers up and down her spine with a few words.

She might have changed in her years away, but Gray had, too. When she'd first arrived home, that steady reality that everyone's life had moved on, growing and evolving with the natural force of years, had seemed daunting.

Like she'd missed something important, all while feeling put out no one had sat around waiting for her.

But the time since had taught her a different view. And that new perspective meant everything.

"I asked you the other day what you remembered of us."

If he was bothered by her subject change, he didn't show it, only nodding at her statement. "You've asked me a few times, actually. You phrase it differently every time you ask, but the underlying meaning hasn't changed."

"And?"

"And you remember something I don't."

"I remember something big, Gray."

For the first time she doubted herself, but even as she questioned her next step, she knew she had to make it. There was no way for them to move forward if she didn't do this.

Because if she didn't take that first step toward him with as much transparency as she could find, the only thing they'd do tonight was have sex.

With that foremost in her thoughts, she slipped out of his hold, turning to face him. With deliberate movements, she took his hands in hers, hopeful she could not only say all she needed to but do it in a way that didn't hurt the recovery—no matter how slow—that he was making.

She had no idea if there was a future waiting for them, but there wasn't a chance of one if she didn't face it fully. And that was true for him, too.

Hadn't that been at the heart of all they'd lost a decade ago? In all the anger and sadness she'd carried since their breakup, the way he'd broken things off had hurt the most. Something had spooked him, whether it was directly about her or indirectly about her due to his father's presence, Harper still didn't know.

Maybe she never would.

But Gray had never given her the real reason he was ending things.

She refused to do the same to him in return, keeping knowledge that affected both of them to herself.

"I'm sorry if this comes as a shock, but we're

not a couple any longer. We haven't been for a long time."

She saw a whisper of truth register in his eyes even as he shook his head. "That's not right. You know it's not. We talked about how we met at Doc Andrews's practice. That time we ran off the town square at Christmas to make love in the bakery. The plans we made in college."

"Yes, those are all true. We did those things."

She kept her voice light and deliberately, carefully calm. But now that they were in this she had to keep on.

"But all those things happened a while ago."

"Well, sure they did. We were kids then."

"What about in the years since?"

That whisper gathered strength, his brow furrowing. "But we're together."

"I'm sorry, Gray. I'm sorry I can't tell you we are. But I moved to Seattle ten years ago and have made a life there. Without you."

"Why can't I remember this?"

She reached up, brushing at some hair that had dipped over his forehead. "You will remember it. When you're ready."

The pain in his eyes deepened, even as they went wide in shock. "Oh, Harper, I didn't hurt you this week, did I? I've taken advantage. I—"

She shook her head, all while squeezing tighter with the hand that still held one of his in her grip. "No, you haven't."

"But I've touched you and kissed you. Hell, I've manhandled you."

It was the anger in his words—completely misplaced in retrospect of what they'd shared—and it shocked her enough that she stepped back, dropping their hands.

"Why would you say that?"

"I've walked up to you whenever I wanted, just like now when I came out of the bedroom. I've kissed you and, hell, I chased you around the kitchen table the other day."

"You did not chase me, Gray McClain."

"But you were moving away from me and I didn't understand it. I didn't ask you why."

"Gray. Stop."

He held up his hands, as if afraid to touch her. "I'm sorry if I took advantage."

"You didn't take advantage of me." She moved in close, wrapping her arms around his waist, insistent on making her point. "But I can't be with you tonight if you don't know the truth about us."

"Harper, we can't be together at all." He still held his arms out, away so they weren't touching. "We're not together."

It was the moment they'd been running to and away from since she got home to Rustlers Creek.

"Do you want me?"

"That's irrelevant."

"Actually, I think it's highly relevant." She pressed her chest against his and laid her lips against his Adam's apple, the solid hammer of his pulse sweet agreement to her point.

"We can't do this." Sexual tension laced his voice and Harper knew she'd won.

"Gray. Please don't walk away in some sort of misguided valor. You did that once before and it left us both lonely and alone. Take what's here." She shifted her lips, trailing kisses long his jaw. "Be with me."

She felt his hesitation for the briefest moment in the further tightening of his jaw before those arms came around her like tight bands of agreement.

Whatever had come before no longer mattered. And the remembering he still needed to do would come in time.

But they were going to take now.

Together.

GRAY'S HEAD SWIRLED and not because he'd been injured a week ago. Harper was in his arms, kissing his throat and jaw and accepting what was between them with sweet surrender.

And still, he held back, so damned unsure of himself.

He loved her.

That was rock-solid in his mind, and no number of missing memories could or would change it.

Only how could he be so misguided that he didn't remember or know they were no longer together?

And why?

He loved her, damn it. Why would he have let her go? Because despite the lack of memories that told him why, he knew his decisions were at the heart of it.

Fuck if he could remember them.

His mind raced through what she told him and all the possible reasons why, all while bearing up under the sweet torture of her lips. It was only when she tilted her head and looked up at him, her body still pressed to his, her arms still firm around his waist, that his racing thoughts finally calmed.

"You can figure out the whys later, Gray. For now, can we just be?"

It was invitation and forgiveness, encouragement and benediction, all at the same time.

And it was Harper.

The needs of his body finally overcame the confusion of his mind, and he gave in fully, bending his head to meet her lips. They'd kissed several times over the past few days, but nothing with this degree of power. Nothing with this shocking level of promise.

And wasn't that a marvel?

His belief that they were together had been reframed by her revelation that they weren't, and in that knowledge he felt his shifting reaction to being with her.

The slim frame in his arms, both tiny in height as he'd remembered but filled out with a woman's shape. The confidence in her kiss, embedded with a woman's prerogative to choose the sharing of their bodies instead of trying to hide the physical aspects of their youthful relationship.

This was new and exciting and as profound as the comfort in remembering. But it was her invitation to take that finally, fully landed.

Pressing, urgent need quickly overrode any focused thought, and he bent down to sweep her into his arms, lifting her up to walk them to the bedroom. She laughed, her arms wrapping around his neck as her lips found his jaw again. "Show-off."

"Consider me the soul of expedience."

A fact he proved with the quick discard of his clothes beside the bed and the slower, more focused removal of hers as he came down beside her. Their casual wear at the cabin—T-shirts and jeans—aided in the speed, and he gave thanks that, other than a lone button on each of their waistbands, their clothes were gone in moments.

With both of them finally naked, Gray looked his fill. What he'd only felt in his arms or against his chest up to now was on full display and he reached out to trace the weight of her breast, his thumb teasing one nipple as he rediscovered her.

As he rediscovered *them*.

The tender exploration of one breast expanded to two and Gray stretched out beside her, light touches growing more urgent as they shared secret smiles, breaths growing heavy with the increasing demands of their bodies.

Gray continued to stoke the fire, quickly realizing it was out of his control when Harper turned the tables on him. The hands that stroked a sensual path over his chest and shoulders moved on lower, teasing the muscles of his stomach before taking his cock fully in hand.

Mindless need overtook him as her palm pressed his flesh, setting a rhythm that was achingly familiar.

It took his breath and he tried to hold on to the moment, so desperate to make this last. To draw out every bit of pleasure, both remembered and brand-new. It was only when Harper laughed, a deep, delighted sound that seemed to echo around them, that he came back to himself.

"What's so funny?"

"My sister."

"Excuse me?" His attention caught hard at that one, suddenly conscious of what they were doing and the mental intrusion of her family in the room. "You want to catch me up?"

"I was just thinking that I couldn't wait much longer. And then I thought about condoms, which I forgot completely. And then I thought about the box my sister neatly deposited in the junk drawer in the kitchen. She called it a 'just in case' present."

"You have condoms?"

"You don't?" Her eyebrows rose and he couldn't hold back the blush that crept up his neck. He might not remember everything about their relationship—or lack of one—but a memory came rushing back with startling clarity. "I haven't been all that focused on this aspect of my life for a while. And it's not like they're hard to find if you need to make a quick run to the drugstore."

It was a strange admission, layered over so

much more he didn't say. Lack of focus on that area of his life also meant he was alone.

But Harper gave no indication she cared about any of that, her expression never changing as she scrambled to sit up.

"Then I'm glad my sister is both nosy and pragmatic."

Before he could stop her, she'd slid from the bed, her naked form scampering out of the room. He couldn't deny the sweet view, even as his body stretched tighter with desire at the visual picture she made.

All while deftly ignoring the truth he'd inadvertently shared.

And then the moment was gone, her triumphant return to the bedroom evident in her raised hand and the shaking box of condoms. "God, I love my sister. She brought dinner *and* an economy-sized box of condoms."

Gray eyed the box. "I think I love her, too."

Harper's carefree laugh was back. "And to think I was irritated she's been all up in my business. Clearly I owe her an apology." She dug into the box, dragging out a strip of wrapped condoms. "A big one."

Gray couldn't hold back his own laugh as he reached out and tickled her ribs, pulling her close so that she sprawled on top of him. Which made the serious question that spilled out a surprise.

"Does it bother you?" When he saw the question on her face, he continued. "The being on display. The knowing looks."

It seemed like an odd departure, stopping to ask questions in the middle of sex, yet it was important to him to know the answer.

Her smile was sweetly thoughtful. "Hadley and Charlotte are doing it out of love. And of course they're interested in what's been going on between us. I would be if the situation was reversed."

"Because we were broken up?"

"Yes and no. Partially, I'd want to know because I'm nosy, but nosy in a way that comes from a good place. I want to see the people I love happy." That soft smile faded completely. "It's taken me some time to remember that, but I'm glad that I have. It was easy, while being away from here, to forget that the same reasons people are so interested is because they care."

"But are they worried that I'll hurt you again?"

She laid a hand on his cheek, her gaze softening. "Do you remember how we broke up?"

"No, not exactly. But I know it was my fault. That I broke us up."

"Yes and no. You might have done the actual breakup but I'm the one who left. Ran away, really. I've thought about that, you know. Could we have salvaged things if I'd stayed?"

The frustration that had dogged him for a week at those stray memories that never seemed to land felt deeper now. Less like frustration and more like a sort of mental agony that the things in his life that were the most important to him were locked away, inaccessible.

How could he make any of this right if he didn't know? Sure, he might know he was responsible for their breakup, but he still had no idea why.

"I don't know, Harper, I really don't. I'd like to say we could have, but I don't know why I sent you away. I can't imagine why I'd do that."

"Maybe it doesn't matter any longer." She stilled. "No, that's not quite right. It matters, but maybe it doesn't have to mean everything any longer. Life's conspired to put us back in each other's way for a bit. Maybe it's time to simply take the present as it comes and stop worrying about what came before.

"After all"—she smiled—"you've been freed from it with that concussion of yours."

He had no idea how she did it, but she'd somehow managed to make him feel carefree, all while bearing up under the heavy weight of misplaced memory and very real, tangible guilt.

"I want this, Gray. Today. Our present time together. I want this and I want you."

"I want you, too."

"Then why are we waiting?"

He pulled her close once more, kissing her as his hands once again traced loving designs over her flesh, and he murmured, "I have no idea."

This was Harper.

And for right now—this moment—she was all that mattered.

HARPER KNEW THE decision to have sex with Gray would be emotional. But she had no idea how much of it would be about discovery. Shiny and new, despite all they'd shared years ago.

Her recollections of sex with Gray had developed something of a hazy quality over the years. While they'd always been memorable and deeply pleasurable, she realized now that she'd forgotten the sheer physicality of making love with him.

The size of his body. The scent of him, so desperately perfect as she buried her nose in the crook of his neck. The light sheen of sweat over his skin that spoke of mutually shared effort in the pursuit of pleasure.

It was almost too much.

It was perfect.

Her position covering Gray's chest gave her an excellent place to begin her exploration of all that perfection, and she pressed a kiss to his neck before beginning a journey down his body. The firm contours of his chest and the thick bands of his stomach muscles were a feast for her senses, her hands tracing each before her mouth and tongue followed the same contours.

Harper took particular pleasure in the way his stomach cratered when she ran the tip of her tongue along one of the ridges of his muscles. Still, she continued on, finding the goal of her sex exploration ready and waiting for her. In a show of appreciation, she lapped at the straining head of his cock before taking him fully into her mouth.

His hard, low moan was like sweet music, and

she kept steady pressure at the base of his erection with the play of her fingers while she pleasured him with her mouth. Every erotic fantasy she'd indulged in over the last decade had some version of this moment in it, but despite her every imagining, nothing prepared her for the sexy, sultry power that rolled through her in deep, sensuous waves.

He exhaled her name on a heavy moan as his large hands covered her shoulders. She felt the determined strength in his hands as he coaxed her back to where she'd been, sprawled across his chest.

"You're a vision," he murmured, his blue gaze unfocused with desire. "And a vixen."

She smiled at that, another wave of that sultry power roaring high. "A lovely compliment to be sure."

"One I mean down to my very soul."

She wanted to laugh, but that easy humor that had flowed between them had already vanished, the sexy, driving needs of their bodies taking the lead.

Harper heard the light rip of foil as he opened one of the condom packets, and in the work of a moment, he had it on and had settled himself between her legs, his broad palms splayed across her thighs where she straddled him.

Pleasure shot through her as she felt him poised at the entrance to her body before sharp, edgy need replaced the growing anticipation.

With the steadying pressure of his hands on her hips, Harper lifted herself up and rode his length in long, languid strokes. They found a rhythm—a sweet memory that hadn't changed in all this time—and pushed one another on, higher and higher, pleasure their sole objective.

Harper had chosen this.

This moment.

This act.

This man.

And as her release stole over her with all the power of a summer thunderstorm, she threw her head back and filled her soul with the ride.

Chapter 18

Gray rolled over onto his side, reaching for Harper in his sleep and coming wide-awake when his hand met nothing but an empty sheet.

Had he only dreamed of having sex with her?

As he came fully awake, her scent flooding his senses, he knew it wasn't a dream.

But where was she?

He shifted to sit up, delighted when her naked form filled the doorway, two plates held high in her hands.

"What are you doing?"

"I made us a few sandwiches with the left-overs Hadley put in the fridge."

"You made us sandwiches?" He heard the bemusement in his tone and knew the question was ridiculous in light of the obviously full plates she carried, but he couldn't hold back his surprise.

Her smile wavered slightly, and he heard the marked notes of embarrassment in her voice. "I was hungry."

"Whatever you do, please don't mistake my idiotic questions for anything other than shocked happiness."

"I've never eaten after sex. It seemed like the thing to do when I remembered all those leftovers in the fridge."

"A talent your sister has in spades."

He reached for the plate in her hand, stopping when he caught sight of Harper's face.

"She cooks for you?"

"She's always foisting something off on me. I think she's secretly convinced herself I'm going to starve if she doesn't make it her mission to feed me. Since I'm over at her and Zack's place pretty regularly to see to the stock, if she knows I'm there she usually finds a way to leave something in my truck."

"That is so my sister." Harper took a seat next to him on the bed. He was absurdly delighted when she settled in, still naked and seemingly uninterested in changing that state.

Gray had no idea what he'd done to deserve a sandwich and a naked woman, but he wasn't going to argue with the fantasy that had suddenly become his life. With that happy thought fresh in his mind, he took a bite of his after-sex snack, groaning at the mix of sweet barbecue and fluffy homemade brioche bun.

They ate in contented silence for a few minutes before he remembered the way they used to share meals when they worked at the vet's. "You and your sister like to feed people."

"It's Hadley's true gift."

"It's yours, too. The way you used to bring me food when we worked together in high school. I knew what you were doing."

"Did it hurt your feelings?"

"Over the food?"

He thought about the way she used to share what she had, always full of one reason or another why she had extras. The stories usually revolved around her sister's emerging cooking skills and items Harper either disliked or heaping servings of food Hadley had forced on her, knowing they were favorites.

He shook his head, those long-ago shared meals some of the sweetest of his life. "Nope."

"I was always worried I might be embarrassing you."

He wiped his mouth with one of the napkins she'd brought in. "I don't recall feeling embarrassed. I only remember feeling full. Hadley's future talents were evident then. And I've still never had gingerbread like hers."

"Hands down the yuckiest cookie on the planet. Unless, of course, you count chocolate chip cookies, basically the best cookie in the world, ruined with the addition of walnuts, the worst nut in the world." She shivered, her slim shoulders shaking. "Yuck."

"There are people that would fight you over that opinion."

"Those people are wrong."

The sheer conviction in her tone had him laughing. "I thought you were the queen of algorithms. Taking what people liked and blending it into something even better."

"I can't do jack with walnuts."

She'd put a pretty good dent in her sandwich, but there was still about half on her plate when she set it down on the end table on her side of the bed before turning back to him. "I can do quite a bit, however, with appreciative men who have been fed a hearty snack and are more than ready for round two."

She glanced pointedly down to his own naked form, clearly pleased when he stirred in response to her frank perusal.

"I didn't realize sex worked on algorithms."

She took his plate, nestling the empty one under hers, before turning back to him. "Algorithms are nothing but a basic set of instructions."

Gray frowned at that, memories of some of what he'd seen covering her computer screen suggesting anything but simplicity. "You make that sound easy."

"Because it is. All an algorithm is"—she traced

a line over his pectoral muscle with the tip of her finger —"is a process that's followed in making calculations."

"I still think you're oversimplifying it."

"Let me make it easier to understand then." She shifted her focus from where her hand pressed against his chest to stare up at him. "If I did this, for example . . ." She traced the line of his nipple, a shot of heat flowing through him, before she continued on down the center of his chest to his stomach.

Memory at the way her tongue had run over his heated flesh less than an hour before added to the feel of her touch, and Gray felt that answering response tighten his body further.

"You provide a predictable response to a specific order of operations."

"Now I'm predictable?"

Her smile went from witchy to teasing in a flash. "In bed you are."

"So algorithms are like sex?"

"Only if you follow the proper steps." Those clever fingers continued on but Gray refused to give her the upper hand. Flipping them both so that he had them stretched out flat on the bed, facing each other, he'd already positioned his fingers at the heated core of her.

"You mean if I did this . . ." He mimicked the motion of her lone finger over his chest, instead using the tip of his finger to trace the seam at the entrance of her body. The clutch of her fingers at his shoulders indicated he'd followed the *exact* proper order of operations. "I'd get a specific response."

"Yes. And if I did this . . ." She slid her hand between them, drawing a similar stroke from the base of his erection to the tip. He felt his eyes threaten to roll to the back of his head at the erotic foreplay. "You'd respond just as you have."

The teasing byplay, the stroking over sensitive flesh, the fun encouragement of what she did for a living as a tool of pleasure—Gray absorbed it all deep into his skin as touch after touch produced increasingly breathless results. And as those moments finally culminated in an explosion of pleasure between them, they clung to each other, holding tight as the world turned to starlight around them.

GRAY WASN'T SURE if he'd ever felt better in his life. Bright Montana sunshine speared down through the high stable windows as he and Harper worked inside, scooping fresh hay into Cabernet's stall.

He hadn't slept, a state that hadn't affected his checkup with the doctor. She'd pronounced him well on the road back to health and cleared him for work and regular activity. He'd assured her that the headaches were lessening every day, with today the first where he'd barely even noticed it.

At the doctor's mention of regular activity, he'd seen Harper's subtle blush. He couldn't resist reaching for her hand at that, well aware she'd carried the lingering concern they'd jumped the gun on his healing by sleeping together. He had no doubt the doctor noticed the simple affection and knew *exactly* what it meant, but she gave no indication as she tapped a few last notes into her tablet.

The doctor visit was followed with the trip to Rick Pruett's stables. Jackie had met them there with a horse trailer she'd borrowed from a contact she knew from the riding world, and they'd spent an hour working with the horse, calming him all while encouraging him.

Such an innate sense of certainty filled him, Gray thought as he shoveled the thick hay, determined to make a welcoming home for Cabernet. A feeling of rightness that there were good things on the horizon. For him and Harper. For his health. And for his work and his dreams for the rescue.

And while he knew a night of good, healthy sex could put a man in a fine mood, what he felt was so much more.

The memories of why he'd sent Harper away still hadn't surfaced, but he'd reflected on the two of them all day. The revelations the night before when he'd discovered what he'd done all those years ago, along with her admission that she'd run from their breakup.

You might have done the actual breakup but I'm the one who left. Ran away, really. I've thought about that, you know. Could we have salvaged things if I'd stayed?

Would her staying in Rustlers Creek have changed anything?

There was no way to go backward, but it did make him wonder what that path would have looked like.

What they would have looked like.

And as he shoveled one more layer of hay, Gray admitted the truth. He could imagine all he wanted, but they both had to deal with now. With the lives they lived now, a result of the choices made all those years ago.

Just as he couldn't go back and change Cabernet's accident, he couldn't go back and un-break up with Harper.

He'd started the rescue with the innate belief that he could give injured horses new lives. Different lives that gave them a future, steeped in the knowledge that blindness didn't change their quality, their worth or their deserving a good life.

Didn't he and Harper deserve the same?

However motivated, he'd made decisions for the two of them once before. And he was more than aware that there were two of them in this right now. But somehow, even with the lack of memories, Gray knew two things.

He did deserve happiness and a chance at the life he truly wanted.

And if she would find a way back to him, Gray would spend every day of his life showing Harper that they were a team.

One well worth fighting for.

HARPER HAD BEEN impressed the prior week when Gray and Rick had led Cabernet out of the stables and into the paddock, patient with the horse, their steps gentle. But watching Gray work with Jackie Delaney was like watching two masters of their craft.

Zack's ranch hands hadn't fully finished the railing on the corral the day before, but Jackie had assured her it didn't matter as they wouldn't allow Cabernet to run loose for some time. So Harper had taken a seat at the picnic table still outside from the night before and watched, fascinated, as Gray and Jackie slowly led the horse through a series of increasingly complicated exercises.

Although she had little knowledge of working with animals beyond the basic grooming work she'd done in her high school job, she did recognize the blend of encouragement and patience that would build trust with the horse. She'd been equally fascinated as Gray and Jackie had discussed how they'd introduce a companion horse to Cabernet, offering added support and comfort to the animal as part of his settling in.

"It's impressive work."

Harper turned to see her father, delighted that he'd shown up. "Dad!" She jumped up to hug him before pulling back to look at him, never leaving the circle of his arms. "You playing hooky?"

"Shhh." He lowered his voice in a conspiratorial whisper. "I'm visiting a future internship site for our FFA students."

"Well of course you are."

They stood and watched for a few more minutes before her dad gestured them back to the table. "Do you have a few minutes?"

"Of course."

"We haven't had a chance to talk much since last week. Since you found Jackie at the house."

It was her father's classic approach to any problem. He simply addressed it head-on.

Had she ever realized what a gift that was? To have a guiding force in your life who talked to you and treated you with direct thoughts and conversations that were the epitome of mutual respect.

"I know we haven't and I'm sorry for that. But I want you to know how happy I am for you." She reached across the table to take his hand. "Shocked at first, I'll admit. But that's just because I've had to reframe you a bit in my mind."

"Reframe me?"

"Yes, as a healthy, happy adult who wants to be in a relationship as much as the rest of us." Harper stared down where their hands joined before looking back up to meet his gaze. "I'm sorry it took me much longer than it should have to understand that."

"I think you've come around pretty quick. And I'm not sure it matters very much any longer."

She heard the slightest catch in his tone but really knew something was wrong as his gaze shifted to where Gray and Jackie worked with Cabernet.

"What's happened?"

"Jackie doesn't want to date me."

The urge to shout was strong, but Harper had already seen what startling the horse could do. She didn't want to be responsible for a repeat performance.

But what the *hell* was her father talking about?

"You're crazy about her. And she'd be just plain crazy not to be interested in you in return."

"I guess that's where we're at, then."

It was hard to miss the sadness that grooved lines into her father's face, especially in the tension around his mouth, but she heard a different note in his voice. "You haven't given up, though?"

"I'm trying not to."

"Try or do, Yoda?"

He smiled at that, those grooves fading a bit. They'd been *Star Wars* junkies since she was small, and a few words of wisdom from Dagobah's resident teacher could usually make one of them smile.

"She's got a lot of history. From before moving here. And"—he stilled, considering—"it's not my place to say. But the past is rearing its ugly head on our future."

While her concerns were deeply embedded in Camp Dad, Harper knew a bit about the lingering pain that could stay with you.

"Sometimes we hold on to that past a little too tight."

And although she didn't want to make this

about her, she did want to assure her father that some of the sadness she'd carried for so long had faded. "I've had to admit to doing that myself. It's a humbling realization to understand that some of the morass and sadness that you're living with is at your own hand."

"You and Gray?"

Images of the night before—hell, all the moments they'd shared since she'd returned home—flew through her mind on a loop.

Until she understood the admittance was really very simple.

"Me and Gray."

"The two of you had something special. Truly special. I hope you can find your way back to that."

She didn't need her father's approval, nor did he need hers. But as he laid a hand on top of their joined ones, Harper had to admit just how good it felt to have it and to give it in return.

"She's a special woman, Dad. I hope you find your way, too. I hope both of you do."

GRAY STOOD BESIDE Cabernet's stall and considered all he'd learned about the animal in such a short time. Cabernet's racing background—and the innate pride that came with being a champion—had come out pretty quickly as he and Jackie had worked with their new charge throughout the afternoon.

Sensitive and skittish at first, Cabernet had preened under the continuous praise and handling, giving them both a thrill when he tossed his mane after a shared exercise between the three of them that the horse successfully navigated on the second try.

Jackie was so excited by the progress she'd wanted to run home to get her things, determined to stay in the stables for the night. He'd done his best to encourage her to come back the next day, but she wouldn't hear of it, claiming she was too excited to continue getting to know their new addition.

"A very good day, indeed," he murmured as he patted Cabernet's neck before giving the horse a sugar cube.

The doctor in him didn't want to overindulge, but the caregiver knew a little extra love and attention—especially after a day full of change—would go a long way to settling Cabernet.

When the horse ultimately moved on to the pail of oats Gray had set out, he stepped back to give the horse some quiet time—an equally important element of Cabernet's settling in.

And turned to find his father standing a few stalls away.

"I didn't mean to startle you," Burt said.

It was a fair gesture, one layered in genuine apology, so Gray had no idea why he was bothered.

Or why that same skittish sense he'd tried

to smooth all afternoon in Cabernet seemed to light up his nerve endings from the top of his head to the tip of his toes.

Danger, it said, despite Burt's wide smile.

"What can I do for you?"

"I heard in town that you had an accident. I wanted to come out and check on you."

That oily sensation didn't quite recede, but Gray couldn't sense any missteps in his father's words. And it wasn't like he'd made it a priority to call him up and tell him what was going on.

Proof that their relationship wasn't great? Or more evidence he still didn't remember everything?

The answer to that nagged at him, the headache that had finally subsided over the past day coming back in full force.

He needed to remember this.

More, he needed to *know*.

Because the man standing opposite him looked like he cared, his smile warm and his stance relaxed, but Gray couldn't shake the sense that it was all a mirage.

"How'd you hear about it?"

"I was over at the Branded Mark, having a beer. I'd nearly left when I heard a few of the Wayne hands talking about how you'd taken quite a hit. The fellas seemed real concerned about you and I wanted to come see for myself."

More details that made sense. His injury wasn't a secret, and it sure as hell wasn't to the guys who worked for Zack, based on all the help they'd provided yesterday.

But were they really worried about him?

He'd figured he'd shown himself up well the day before, helping where he could to get the stable details finished. He still wasn't hefting a lot of weight due to his injury, but he'd stained wood inside the stalls with several other men and no one seemed all that upset about him.

Would they go out and talk about him last night?

"I'm on the mend and already saw the doctor. She's happy with my progress."

Burt shuffled a bit closer, his hands still in his pockets. "I was sorry to hear you went through this. A knock on the head's nothing to mess with, son."

"Like I said, I'm feeling better now."

Burt glanced around the stable, his eyes wide as he took it all in. "This is quite a setup you've got here."

"It's small, but it'll cover what I need."

"That's nice to hear. A man knows he's raised a good boy when he can talk about having enough."

Once more, Gray tried to process through the dissonance of his father's words and his presence, increasingly irritated at himself that he couldn't relax and have a simple conversation with his father. Burt had been kind enough to come over and ask after him. He was clearly concerned.

"Why don't you come in and I'll show you around."

They walked around the stables and Gray pointed out the various features. He'd never remembered his father being a particularly big animal lover, but he asked several questions about the care and feeding of the animals and their overall prospects for good lives.

Gray used Cabernet as an example—a former racing horse that needed a place to live out his days—when his father's eyes lit up.

"You think about breeding him?"

"I'm not—" Gray stilled, breaking off. "That's not the purpose of the rescue."

"Might not be the main purpose, but you could try for a bit of business on the side. Blind isn't dead below the waist, you know." Burt cackled at his own joke.

"I guess that's an idea but not with this one. Cabernet's a gelding."

"Why the hell would you want a pussy horse like that? Maybe you should've put him down instead of paying all the money to feed him and keep him comfortable."

"Sort of the opposite of a horse rescue."

Burt nodded and clucked his tongue. "Sure, sure. I suppose."

He supposed?

Before Gray could formulate some sort of answer to that, his father continued. "So listen, I'm real glad you're doing better. You look good, too and you've got some great things going from the sounds of it. I also came here because, well . . ." Burt glanced down and kicked his foot against an empty stall door. "Well, it's embarrassing to ask my son, but I'm on some hard times and I need a hand."

Those subtle warning signals amped up again, the definite sense of being played growing more and more evident with each word his father spoke.

"Come on, Gray, what do you say?"

And then Gray saw it.

The moment Burt lifted his gaze from his restless foot and before he had the wherewithal to tamp down the hard glint that shone in his eyes.

And along with that recognition, Gray felt the dam of memories open in his chest on a raging flood of anger.

"Why are you really here?"

"I told you why. I wanted to see you."

"Lie to me one more time, old man, and I'm kicking your ass off my property."

The words were out—and the residual fury that he'd harbored since his youth along with them.

"Fine. I need some fucking help. Is that what you want to hear?"

It wasn't what he wanted to hear but it was the proof of what he'd sensed all along. There wasn't any concern about Gray's health or his ranch or his work. This visit was all about Burt and whatever needy scam he'd decided to come and run.

"Gray! Dinner!" Harper's voice was light as

she headed into the stables. He saw her coming, that slim form, the late afternoon sunlight glinting off the auburn in her hair and the happy smile, as if in slow motion.

And then he saw his father's smile.

Greedy.

Calculating.

And far too delighted to see Harper walking toward both of them.

It was in that moment that it all came crashing back. Just like the doctor had told him it could, every dark, bitter memory he'd ever had about his father streamed through his mind.

Along with the fight they'd had that last day before he'd broken up with Harper.

He and Chance had gone to the Branded Mark for a few beers and his father cornered him between the dartboards and the hallway to the restrooms.

"You've been getting awfully cozy with that Allen girl."

Gray heard the speculation. "What of it?"

"It's nice to see you moving up in the world. Though I'm surprised her father, the educator"—Burt made air quotes as he referenced Marty Allen—*"allows you inside his house."* Burt's careless grin took on a dark quality. *"You fuck her there?"*

Gray saw red—literally a bloodred filter that smashed down right over his eyes. The only thing that held him back—and that was a slim only—was the knowledge the old man wanted him to take a swing.

"Classy as always."

"*Fuck classy.*" Burt dug the pack of cigarettes out of his front shirt pocket. "*She's your ticket to something better. You play your cards right and you'll have a good little life. You can give me one, too.*"

"*Why would I give you anything?*"

Burt had the audacity to look surprised at that as he lit his cigarette. "*I'm your father.*"

"*A sad mistake of biology.*"

The not-so-subtle baiting shifted into genuine anger. "*You don't fucking talk to me that way, boy.*"

"*Then stay the fuck away from me. And don't you go anywhere near her.*"

Chance had found them then, coming up behind Gray and pulling him away. His friend's voice had remained low, keeping Gray moving with the quiet insistence that his father not only wasn't worth it, but he didn't need to put Burt McClain's antics front and center of the gossips.

It had been enough to get Gray out of the bar, and he'd headed home that night, miserable and sick over his father's words.

And revolted that Harper—his beautiful, precious Harper—would be tainted by it for the rest of her life.

He'd already begun to worry that staying in Rustlers Creek would harm her professional prospects. Every time he brought it up, she pressed the idea they could go other places, his skills in such high demand he'd be a shoo-in for opportunities, but he already had a line on taking over Doc Andrews's practice and hadn't yet believed he was cut out for something bigger.

Hadn't seen his abilities with the same sheen of optimism that she did.

So he did the only thing he believed he could do to keep her safe.

He ended them.

The words haunted him still, the only ones he could think of to send her away.

And he now understood why his mind had worked so hard to block them out.

We have no future.

With a steady, relentless focus on his father, Gray pointed toward the exit. "Get off my property."

"What do you mean get off? I need your help."

"Help you thought you'd swindle out of me, hoping I was so dizzy from my head injury you could get it past me." Gray stared his father down. "Right?"

"Them boys said you were shaken up and hurt pretty bad."

"I just saw them yesterday and I was fine. Why would they—" Gray stopped. "How long have you been planning this?"

"I just need some fucking help!"

"Get off my property."

"Trevor Beaumont's property."

"*My* property." Gray moved up into his father's space, again reminded how the solid, strapping man of his youth had faded. "So get the fuck off of it."

Burt made a good show of trying to stare him down, but eventually realized he wasn't going to get what he came for. With a heavy string of curses, he finally turned and headed out of the barn.

Gray had half a mind to follow him, but to what end? The man would slither back when he got up the courage again anyway. He always did. And other than kicking up some dirt as he left, there wasn't a hell of a lot Burt could do unsupervised.

He turned to see Harper, still standing quietly by Cabernet's stall, petting the horse where he leaned over the top, nuzzling her neck.

To *him*—Gray—Burt couldn't do a lot of damage. But the same couldn't be said for Harper.

Just like the same couldn't be said for his mother.

Even after all the years apart and all they'd shared in the past month since she'd been home, he now knew that even if he could, there was no way he'd go back and make a different decision.

Because it was the same one he needed to make now.

This town wasn't for her.

This life wasn't for her.

And she needed to be very far away from all of it.

"I'm sorry you had to see that."

"Oh, Gray." She pushed off the stall door immediately, walking toward him, but he moved back, dancing out of her reach.

He saw the hurt—felt it slice clear through his midsection—but he stayed in motion.

And he stayed away from her.

"You've done your job. I'm healthy and I'm healed. And I have all my memories back."

"Gray, stop this. Please."

"It's time for you to go."

"Please talk to me. Don't do this again. To me or to yourself."

We have no future.

"Please, Harper. It's time for you to go."

Chapter 19

Harper stared at the emails that had come in earlier that afternoon, and for the first time since she drove away from Gray's property had the overwhelming urge to cry. Her three Coffee 2.0 locations in Seattle had beat all expectations for the month and they'd stolen four share points from the surrounding shops on nearby corners in each neighborhood where they did business.

Her idea was successful.

More than successful, if the email that had followed the sales results was any indication. A local venture capitalist in the Pacific Northwest wanted to front four more locations in Seattle's suburbs and also fund a test location in L.A. The guy was eager and excited and believed in her business plan with a fervor that was as exciting as it was slightly unnerving.

And, obviously, tear-worthy if the hot tracks running down her cheeks and blurring her vision were any indication.

Even being away from home for nearly a month, she was successful. She'd done the work and solved a problem and was making money at an endeavor that, by all rights, was risky.

Who bought coffee shops on a whim?

Worse, who bitched about it when the gamble paid off?

God, what was wrong with her? Because she hated pity and she *really* hated self-pity.

And she was full to the brim of her fucking successful coffee cup with that hateful emotion.

A reality that only made the tears stream harder.

She was a woman in touch with her feelings, and tears had always come easy. But a sort of cold numbness had overtaken her when Gray asked her to leave, and she'd simply operated on autopilot.

She refused to go down this path again.

Wasn't that what she'd finally figured out these past few weeks? How much time she'd lost, pining away for something that couldn't be.

She loved Gray and she had every belief that he loved her. But unlike some couples who were lucky to keep that love and watch it grow, they were destined to remain at the misguided crossroads of good intentions.

His, most specifically.

His stupid, bullshit, ridiculously childish intentions. And her self-righteous anger would have been valid if only she hadn't seen the raw, vivid marks of abuse that were so clear when in the presence of his father.

Marks made on a child and still carried by the man.

She'd known the problems from the start. Those meals she'd brought to Doc Andrews's breakroom had been given in the knowledge that Gray had none.

But she'd never fully understood what that forced depravity did to the way Gray saw himself.

He was kind and caring and more than capable of handling Burt McClain. She could see where the man would have been a scary figure years ago—and even more so to a child—but the husk of a man she'd seen today wasn't capable of eliciting much beyond an angry sort of pity.

And wasn't that the rub?

What had harmed them a decade ago—even when it shouldn't have—still had that power over Gray.

At the light knock on her door, Harper dashed at her tears before hollering, "Come in!"

Hadley stood in the doorway, framed by the hallway light, her expression a mix of sadness and sympathy that struck a hard chord in Harper's chest.

"You doing okay?"

Of all the people she did not need pity from, her sister was at the top of the list. Especially since Hadley had found a way to work past her problems and still come out on top. So she'd come in here, try to comfort Harper with sweet smiles and doe eyes, and then she'd leave and walk down that hall and sleep with the man she loved tonight.

Hadley had somehow figured out how to make her whole fucking *life* work.

Success and love and home and forever.

And it was for all those reasons—and Harper's own set of childish hurts and resentment of piteous glances from others—that she found a very soft place to hurl each and every one of them in her sister's face.

"Do I look like I'm doing okay?"

Hadley's sympathetic smile never wavered as she came into the room and took a seat on the edge of the bed, curling her legs underneath her. "Want to talk?"

"Not particularly."

"Do you want to punch something? Zack has standard-sized boxing equipment in the gym downstairs."

"Why?"

Harper had no idea why her extraordinarily fit brother-in-law, who did a job that was the epitome of working out for a living, needed a gym room in his home.

"No idea, since he and I both avoid the gym like the plague."

"Must be easy to do when you have a gazillion rooms."

Harper let up a small mental cheer as she saw a slight wavering in that warm, sympathetic front. "I'm sorry you're crying. Want to tell me about it?"

"What do you want from me, Had? You're doing such a great job reading my body language. Do I have to actually yell at you to get the fuck out for you to finally move?"

In more than three decades of sisterhood, it wasn't one of Harper's better digs, but it did the job.

Hadley uncurled her legs and climbed off the bed. "Fine, then. I'll leave."

Harper nearly let her go. The fight felt half-hearted at best and she really did want to be left alone. Only try as she might, something happened when she saw her sister, silhouetted once more in the hallway lights.

Because there was a man waiting for her at the other end of that hallway. The one she had wanted and had fought for and had won back into her life.

And Harper couldn't say the same.

"Excellent. Go fuck your perfect husband in your perfect house in your perfect bed and leave me the fuck alone."

Hadley stilled at the verbal assault, her back arrow straight as she continued to face the hallway. Harper got the distinct sense that she, too, was warring with jumping into the half-hearted fight or just calling it a day and walking away.

Which made the whirling dervish who twisted around, racing back into the room, something of a surprise.

"Yeah, Harper. I got my hot man who is waiting to fuck me down the hall. You know how? Because I fought for him. I fought for us. I didn't at first and that's on me, but I'm watching you and seeing you miserable, which I've watched for the past fucking decade, by the way, and I know that you could go after this. That you could do something about this. So quit taking that out on me."

The hot tears turned into blind, raging sobs and Harper simply crumpled with it.

Because every word her sister had screamed at her was right.

And she had no idea how to fight. How to get what she wanted when it came to Gray. How to push just hard enough that he saw reason instead of curling up into himself and pushing her away.

She didn't know how to do it.

What if she did push and prod and he walked away anyway? Wasn't that part of what leaving had been about all those years ago? Sure, she'd had good job offers coming out of school and a few were in Seattle. But she'd had them in a lot of other places, too. And she'd even had a few offers that would have allowed her to live any place in the country so long as she had an internet connection.

Yet she'd run anyway. She'd taken one that sounded interesting and challenging and where they'd deliberately told her in the interview that she'd work eighty-hour weeks.

Because staying, knowing she might push and plead and try to keep Gray in her life and still come up empty, had scared her more than running.

The sobs came harder as Hadley sat down beside her on the bed, pulling her close and wrapping her up in her arms. They sat like that for a long time, the sobs fading for a bit, only to come back on another hard, bitter wave.

And her sister sat and held her through it all.

It was only when Harper had finally tired herself out that Hadley spoke.

"I'm sorry I was ugly with my words."

"You were truthful. I was ugly."

"We were both ugly."

"And I really don't resent that you have a hot husband you get to sleep with. I love you too much to hate you for that."

"Thank you." Hadley squeezed, tightening the hug. "I think."

"I don't know what to do about this."

"I don't, either. But give yourself some time. You're allowed to be angry, Harper."

While it was lovely to be given permission, in hearing the words she knew they weren't really what she was looking for. Lifting her head off Hadley's shoulder, she looked at her sister.

"I'm so tired of being angry. Or sad. Or some combination of frustrated or discouraged or unsatisfied with my life. I've tried so hard to make it better."

"And you'll try again."

Hadley stopped, closing her mouth before she seemed to think better of it.

"I said something a few weeks ago that upset you. About trying to butt in and orchestrate things."

"I was a bitch that day."

"Yeah, but you had several good points. And because of it, I tried to remember that this is your journey and I can cheer you on, but I can't walk it for you."

"Why would you want to?"

"I'm a big sister. I'm wired that way." Hadley brushed a tear off her own cheek. "But what I realized is that not only is this not my journey, but that you needed to come back, Harper. You needed to come here and see him and let whatever was going to happen between the two of you happen."

"So I could fall back into old patterns?"

"So you could exorcise the ghosts. You're not twenty-two anymore. And you needed to experience Gray as a grown woman with a grown woman's perspective."

"To be hurt again?"

"No, sweetie." Hadley smiled, only this time there wasn't any trace of pity or sadness. There was only undying love and support. "To find yourself again."

MARTY LET HIMSELF into Gray's stables, unsurprised to find a low light burning at the back. Zack was the one who'd tipped him off to Jackie's new sleeping quarters, his son-in-law's visit with Gray a few days before producing that bit of news.

And it had been Harper who'd shared the news that she'd moved back into the Wayne and Sons ranch. He was sorry for it—more sorry than he could have imagined—but he also knew there were deep hurts there that needed time to heal. He'd toyed with visiting Gray a few times in hopes of speeding up that process, but had ultimately opted to leave the idea of a face-to-face alone for a bit longer. He already knew Harper's side of the story and recognized that her trust in sharing the details also meant that he didn't have a place to step in.

Not that his grown children needed him to step in.

Just like he didn't need them for this.

But he did need Jackie. And he was done waiting for her to come around.

"Hello?" Her voice rang out from the far end of the stable. "Gray, is that you?"

"No, it's not Gray."

Jackie's head peeked around the last stable, her mouth opening into a small O before she said, "Hello, Martin."

God, he loved how she said his name. He'd never been a big fan of his formal, old-fashioned moniker, always feeling like it was too formal. But on her lips, it felt regal, almost

Special.

Which was how she made him feel.

"What are you doing here so late?"

He continued on down the main aisle through the stable, his gaze never leaving her face. So much depended on these next few moments.

Would he stay?

Or would he finally accept that he needed to go, leaving her and this lovely dream of being together alone.

"I came to keep you company."

"How'd you know I was here?"

"You forget I'm hooked into the cowboy grapevine with my son-in-law. He mentioned you were here and that the horse intake has been going quite well. I think Zack's a little mad at me I never recommended you for his stables."

"Is he having an issue? I can always help."

"That, Jackie Delaney. Right there. How can you do things like that and not make me love you?"

She chewed her lower lip, her gaze still locked on his. It was that look—that steady gaze that seemed to drink him in—that gave him the hope this might work.

"You said that the other day. In your office. You told me you loved me."

"Because I do."

"You don't know me."

"Of course I do."

"No, Martin, you really don't."

For all the arguments she'd made so far, this one found some purchase. "Are you suggesting we've moved too fast? That two people who've known each other for thirty years don't know each other well enough."

"We don't know each other *that* way."

"What way?"

"Intimately. And not the sex intimacy, but the sort of intimacy that comes from being close friends."

Marty considered her words. "I seem to remember a guidance session about fifteen years ago when Amanda Brockmire got pregnant. You and I discovered her crying behind the bleachers as we were closing down the gym after a basketball game."

"You were so kind to her that night. She was scared and frightened and you helped her."

"You were right there with me, helping me through it. And at the end, after we'd dropped her home, you said something to me in the car."

Her gaze had hazed with the memories, even as she kept her focus steady on him. "I said that no matter what decision she made, she'd never be a child again."

"That was intimacy. So were the preparations we made each year for the field day events and how carefully we selected the games so everyone had an opportunity to compete. You told me you wanted to make sure everyone had a ribbon, not just to have one but because they had an obstacle they could conquer."

"What does this have to do with us?"

"Because it's *us*, Jackie. You and I had a relationship with each other, a real, deep friendship, long before we moved on to something else."

"I'm not your wife," she whispered. "And you love her and I can't change the fact that I had feelings for you when she was alive."

"Is that your only argument?" When she only looked confused, he added, "For us not being together."

"Well, yes, I suppose." She stopped, her mouth quirking into a skeptical line. "But it's not an argument. It's the truth."

"It's immaterial. My wife loved Nicolas Cage the entire time we were dating and married."

"That's not the same thing."

"It sort of is."

"He's a celebrity." Jackie waved a hand in the air. "She had a crush, nothing more. That wasn't real."

"I don't know about that. Especially when we flew to an event in California and she got to meet him."

"How did that happen?"

"A long story with some fuzzy specifics I don't quite remember but having something to do with a contest she entered for a red-carpet getaway for one of his movies. The point I'm making is I am 100 percent certain Maria was both attracted to him and imagined sleeping with him when she met him."

"He's a celebrity. It was a crush. She wouldn't have acted on it."

"Neither did you."

"It's not the same."

"How?"

"It's—"

Marty moved forward then, aware that he wasn't going to get another shot. And as he pulled her close, he took his first easy breath as her arms wrapped around his waist. "That's a really dumb story to make as a comparison."

"You going to teach me a lesson and hit me like Cher hit Nicolas Cage in *Moonstruck*?"

A small smile creased the corner of her lips. "And tell you to snap out of it?"

"You could, you know."

"It really isn't the same."

"Don't you see, though? It's exactly the same. We're not guilty for the things we didn't do. We're not beholden to some cosmic justice because we wanted something we didn't think we could have."

"But you loved her. Deeply. And she died."

"And it gutted me in every way. And then I discovered I had feelings for you. And you, Jacqueline Delaney, are very much alive and very much capable of giving that love back to me. Assuming you want to."

"Oh, Martin." Tears shimmered in her eyes and he reached up, catching one on his thumb. "I love you. And I want that more than I can say. I just—"

No more *justs*, Marty thought as he leaned down and captured her mouth with his

No more excuses.

No more waiting.

Life was too short and he'd spent too much of it marking time. He didn't want to wait any longer.

And as her arms tightened around his waist, her mouth opening to allow him better access, Marty knew he'd finally found what Maria had wanted for him all along.

Someone wonderful to hang on to.

"WAYNE, YOU ARE a freaking cowboy god." Chance's voice wavered with the notes of a happy buzz as he extended an empty tumbler across Zack's office desk. "And if you're willing to keep pouring that elixir straight from the heavens, who am I to say no."

"You can thank my wife for it. It was a Christmas present."

Gray was still nursing his own glass of super premium bourbon, able to do little beyond staring into its amber depths.

He'd initially been called out to Wayne and Sons to look at one of the newer calves, and Chance had already been there, talking with Zack about a new salesman he was considering hiring. Zack had ultimately invited them both to stay and enjoy a few drinks.

Gray had almost said no until he'd seen the

sheer awe in Chance's expression as he caught sight of the bourbon. Then he'd figured what the hell. All he had waiting for him at home in his small cabin was the lingering memory of having Harper there for a week. He could envision her in every single part of his house, and it was torture.

And he'd slept on the couch for five days because he still couldn't return to his bed. The memories of making love with her were vivid enough without lying in the place where it happened.

"Well, look at you booze hounds." Charlie Wayne's voice echoed off the small walls of the office as the older man ducked his head into the room. "You bastards are drinking the good stuff without me."

"Come join us." Zack waved his father in, but Charlie's good-natured smile never wavered. "I actually came to find you and see if you could help me for a minute. I'm working with a few of the hands on the herd's schedule for the next few weeks, and Carter's not around to ask when the south pasture was last rotated."

Gray pictured the large maps of the ranch they kept in various places and could see Charlie leaning over them, talking about herd rotation, land resources and water management. Zack had mentioned more than a few times that he valued his father's inputs and could use them around the ranch, and it was good to see Charlie passing that knowledge on to others.

"Excuse me for a few minutes?" Zack asked. Chance and Gray both waved him on, and Zack added, "Keep enjoying the bourbon and don't wait on my account. I've got one more bottle secreted away in here."

Charlie let out a short expletive before laughing at something with Zack as the two of them walked away, leaving Chance and Gray to their glasses and that very tempting bottle.

"That must be nice."

"Hmmm?" Gray glanced up from his glass.

"Zack and Charlie. To have a man like that for a father. To have an actual relationship with your dad. Zack's lucky."

"He is."

Chance held up his crystal tumbler, his casual gaze on the amber liquid not at all able to hide his focus on the conversation. "I've kept my mouth shut about you and Harper because you don't need someone so far up your ass they're coming out your throat."

"That would be correct."

"But you're my friend, Gray. One of the few men I call friend in the world. And if you're going to let your father fuck up what you have with that woman, you're not the man I thought you were."

The first small embers sparked under his skin. "She and I can't be together."

"No, you *think* you can't be together. There's a difference."

"Like you and—"

He was nearly about to poke Chance about Charlotte when he stopped himself. Whatever Chance was driving at, it came from a good place.

And a low blow was well, low, and entirely un-necessary.

Even if Chance did answer the question for him.

"Like me and Charlotte?" He shook his head. "It's not the same."

"Maybe it could be."

"A broke cowboy doesn't need to be courting the daughter of the king of all the cowboys. It's not done." Chance stared into his tumbler once more before returning his gaze to Gray. "But you, my friend, are hardly in the same situation. So what the hell are you waiting for?"

"She deserves better."

"You ever think about the fact that you do, too?"

GRAY FIGURED HE'D curse himself later for ignoring Zack's generosity and only drinking one glass of the Pappy, but his admirable restraint did allow him to drive home. A fact Chance thanked him for as he tumbled from the truck to his front door.

Even though he was happy to avoid a hangover on the heels of his recently healed concussion, Gray knew the evening was good for Chance. His friend might talk a good game, but he carried a sizable suitcase of his own baggage over his father, and the opportunity to talk with others who could help him build his business and work toward his dreams meant something.

Dreams. And the hopes that went with them,

Gray thought as he headed back over the interior roads of the Beaumont property before crossing onto what was now his.

And much as it pained him to keep going over the scorched earth of his own actions, he had to acknowledge that Chance knew what he was talking about.

If you're going to let your father fuck up what you have with that woman, you're not the man I thought you were.

Was that what he was doing?

Because over the past few days, what had started as an act of protection for Harper felt an awful lot like running away from her.

He'd sent his mother away once, and even after all this time, he still knew it was the right thing to do. But this? This felt like his own running away and it didn't sit well at all.

Did he really want to do that any longer?

Especially because he'd been given the strange and unexpected gift of forgetting his past for a while. Chance had to live with the reality of Trevor Beaumont's bad choices, but Gray had been lucky enough to live in a carefree place where Burt Mc-Clain hadn't existed for a while.

He pulled into the long dirt path that led to his cabin, his headlights catching on the back of an SUV. He'd no sooner recognized it as Hadley's car than he caught sight of Harper, stepping out of the driver's side door.

His breath caught as he looked at her, slowing

to pull up beside the SUV. Even in the deeply un-flattering fluorescent lights of the garage overhead, she looked luminous standing there, a shy smile on her face.

He parked and jumped out, crossing over to her. "You been here long?"

"About ten minutes."

"We probably followed each other here from the Wayne Ranch. I just dropped Chance off."

"I heard the news you were carousing in the barn. It spurred me into action." She shifted from one foot to the other. "Well, that and my fight with Hadley."

"I'm not sure my glass of bourbon qualifies me for carouser status, but I am glad you're here. I am sorry that you and Hadley fought."

"I'm not. Turns out a good old-fashioned battle between siblings clears the air and the tear ducts."

Harper glanced across the small parking area off his driveway. "We all seem to be crisscrossing town tonight. It looks like my father is out in the stables with Jackie."

"Looks like. Does that bother you?"

"No. Well, if she doesn't figure out how great he is and start dating him again, I'll be bothered. But let's hope they figure it out."

Although he wanted to believe she was there for a different reason—a good one—she'd made no move to touch him or ask him how he was doing.

"The weather's been beautiful these past few

days. How's Cabernet doing with his training?" she asked.

"Adjusting better every day."

"And you? How are you doing?"

"Not as well," he admitted.

"Yeah, me, either. I've been thinking a lot."

"About?"

"Running away."

It was jarring to realize how closely her comment mirrored the thoughts he'd just had on the drive back to his house. "You mentioned that before, and I never got to tell you what I thought about that. Or how maybe I've been doing the same."

Her eyebrows lifted but she didn't say anything, only stared at him expectantly.

"I don't think you ran. I think we do the things we need to do to feel safe. To heal. To feel in control." He took a deep breath as Chance's words ran through his mind once more.

You think *you can't be together.*

Was Chance right? Had he convinced himself of something that wasn't true?

Or that didn't need to be.

"I'm the one who ran. All those years ago, Harper. I ran away from what we had, instead of having the faith that it was strong enough to see us through."

"And then you did it again last week when your father was here."

"I did."

"Are you ready to stand still?"

"I think I am."

Wonder filled him at that truth and, with it, he corrected himself. "I know I am."

She stepped toward him, her smile growing as she closed the distance between them. "Then I can give you what I brought with me."

"A kiss?"

"Among other things."

He took that as acquiescence, pulling her close and pressing his forehead to hers. "I love you, Harper."

"I love you, Gray."

She lifted her head as he bent his, their kiss hot and wildly intoxicating. He gave himself a moment to drink his fill, the taste of her far richer than any bourbon.

The feel of her in his arms like heaven.

Could it possibly be this easy?

But as he stared down into her eyes, Gray recognized the truth. Everything had felt far too hard for far too long.

Maybe it was simply long past time he accepted what was.

Which made the fact she was pulling away nearly painful.

"Where are you going?"

"I told you, I brought you something."

He reluctantly let her go, and she marched around to the passenger side of the SUV, pulling out a handled bag from the front seat.

Curious, he couldn't imagine what she'd

brought him. It was only when she pulled out a small plastic bag that he finally understood. "You brought me gingerbread?"

"With icing." She held out the bag to him. "They're all for you."

"That's because you don't like them."

"But I do like you." She stepped up and laid a hand on his chest. "Isn't that all that matters?"

Gray pulled her close, wrapping her tight in his arms, the cookies crushed between them. She was right.

It was all that mattered.

Author's Note

I've always wanted to write an amnesia book. It's one of my favorite tropes to read and it's been the type of story I've wanted to tell for a long time. But as with most things in writing, it takes just the right couple, with just the right story, to sometimes find the fit.

For me, Harper and Gray were that fit. I loved the idea of playing with who they were before, who they'd become, and maybe that precious opportunity to figure out who they might have been if their circumstances were different.

I know I've taken some liberties with amnesia, though I did try to ground Gray's behavior in as realistic details as possible. I hope you'll forgive any license I took in benefit to the story.

And I hope you'll laugh as I did to find one final tidbit while researching. While the three main causes of amnesia noted in the book are accurate—head trauma, psychic trauma that the body blocks out or deteriorating health—the actual frequency of amnesia occurrences is far more prevalent in TV, movies and books than in real life. Something to be quite grateful for, don't you agree?

NEW YORK TIMES BESTSELLING AUTHOR

ELOISA JAMES

The Wildes of Lindow Castle

Wilde in Love
978-0-06-238947-3

Too Wilde to Wed
978-0-06-269246-7

Born to Be Wilde
978-0-06-269247-4

Say No to the Duke
978-0-06-287782-6

Say Yes to the Duke
978-0-06-287806-9

Wilde Child
978-0-06-287807-6